THE
HEN PARTY

Kath Kincaid

Hodder & Stoughton

Copyright © 2001 by Kath Kincaid

First published in Great Britain in 2001
by Hodder and Stoughton
A division of Hodder Headline

2 4 6 8 10 9 7 5 3 1

A CIP catalogue record for this title
is available from the British Library

ISBN 0 340 76881 9

Typeset in Centaur by Hewer Text Ltd, Edinburgh
Printed and bound in Great Britain by
Mackays of Chatham plc, Chatham, Kent

Hodder and Stoughton
A division of Hodder Headline
338 Euston Road
London NW1 3BH

In memory of
PERCY
Prince of Dachshunds

Chapter One

Five women, all from Liverpool. Four nurses and a
schoolteacher. Three Catholics, a C of E, an agnostic.
One pretty, one plain, two somewhere in between.
Tracey, the only virgin, is staggeringly beautiful. One
of the women has had a child. The schoolteacher, Pauline, the eldest at thirty-five, is unhappily married. Another is divorced, one not long married, one single, and
Emma, twenty-four, is getting married next week to
Matthew who works in a bank. Hence the hen party. Not
a normal hen party, but one of that newfangled sort
which would be held abroad.

Four of the women, with their responsible jobs, feel
weighed down by the cares of the world. They take their
work very seriously. It prays on their minds when they are
away from the hospital or the junior school where Pauline is assistant head. They find it difficult to laugh and let
themselves go, have a good time. On them rests the
health and well-being of vulnerable, sick and damaged
people, or the education of the young. Perhaps it was this
sense of responsibility that had drawn three of the nurses –
Emma, Tracey and Rosemary – to each other in Liver-

pool General Hospital where, unlike the majority of
nurses, they lived to work rather than – more sensibly
– worked to live.

The fifth woman, Donna – the plain one – is a bit of a
failure as a human being, as well as a hopeless nurse. The
other three, feeling sorry for her, had taken her under
their collective wing.

A hen party abroad isn't anyone's cup of tea. They
would have preferred to have gone to dinner in a quiet
restaurant in Liverpool and talked shop.

But Emma, easy-going to a fault, had been talked into
it by her mother. An only child, no expense was being
spared with the arrangements for the wedding. Mrs
Harrison was shameless in her desire to impress Matthew's
relatives, her own relatives, her friends, her enemies, the
neighbours, and the entire area of Childwall where they
lived, with the extravagence of the proceedings: the
white stretch limo almost as long as the road, the flowers
being specially flown in on the day from the Channel
Islands, the five-course sit-down meal for over a hundred,
the free bar open all day . . .

Mrs Harrison looked forward to her daughter's wedding being a talking point for years to come, a benchmark
against which all future weddings would be set.

Matthew was going for the weekend with his mates to
Lloret de Mar for his stag night. Therefore, her Emma
must also have a weekend away. Mrs Harrison would feel
uncomfortable and embarrassed announcing she was
merely having a meal in town when nowadays it was
the fashion to fly somewhere dead fashionable.

'Your dad'll pay,' she said, and Emma's dad winced,
having thought he'd finished forking out for the horrendous cost of joining two young people together in

Holy Matrimony, apart from the open bar on the day. He winced again and hoped he would avoid a heart attack when the time came to settle up.

Excluding Donna who didn't give a toss, the women didn't want to go to a foreign place with exotic smells and dark-eyed, sexy men. It didn't suit their mood. They weren't hedonists, but conscientious members of society with a duty to those less fortunate or more needy than themselves.

They decided on Dublin, where the population were Christian and spoke English and they wouldn't feel too strange. If they travelled late on Friday and returned early Sunday after the Catholics had been to Mass, they wouldn't be away long. They were looking forward to Sunday before they'd left the confines of Liverpool, vaguely aware of how pathetic this attitude was. Pauline had books to mark, question papers to prepare. Tracey and Rosemary were studying for their Midwifery Certificate, Emma worried how the hospital would manage without her. Donna still didn't give a toss.

It was October and already dark when the plane landed in Dublin. They caught a taxi to the hotel, a comfortable, medium-grade establishment in the centre of the city, arriving just in time for a late dinner, after which they decided to go to bed. All felt exhausted and longed for sleep.

Pauline, who was Emma's cousin and used to babysit her in days gone by, was annoyed to find herself sharing a room with Donna, for whom she'd never cared and privately considered as ugly as sin, with her long, thin, wormlike body and permanent scowl. It never ceased to amaze her that someone who was a ward sister and had no doubt witnessed the effects of cigarettes on numerous patients in her care, chain-smoked when off duty, and possibly on duty for all Pauline knew.

Donna fell asleep with a cigarette stuck in her mouth which Pauline had to get out of bed and remove. As soon as the cigarette had gone, she started to snore and Pauline's longing for sleep was seriously hampered by a sound similar to a jet engine revving up all night long interrupted by the occasional fart.

It was for this reason that next morning Pauline was the only one awake in time for breakfast. She ate alone, feeling sullen, virtuous, and excessively tired.

By the time everyone had showered, dressed and made-up, it was quarter past eleven. They sat around in the lounge, wondering what they were supposed to do to enjoy themselves.

'We're letting women down,' said Tracey. 'We should be getting pissed out of our minds, telling dirty jokes, going to discos, copping off with fellers.'

Everyone shuddered.

'It's raining,' Rosemary said gloomily. 'We can't even go round the shops.'

'Perhaps we'll enjoy ourselves tonight,' Tracey said half-heartedly.

'We're going to a party tonight,' Emma reminded them.

Pauline pricked up her ears. 'What party?' she demanded. No one had mentioned anything about a party to *her*. She sometimes felt excluded from the nurses, who made decisions at work and forgot to tell her.

'I could have sworn I told you, Pauly.' Emma frowned. 'We're meeting Eileen O'Brien in some pub called Maloney's at six o'clock. She worked at the hospital until last year. When she heard we were coming, she insisted on throwing us a party.'

'It's the first I've heard of it,' Pauline said sulkily. She didn't want to go to a party. She would have preferred to fly home and get on with her work.

They decided it was late enough to order lunch. Then, as it was still raining, they went to the pictures for something to do. It was a multiplex cinema and everyone fancied seeing a different film. To be fair, they spent the next two and a half hours watching a comedy that no one wanted to see surrounded by several hundred noisy and enthusiastic children, it being Saturday afternoon.

The rain had stopped by the time they came out, but the shops were closing. They had coffee then caught a taxi to Maloney's, which the driver informed them was on the outskirts of the city.

It was already growing dark some fifteen minutes later when they were dropped off outside a dingy, run-down pub. Emma, Rosemary and Tracey, were concerned that they had so far seen little of Dublin. Donna didn't give the inevitable toss. Pauline was glad, the less she saw of Dublin the better, and if she could avoid the party without appearing rude, then she would.

Inside, the pub was even dingier than outside – there was actually sawdust on the floor. Half a dozen men were already propping up the bar when they went in. They and the burly barmaid regarded the newcomers with a mixture of rude interest and hostility.

Pauline offered to buy the first round: three orange juices, a gin and it for Donna, a glass of wine for herself. They discussed the film, agreed it was awful, and wondered what they were doing sitting in such a disgraceful pub when they could have been in a much nicer one in Liverpool.

'This place is a dump,' Donna declared loudly.

Tracey bought a second round the same as the first and they mused aloud why Eileen O'Brien was so late. She'd always been reliable in the hospital and, talking about the hospital, did they know what had happened the other night in Casualty? Two guys had a fist fight and a woman had joined in. They'd all ended up in a worse state than when they'd arrived.

Emma wrinkled her nose. She was a pretty girl, small and delicate, with baby-blonde hair and an appealing lisp. 'I hated being on Casualty. I prefer Orthopaedics any day. Hardly anyone dies. I hate it when patients die.'

Pauline remarked that in that case, wasn't she too soft to be a nurse?

The others hastened to disabuse her. 'Emma's a wonderful nurse. All the patients adore her. They can tell she really cares.'

'Everyone hates me,' Donna said gloomily. 'I have difficulty building up a rapport with me patients.'

No one hastened to disabuse Donna. Perhaps, Pauline thought cynically, her patients resented having tobacco fumes breathed all over them when they were sick.

The conversation turned to the under-funding, or possibly over-funding, of the National Health Service, the shortage of this, the abundance of that. Pauline told them about the large classes she had to teach, the pressures she was under, the fact that none of the other teachers worked as hard as she did.

From behind the bar, the burly barmaid glared contemptuously at the five women. 'Will you look at that crowd of slab-faced bitches,' she snarled. 'Not a one of them has smiled since they came in. I feel depressed in the same air space. Where do they think they're at, a wake?'

'There's three of 'em can't even take a proper drink,'

6

remarked a man. 'Orange juice!' He pretended to be sick. 'And did you hear them slagging off this pub earlier?'

'They make the place feel seriously cold,' remarked another. 'Any minute now and there'll be icicles round the winders.'

'Life is for enjoying, not enduring, as my ould grannie used to say.'

'Tell *them* that,' the barmaid sniffed.

'Are they lesbians, d'you think?'

'I shouldn't be surprised. Five women together and not a man in sight.'

'I've got an idea.' The first man reached into his pocket and brought out a bundle of Irish pound notes. 'Had a win today on the horseys. Give them poor, sad ladies a pint of Paddy's Brew. Tell them it's on the house and it's only Irish lemonade. It'll put a sparkle in their eyes and a smile on their miserable gobs. Otherwise, any minute now they're likely to cry themselves blind and they'll have us crying with them.'

The pub was gradually getting fuller and the strangers did nothing to encourage the usual riotous Saturday night atmosphere. So far, no one had felt inclined to sing and the piano remained untouched.

The barmaid grinned. 'Paddy's Brew is fifty-seven per cent proof. What happens if one of 'em has to drive back to Dublin?'

'They came in a taxi, I saw them get out. They can catch a taxi back.'

They all agreed that the lemonade was very nice, very drinkable, lovely and sweet and tangy, and extraordinarily refreshing.

'As rejuvenating as a tonic.' Pauline treated them to a rare smile. She suddenly felt like dancing. This was accompanied by a strange sensation that she eventually diagnosed as happiness. It was so rare that she was happy, that the feeling worried her. It made her feel vulnerable, being happy in a public place. She would sooner be happy somewhere private, such as her own home, where she could take the happiness out and examine it, experience the feeling in quiet solitude until she got used to it. There was no one at home at the moment, her husband, Dennis, having managed to get himself invited to Matthew's stag night. Dennis was in Lloret de Mar, no doubt dancing cheek to cheek with a dusky señorita whom he would take to bed that night if he could.

It reminded Pauline that she couldn't go home, not easily, because she was in Dublin. The hotel then, she'd go back to the hotel and take her young charges with her, apart from Donna who could do as she liked. Oh, there was a lovely, fluttery feeling inside her head, like one of those paperweights that shook into a snowstorm.

She discouraged the others when the idea of a second glass of Irish lemonade was mooted. There was something funny about it. It had made her feel happy and too much happiness was dangerous. Tracey had developed a squint and was grinning inanely. Emma looked as radiant as a bride, somewhat appropriately, but Pauline doubted if it would last until next Saturday. It occurred to her that it was a long time since Rosemary had gone to the Ladies.

Donna told Pauline to mind her own business when it was suggested she desist from another lemonade. She went over to the bar where, for some reason, angry words were exchanged.

'They didn't want to sell it me,' Donna said indignantly when she came back and plonked the glass on the table. She lit the inevitable cigarette, made a face at the barmaid, and drank half the glass in one go as a gesture of defiance. So far, Donna showed no inkling of the slightest good humour, let alone happiness, but she was a hard nut to crack.

'I think we should go back to the hotel,' Pauline announced.

'Aren't we waiting for someone?' said Emma.

No one could remember who it was nor, as it turned out, could they remember where they were staying, other than it was a grey building in a wide street and their rooms were on the fifth floor.

'I'll ring for a taxi and ask the driver to take us to that cinema we went to,' Pauline said sensibly. 'We can find our way back from there. I'll look for a phone.' She felt naked without her mobile, but they had recklessly decided to leave their mobiles behind along with all their other troubles.

She went over to the bar, a rather more difficult procedure than she would have imagined because her knees seemed to have turned to jelly. One of her hands was also having difficulty finding the other. She leaned on the bar and almost missed. 'Excuse me,' she said courteously to the barmaid. 'Where's the phone?'

'Haven't got one,' the barmaid said abruptly.

'But I need to tall a caxi!'

'You'll just have to stand outside and hail a taxi when it passes.'

'I see. Thank you mery vuch.' Pauline returned unsteadily to her seat.

'Now you're being cruel,' the man who'd paid for Paddy's Brew remarked to the barmaid. 'There's a phone round the back. Those poor wee lasses could wait outside a month of Sundays before a taxi passes this way.'

'Don't care,' said the barmaid nastily. 'I don't like the look of 'em. They're tourists. I can't stand tourists cluttering up the Dublin bars.'

The man couldn't recall a single tourist having cluttered up Maloney's in all the years he'd been cluttering up the place himself. He decided to keep his gob shut, preferring to stay on good terms with the barmaid.

Back at the table, Pauline said in a schoolmistressy voice, 'You two wait outside and keep your eyes open for a taxi, while I collect Rosemary from the Ladies.'

'What about Donna?' Tracey enquired.

'What about Donna?' Pauline growled. She had no intention of looking after Donna.

'She's either dead or paralysed. I can't tell which.'

Donna looked as if she'd been sprayed with starch and steam-pressed by an Amazon. Her mouth had fallen open, making a perfect round hole into which Pauline felt the urge to shovel something horrid. A cigarette trembled precariously on her bottom lip. Pauline reached over, removed the cigarette, and none-too-gently closed the open mouth. Donna's teeth met with a loud crack, her head fell on to her chest, her upper half fell on to the table. Glasses shuddered.

The three women began to giggle helplessly.

'I think we should leave her,' Pauline said eventually, tears streaming down her cheeks. 'Let her find her own bay wack.'

'We can't possibly,' gasped Emma, the humanitarian.

'Okay, then we'll take her. Come on.' Pauline seized Donna's collar, pulled her off the chair, dragged her towards the door on her heels, and dropped the long, lanky figure on to the damp pavement outside. She returned to the pub to look for Rosemary.

The single cubicle in the grubby and unsavoury-smelling Ladies was engaged. Pauline knocked. 'Rosemary!'

'Yes,' a dreamy voice replied.

'Open the door. We're going.'

'Don't want to go, Pauline,' said the same dreamy voice. 'It's beautiful here.'

'You're in a lavatory, dear. It can't possibly be beautiful.'

'Oh, you should see the back of this door! It's glorious. The pictures keep changing all the time. I'd like to stay here for ever.'

'Open the door and let me look, then.'

'No.'

'Why not?'

'If I open the door, it might spoil the pictures.'

Pauline dragged over a chair with only three good legs and propped it against the door. She climbed the chair and looked over. Rosemary was sitting on the lavatory and gazing at the back of the door, her eyes glazed with wonder. She was an absent-minded girl burdened with too much imagination, not long married herself to a fireman called Gary. She didn't look up when Pauline spoke. 'The door looks even better from the other side, dear.'

'Can you see deserts and mountains?'

'Yes,' Pauline lied shamelessly. 'And trees and lakes and fantastic sunsets. Oh, and a field of poppies, like in *The Wizard of Oz*. Why not open the door and come and look?'

'I think I prefer me own pictures, thanks all the same, Pauly.'

Had Pauline not been feeling so gloriously happy, she would have battered down the door and led Rosemary out by the ear, but in her present state she couldn't see the harm in leaving a young woman in the dirty lavatory of a run-down pub in a country she'd never been before. People were too nice to hurt each other, she thought. 'If that's what you want,' she said, shrugging.

The man who'd bought the drink opened the door to let her out to where the others were waiting. 'I shouldn't bother with a taxi, luv,' he hissed, overcome with guilt. At least it had turned out a fine night for four drunken ladies to be lost in – had he not already partaken of a few pints of Guinness too many, he might have remembered there'd initially been five. He averted his eyes from the long lady lying on the ground who'd insisted on a second pint of Paddy's Brew. 'If you walk down the hill you'll come to where the buses run. It's a steep hill and it winds a bit, but you'll find that way just a wee bit quicker than hanging round for a taxi.'

'Thank you.' Pauline spied the hill, deserted and badly lit. The onus of responsibility lay heavily on her shoulders and she had begun to think of herself as in charge of a school outing, though an unusually cheerful one for a change. She was actually enjoying herself. Clapping her hands, she cried imperiously, 'Quick march!'

They followed unsteadily, Donna bringing up the rear on all fours. When this proved agonisingly painful, she seized a passing tree and hauled herself upright. But her head hurt, she could hardly see, her heart was pounding dangerously, her legs refused to straighten. A car passed, going the other way, and the three children in the back, screamed in terror when they saw the stooped, grotesquely misshapen figure stumbling along the road, like something out of a horrible fairy tale.

Not long afterwards, Donna fell sideways into a hedge which proved so comfortable she decided to stay, and the party continued their dogged journey without her.

'I can hear a cat miaowing,' Emma remarked. She loved animals and the piteous sound tore at her heart. She wanted to weep. To her left, loomed a large, dark church with a small graveyard in front from which the cries came. The tall iron gate to the church opened when she pushed it. 'Don't worry, puss. Emma will rescue you,' she called, closing the gate behind her.

It wasn't noticed that the group had been reduced to two, Pauline ahead, swinging her arms. 'The grand old Yuke of Dork, he had ten thousand men . . .' she bellowed tunelessly.

Tracey felt pleasantly dizzy and longed to sit down. Pauline was walking so quickly, it was hard to keep up. A few times, Tracey had suggested they rest a minute, but had been ignored. It seemed it would take a bomb to stop Pauline singing and marching ahead like a clockwork soldier wound up by a maniac.

By now there were more people around, more houses, more traffic. They had almost reached the bottom of the hill and were approaching civilisation. Ahead, a bright light spilled on to the pavement which turned out to be a tiny theatre where posters informed her *Lady Windermere's Fan* was being performed that night.

In her teens, when the world had been a more carefree place and she'd had few worries, Tracey had been a member of an amateur dramatic society, though they had never done anything as classy as Oscar Wilde. She tried the double doors. It was years since she'd been inside a theatre. At least she could sit down even if she only stayed for the first act.

Pauline arrived at a bus stop, surprised to find herself alone. She could have sworn there'd been people with her when she'd left wherever she'd left. Still, it didn't matter that it was so hard to remember anything when she felt so ecstatically, so deliriously happy.

Chapter Two

—————◆—————

Donna had no idea how long she lay trapped in the hedge. She wasn't even aware it was a hedge, just that she was perched on a prickly armchair that was difficult to get out of. Or would have been difficult to get out of had she wanted to try.

She was quite content where she was, thank you. She would have been happy to stay there for the rest of her life. No one was bothering her, no one was asking for more tablets, a bedpan, a doctor, a newspaper, a tissue, a drink, a priest, what day was it, what time was it, what time was visiting, what time did visiting end, what time was breakfast/dinner/tea, when would they be going home, was it raining outside, was it sunny, was it cold, was it warm, am I alive or am I dead?

Dead, Donna decided. I'm dead.

She liked being dead, for the moment at least. It was peaceful. She liked the refreshing drops of that afternoon's rain that were falling through the hedge on to her face. (Though Donna didn't know it was a hedge.)

There were slight shuffling, scuffling noises, as if tiny animals were burrowing down for the night underneath her bony bottom. She liked animals, but not as much as Emma who was crazy about them.

Emma?

Who was Emma?

She must have known someone called Emma when she was alive.

Despite being dead, she longed for a fag. Somewhere about her person there was a bag containing a full pack of Marlboros. She wriggled about, trying to find it, but when she couldn't came to the clever conclusion that it had been mislaid.

Catastrophe!

Her affinity with the hedge was hugely diminished. A fag was far more important. After a long tussle with the branches, she managed to pull herself to her feet where she swayed like a delicate tree in a force-ten gale.

Where was she?

There wasn't a soul in sight and it was awfully dark. A dim, solitary streetlight revealed only a deserted road that sloped away into blackness. It reminded her of something.

Hell!

It reminded her of hell.

Okay, she was dead, which she didn't mind, but going to hell was something which had been a nagging concern ever since she was a small child.

Donna shivered.

Was this it? Was this all she would know for all eternity? Would she never again smoke another fag?

From what she could only vaguely remember, life hadn't exactly been a bowl of roses, but she would have preferred it any day to the thought of a fagless non-existence with only Old Nick himself for company.

She examined where she'd been sitting with the idea of getting back to think things over, discovered it was a hedge, and decided the likelihood was she was alive. It was a relief to find herself pleased, not sorry, though her current situation was somewhat dire.

Why was she here?

Where had she been?

Where was she going?

Why didn't she know any of these things?

If the truth be known, she wasn't even sure who she was, but had a feeling her first name began with a D.

Jaysus! She suddenly felt very sick, as if concrete had been poured into her stomach and had set hard. Her heart was pounding. Her head felt as if it had left her shoulders and was floating several feet above. Her legs had lost their bones and her feet had altogether disappeared, along with her fingers.

Perhaps she'd been involved in a terrible accident and had concussion. It would explain why she had lost part of her memory and some of her limbs.

She rolled herself along the hedge which was bound to end somewhere and she'd find what lay behind it. Hopefully there'd be someone who would give her a ciggie, help sort her out.

The hedge ended. Donna fell flat on her face and the concrete in her stomach cracked in several places. She lay immobile for a while, before looking up and finding herself in the gravel driveway of a large old house with a tiled roof and beams built into the white walls. The lights were on in the downstairs rooms, the front door was wide open, she could hear the babble of voices, the drive was full of cars.

A party!

Donna dragged herself towards the open door and the voices, removing the occasional piece of gravel from her mouth and ears. She crawled over the step, into the hall, where she was met with a grotesque apparition, a barely human being.

The apparition was female, a woman, with blood on her face and stones in her hair. Her clothes had been ripped to shreds, the flesh on her hands was torn. Her eyes glinted with madness.

Donna opened her mouth to scream at exactly the same time as the mad woman.

Jaysus! She was looking into a mirror and the woman was herself.

From somewhere deep in the recesses of Donna's sozzled brain came the awareness that it would be wise not to make her presence known at the party looking as she did. Any sensitive souls present might be seriously harmed. The less sensitive ones might sense danger and kill her on sight.

The voices were all coming from one room. Dishes clinked, cutlery scraped. 'Who'd like more wine?' a man asked. 'This soufflé is delicious, Maeve,' said a woman.

It must be a dinner party and some of the guests were Irish – she recognised the accent. She'd go upstairs, find a bathroom, clean herself up a bit, then creep down again and claim to have been attacked – you never know, perhaps she had. It would explain the torn clothes and the fact she could remember so little. Someone would give her a fag and a lift to wherever she should be.

She crawled up the thickly carpeted stairs and found herself on a spacious landing with fancy paper and gold-framed pictures on the walls between thick, black beams.

There were eight doors, all closed. It was indeed some fancy house she'd stumbled into.

Unlike the hospital, there was no indication on the doors as to what lay behind them. Which was the bathroom? She'd just have to try them, one by one.

After pulling herself to her feet with the aid of the knob, she discovered the first door opened on to an airing cupboard in which huge amounts of pastel bedding and expensive towels were neatly stacked. Behind the second door two small children were fast asleep: a boy no more than twelve months in a cot, a girl about a year older in a white painted junior bed with bunny rabbit transfers on the head. A lamp shaped like a mushroom cast a pale, rosy glow over the room.

Donna's face softened. She would have liked children, but her lousy ex-husband had refused. 'They might turn out as hideous as their mother,' was the excuse he gave.

'Why did you marry me if you think I'm so hideous?' a hurt Donna asked once.

'I dunno. I must have been pissed,' came the reply, which no doubt accounted for the fact the marriage had begun to falter on the honeymoon.

'You're no oil painting yourself.' His beer belly was revolting and getting bigger all the time.

They'd got divorced two years ago with the excuse the marriage had broken down, the legal way of describing their intense hatred for each other.

With a sigh, Donna closed the door and opened the third. A child of about ten was sitting up in bed reading a book through round, hornrimmed glasses. It – she couldn't tell if it was a boy or a girl – had short fair curly hair and was wearing blue pyjamas.

She was about to quickly close the door but the child

had spied her. 'Are you at me mammy and daddy's party?' it enquired.

'Yes.' Donna had a brainwave. 'Your daddy sent me upstairs to fetch him down some ciggies, but I can't remember where he said they'd be.'

'Beside his bed, I reckon. He smokes like a chimney does me daddy.'

'And which room would that be? I've forgotten.'

'At the other end of the landing, the last door. Why are you all bloody?'

'I had an accident. I'll just go and fetch those ciggies for your daddy.' Donna was on the verge of leaving in search of the longed for fags when she heard footsteps on the stairs. Although she wasn't quite herself that night, the instinct for survival remained intact. Something told her it would be dangerous to be found upstairs in a strange house talking to a child she didn't know. She slipped inside and closed the door. Someone went into the next room where the sleeping children lay. Seconds later, the same someone opened the door behind which Donna stood. Donna made an imploring face at the child and the child grinned horribly back.

'Are you all right, sweetheart?' enquired a voice.

'Yes, Mammy.'

'Don't read too long, now. You'll hurt your eyes.'

'No, Mammy.'

The door closed.

'Ta,' breathed Donna.

The child regarded her with interest. It had big brown eyes and long, innocent lashes. It looked very intelligent, though perhaps that was the glasses. 'Who are you?'

Donna didn't know. 'I'm the unknown woman,' she replied truthfully.

'It's a good job I'm not of a nervous disposition, else I might have screamed.'

'You're a wonder, you are. I'm very grateful.'

'There's no need to butter me up. Now as you're here, you can tell us a story. Mammy and Daddy are always too busy to tell me stories. Mind you, he's not me *real* daddy. Me real daddy tells stories at the drop of a hat. He smokes even more than the other one.'

'Could I come back in a minute and tell you the story?' Donna said imploringly. 'I'm desperate for a smoke, you see.'

'No,' the child said sternly. 'I've heard people say that before. You'll only not come back.'

'I promise to come back,' she said, lying through her teeth.

'No! Sit here!' The child patted the bed. When Donna looked reluctant, it said snottily, 'If you don't tell me a story, then I'll scream me little head off and me other daddy'll come running. He's one of the top men in the Gardai and you'll be behind bars within the twinkling of an eye. He'll throw the book at you – he's quite fond of throwing books at people is me other daddy.'

'What's the Gardai?' Donna asked weakly.

'The Irish police force. You're not Irish, are you?'

'I'm from Liverpool.'

'What are you doing in Dublin?'

It was the first Donna knew she was in Dublin. She wondered how she'd got there. And why. 'I don't know,' she confessed.

'You're in a state, you are.'

'I certainly am,' agreed Donna.

The child scowled. 'Story!' it demanded.

'Well,' Donna began, 'once upon a time, there were three bears: Father Bear, Mother . . .'

'For Christ's sake,' the child snorted. 'I'm ten. I don't want to listen to crap stories like that. I can read them for meself. Tell me something different.'

'I don't know any different stories,' Donna confessed. 'I only know the ones me own mam told me when I was little. Would you like to know about things that happened at the hospital?'

'Are you a doctor, then? Or a nurse?'

'I reckon I must be one or the other.' She could remember all sorts of things about life in a hospital. 'Would you like to know about the man who had his leg amputated and wanted it back but we'd thrown it away?'

'What happened?' frowned the child, folding its arms.

'We just gave him the first leg we came to and he seemed happy. Maybe he'd never looked at his legs properly before. He was very fat and couldn't see them if he looked downwards because his tummy got in the way.'

'What did he want the leg for?'

'He was going to preserve it and mount it on a plinth or something.'

'What's a plinth?'

'I haven't a clue. The word just came to mind.'

'What else happened at the hospital?'

'There was this chap who used to put his false teeth in a glass every night and someone added dye to the water so his teeth were bright red for weeks.'

'I've heard that one before.'

'I'm sorry.'

'Tell me something funny about dead people.'

'There's nothing funny about dead people.'

'*I* think there is.'

You would, you bloody little toe rag, Donna thought rather than said. 'There was this child once, about your age, looked like you too. I can't remember if it was a boy or a girl. Nasty little thing he was or she was. Its mammy and daddy didn't cry a drop when it died. The awful thing was, when the body was lying in the morgue, it just disappeared in the middle of the night. It was rumoured the devil himself had stolen it.'

For the first time, the child looked rattled. 'What did the devil want it for?'

'For himself, we all reckoned, to play with. He saw in it a spirit equal to his own. If only it had been nicer when it was alive, it would have gone straight to heaven, like all good children do.'

'You can go and have that cigarette now. I don't want any more stories, thanks all the same.'

'Ta.' Donna got up and waited for the inside of her head to settle down before going over to the door. 'It's been nice meeting you.'

The child didn't answer. It appeared rather worried. Serve it bloody right.

The final door on the landing led to a fine big room with a four-poster bed draped with lemon frills and heaped with the coats of the guests downstairs, several of them fur. Matching curtains graced the two large latticed windows, both open so that the material billowed gently into the room. The furniture was powdery white and the floor covered in fluffy pale green. An en suite bathroom with an ivory suite could be seen through a door to her right.

Donna didn't take in the colour scheme, the frills, the

beams on the ceilings and the walls, the furniture. Her eyes desperately raked the room for fags. She needed a smoke more than she'd ever done before. Her body was as useless without nicotine as a politician without a mouth.

There was a packet of Dunhills and a silver lighter on top of a white chest of drawers.

'Thank you, God,' she sobbed. With trembling hands, she shook a cigarette out of the packet. Jaysus! Where had her mouth gone? She found it eventually, lit the fag, breathed in deeply, and felt the poisonous fumes go down as far as her heels. It was a wonderful feeling, better any day than sex. She felt sorry for everyone in the world who didn't smoke. Fancy missing a sensation like this!

She sat on the bed, smoking furiously to make up for lost time. The first cigarette went. She lit another, then a third.

Halfway through the third, Donna was possessed by an irresistible lethargy. She swung her feet on to the frilly cover and the heap of coats, rested her head on a pillow, took a puff on the fag – and fell asleep.

When she woke up, feeling unusually hot, the bed was on fire and the cigarette was no longer between her fingers. The frilly drapes were burning merrily overhead and bits were dropping off on to the fluffy green carpet where tiny, independent fires had started. As she watched, frozen with disbelief, the billowing curtains touched the drapes, caught alight, and were melted into tatters by the flames. The breeze blowing through the open windows spurred on the tiny fires so that they joined together and became one and the floor was a carpet of snapping, dancing tongues of fire which spread under the furniture, under the bed, up the walls, gobbling up the centuries-old wooden beams, flickering across the heavily beamed ceiling.

It took Donna several minutes to realise what was happening, then to realise it wasn't a dream, but real.

No wonder she felt hot.

She leapt off the bed and ran into the bathroom, filled a glass with water, and threw it on the fire. She did this several times before it crossed her mind that the fire was gathering pace rather than lessening. By now, it needed more than a few glasses of water. It needed a fireman's hose.

There was a telephone beside the bed at that very moment being turned into a melting heap of plastic. Donna opened the door and fire rushed out before her with the speed of light, spreading over the carpet on the landing, licking its way up the walls, circling the pictures in their gold frames, racing down the stairs consuming the wooden banisters in its wake.

The lights in the house went out. There were laughing screams from downstairs, until a man said loudly, 'Can you smell fire?' and the screams became real.

'Ring the fire brigade someone,' said the same man.

'The children!' screeched a woman. 'We've got to get the children! Oh, my God! Look at the stairs!'

The stairs had become stairs of flames, impassable.

Donna calmly walked along the blazing landing until she reached the room containing the child of indeterminate sex.

'Come along,' she ordered. 'We need to get you outside straight away. The house is on fire. Let's go into the next room where the little ones are and we'll take your bedding with us. We're going to turn it into a rope.'

The child followed obediently, sucking its thumb. 'Are we going to die?'

'Absolutely not. It's my job to save lives, not destroy them.' She had the strongest feeling it was she who was responsible for the fire.

'Close the door,' she said when they were in the small children's room. Both were asleep, like little alabaster angels. She pushed a tiny dressing-gown against the crack under the door where the flames peeped through, anxious to enter.

Donna began to knot sheets together. There should be enough if she joined them diagonally. She opened the window and looked down on to a deserted lawn at the back of the house. Then she tied the end of the sheet-rope to the leg of the junior bed which looked strong enough. The little girl in the bed didn't wake up when it was dragged over to the window – Donna had suddenly found the strength of an ox. She let down the rope and it stopped just above the grass.

'Can you climb down there all on your own?' she asked the older child.

'I think so.'

'Someone as clever as you will find it as easy as pie. Let's help you out. We need to be quick.'

There was smoke coming through the door. The walls were crackling. The screaming downstairs had become hysterical. The baby in the cot had woken up and started to cry. Donna picked him up. 'There, there,' she soothed. 'You're going to be all right, I promise.'

It was awkward climbing on to the window ledge with a baby in her arms. Donna's elbows scraped on the wooden frame and on the brick walls as she shinned down, only slowly because she could only use her right arm when she had a baby in the other.

At the bottom, she gave him carefully to his brother or sister, and returned to the rope, climbing it like a monkey in a way she hadn't thought possible. The little girl was awake, sobbing for her mammy. Donna hoisted her on to her back. 'Keep your arms tight around me neck now.'

She was clambering out of the window when the bedroom door flew open with a crash and giant tongues of flame licked greedily into every corner. They licked Donna's face and singed her hair.

There were people waiting at the bottom of the rope this time. Hands helped her tenderly to the ground. A woman, the baby already in her arms, made a grab for the little girl, then turned tearfully to Donna.

'Oh, thank you! Thank you so much. You were so brave. I'll never forget what you just did for as long as I live.'

The older child was standing alone, looking rather lonely, as if no one particularly cared it had been saved. It stared vacantly at Donna through the round glasses.

'You'll get a medal for this,' a man said gruffly. 'Look, let's get away from here. The whole house is going to go up in a minute.'

'Here's the fire brigade at last,' someone said.

'Took their time.'

Donna was helped across the grass to a cooler spot some distance from the house. Neighbours were bringing tea, she was told in a cooing voice. Or would she prefer whiskey? An ambulance would come soon and take her to hospital so that her wounds could be bathed and dressed. Nobody had ever witnessed such bravery before and from a passing stranger, an' all. She must have seen the flames through an upstairs window. She should feel very proud of herself. Why, any minute she could have been burnt to death. Fancy shinning up that drainpipe in the first place! It was a wonder it had stood her weight, almost falling off the wall as it was.

'You poor love,' said a woman. You must be dead on your feet. Look, you're shivering. Can someone fetch a blanket? What's your name, dear? Oh, the brave young woman's lost her voice.'

'I reckon she's in shock,' someone said.

Donna decided she had no alternative but to faint. It would avoid explanations. Anyroad, she felt like a rest.

Chapter Three

—◆—

The cat was black with one white sock and a white shirtfront. Emma found it lying behind a gravestone. It purred joyfully when she touched it.

'Have you hurt yourself? Poor pussy. Let Emma pick you up. You're not very big, are you? You're either a lady cat or still a kitten.'

The cat felt as light as a feather as it snuggled into her neck. Emma stroked it and felt it tense when she touched its left paw. 'I bet you've got a stone or a seed stuck in your pads. Our cat at home is always doing the same thing. His name's Hector. What's yours?'

Emma had never been drunk before and was unaware that she was. She therefore wouldn't have been the least surprised had the cat answered, 'Tiddles', or some other appropriate name, nor if it had reeled off an address when she asked where it lived.

'What are we going to do with you?' she said worriedly. 'I can't take you back to Liverpool. Hector would eat you for his dinner.'

The cat miaowed and licked her chin.

'No, I bet you wouldn't like it. Neither would I. I

can't leave you here, can I? I bet someone's doing their nut worrying where you are. Do you know where the police station is?'

The cat shook its head.

'Oh, well, never mind, I didn't think you would.'

'Is someone out there?'

Emma jumped. The voice had come from a small building half tucked behind the church. A man was leaning out of an upstairs window.

'Have you lost your cat?' she called.

'Well, I have a wee cat, yes, but I didn't know it had lost itself. In fact, it can't have done since you would appear to be holding it in your arms and standing right outside me own front door.'

'It's black with a white front and one white paw.'

'That is indeed Elizabeth. She's called after the queen, the first one. And she told you she was lost, did she? She's a little liar, that cat.'

'She's hurt her paw, the white one.'

'She's only done it to get sympathy. She does it all the time.'

'Don't be silly,' Emma said shortly. 'Are you going to let her in or not?'

'I can't let her in. I'm a dying man and bedridden. It creased me getting as far as this window. You'll find the back door open. Let her in there.'

'I'd like to fix her paw.'

'You'll find a tool box in the kitchen cupboard.'

'Is this a priest's house?'

'It is indeed.'

'For Catholic priests?'

'It is so. And before you ask, I'm a priest meself, Father Jack McKeown, dying as I said before.'

Emma made her way through to the back of the house through overgrown, damp grass which was badly in need of cutting. There were lights on inside and she entered a miserable, old-fashioned kitchen with a chipped tiled floor and some battered units. The fridge looked as if it had come out of the ark, though everywhere had been scrubbed scrupulously clean.

She sat down beside a cracked wooden table and examined Elizabeth's paw. There was a tiny grass seed buried inside the pads. Elizabeth gritted her teeth but didn't complain as it was removed. She mewed gratefully when set on the floor, pushing open a door leading to the interior of the house.

Emma followed and found herself in an equally miserable hallway with a large crucifix on the wall and a plaque of Our Lady over the door. There was holy water on a small table. She dipped in her fingers and made the Sign of the Cross, just for luck.

'Her paw's all right now,' she shouted.

'Thank you very much, young lady. We're both very grateful. Would you like to come upstairs and give an old priest a cuddle?'

'I'd like to do no such thing,' Emma said indignantly. 'I'll come up for a minute, but you're not getting a cuddle, priest or no priest.'

Father Jack McKeown was sitting up in bed propped against several pillows in a small spartan room with linoleum and a rag rug on the floor and a green blind on the window. Apart from a narrow bed, the only other furniture was a bedside table and a chest of drawers with a crucifix on top. The priest wore winceyette pyjamas with faded stripes showing no trace of their original colour. He looked very much alive, with an enormous amount of very white hair which flared in a wire halo around his baby pink face, and glittering blue eyes. He was old, at least eighty, but Emma had rarely seen anyone half his age look quite so healthily cheerful.

'Have you been left to die on your own?' she asked sarcastically.

'Yes, as it happens, I have. Me housekeeper, Kate, did a bunk when I told her I had an appointment to meet me maker this very night. Went screaming out the house like a banshee on heat, she did.' He grinned and patted the bed. 'Come and sit beside me. What's your name?'

'Emma Harrison. Please don't ask what I'm doing here, because I'm not quite sure. Five of us came to Dublin for a hen party, but I seem to have lost the other four. I don't even know the name of our hotel. All I can remember is passing your church and hearing Elizabeth miaow. I could tell she was hurt.'

'It sounds to me as if you're pickled to the gills.'

'What does that mean?'

'That you're half-seas-over, three sheets in the wind. That you've had too much to drink, to put it baldly.'

'Oh, no! I don't drink.'

The Father grinned. 'Don't you now! Anyway, Miss Emma Harrison, you entered the dark blackness to rescue me little cat. You have a stout heart. Are you a Catholic?'

'Yes.' Emma blushed. It was years since she'd been to Mass.

'Then you have a stout Catholic heart. Is it Miss or Mrs Harrison, or that other thing, Ms?'

'It's Miss, but only for another seven days. I'm getting married next Saturday to someone called Matthew.' Emma sighed.

'But you don't want to!' The blue eyes dazzled into hers.

'Of course, I do. What made you say that?'

'People don't usually sigh when they announce they're getting married to someone called Matthew.'

'Sigh? I didn't mean to. Look, can I make a cup of tea? Would you mind? I'll put everything back where I found it.'

'By all means. And, oh,' he said casually, 'while you're down there, would you mind fetching the bottle of Black and White out the sideboard in the parlour? You'll find a box of cigars there, an' all: Cuban, good old Castro. Bring them at the same time and a box of matches while you're at it.'

'Are you allowed to smoke and drink when you're dying?'

He chuckled. 'I can't think of a better time.'

The tea was loose, in a caddy with a proper teaspoon. While waiting for the kettle to boil, she found the whiskey and cigars, put them on a tray, and took them up to the bedroom, Elizabeth at her heels. The cat jumped on to the bed and pressed herself against the old man, who rubbed his hands together, grinning fiendishly, when he saw the tray.

'I'm glad you came, Miss Emma Harrison. Oh, and you've brought a tumbler too. How clever you are.'

'I couldn't very well expect a priest to drink out the bottle, could I?'

'How little you know of priests, my child. Have you made your tea?'

'I'll be back with it in a minute.'

'Look,' she said, returning with the tea. 'You know you said Elizabeth was pretending to be hurt in order to get sympathy? Well, I think you're doing the same.

You're pretending to be on your deathbed so's everyone will make a fuss of you.'

He raised bushy white eyebrows and looked slowly around the room. 'Everyone? So, where is everyone? There's only you, and you're only here by accident, unless you think I stuck something in the dear cat's little paw in order to entice the world and his wife through the gates of me church.'

'That wouldn't surprise me,' Emma said darkly. 'Anyroad, what's wrong with you?'

'You wouldn't understand.'

'Yes, I would. I'm a nurse.'

He blinked. 'A real live nurse! I don't believe it. You're too young.'

'I'm twenty-four. I'm the senior nurse in Orthopaedics.'

'You don't say!' He looked impressed. 'Well, Nurse Harrison, there's nothing wrong with me orthopaedically, but I've got a heart defect – one of the valves is acting seriously temperamental – diabetes, a diseased liver, and little bits of cancer dotted here and there. Will that do? And, oh, I'm deaf in me left ear.'

'Are you sure?'

'Unless the doctor's lying through his nasty yellow teeth, then I'm sure.'

'I'm so sorry.' Emma started to cry. She'd been wanting to cry for ages. She felt very strange tonight. Under ordinary circumstances, she wouldn't have dreamed of talking to a priest as if they were equals. 'Oh, I'm so sorry. You seem so nice. It doesn't seem fair.'

'That I'm so nice or that I'm dying?'

'Nothing's fair,' Emma wept.

'Never mind,' he said consolingly, refilling his already

empty glass and lighting a cigar. 'This is a perfect way to die, with a glass in me hand, smoking a good cigar, and a pretty girl sitting on the bed with me. I'd prefer it if you were in the bed, not on, but a man can't have everything.'

'You're not *really* thinking of dying tonight, are you?' Emma said, alarmed.

'I *am* dying tonight.' He looked inordinately light-hearted for a man whose death was imminent. 'I'm seventy-nine. Tomorrow is my birthday, but I won't see it. It was foreseen a long while ago that I would never reach the age of eighty.'

'Who by?'

'Meself. I have flashes of second sight occasionally. A voice once told me I would never reach four score years. And I was only a titchy lad when I told me ould mammy that men would walk on the moon by the year 2000.'

'Didn't they walk on it much earlier than that?'

'Yes, but I was still right. Think about it.'

'Well . . .' Emma looked doubtful. 'About dying, tonight that is. It's getting late. How exactly do you intend to manage it in time?' She looked at her watch but it didn't make sense. Was she really having this conversation? Perhaps she was dreaming. If she were, she wondered at exactly which point in her life would she wake up? Perhaps she had never come to Dublin. She might not even be engaged to Matthew and getting married next week.

'I shall drink myself into oblivion,' Father McKeown said with a chuckle, 'and never wake up again.'

'What if I hadn't been around to fetch the whiskey?'

'Ah, but I knew you were coming. I knew the Good Lord would send someone to help me on me way.'

'I'm not sure if I'm really here.'

'Some helpful soul brought the whiskey and cigars upstairs and it wasn't Elizabeth.'

'Oh, you!' His complacent acceptance of death was getting on her nerves. Unless he was having her on, which was always a possibility. 'Why do you look so happy?' she asked suspiciously.

'Because I'm looking forward to heaven.'

'You believe in heaven?'

'For Chrissakes, woman. You're talking to a Catholic priest. Of course, I believe in heaven, and all that other guff about the virgin birth and the holy trinity. I'll be having a fine old time in heaven. I'll drink meself delirious and smoke meself blue in the face, but it won't matter because I'll already be dead.'

'What makes you think you'll go to heaven?'

'Because I've led a blameless life.' He put his head on one side and thought a little. 'Well, not entirely blameless, but I've always confessed me sins and said the proper penance.'

Emma made a face. 'I haven't been to confession in ages.'

'I'll hear you now, if you like. But only if you've got something juicy to confess. It's one of the things I'll miss, hearing confessions. Maybe someone could arrange for me to do it in heaven. Or I could eavesdrop down here. You wouldn't believe some of the things people get up to, worse than the stuff you see on television any day. I could have written the scripts for half a dozen blue movies if I'd had the time.'

'You're only trying to shock me.'

He grinned. 'If you say so.'

There were sounds of activity downstairs and a few seconds later a woman came flying into the room, a sharp, skinny woman of about fifty wearing a gabardine mack and a headscarf. Elizabeth dived under the bedclothes. The woman glared at Emma.

'Who are you and where've you come from?'

'I'm . . .' Emma began, but the woman didn't wait to listen.

She turned on Father Jack. 'Look at you! Drinking as well as smoking, yet Doctor O'Leary said you weren't to do either. How did you get your robbing hands on them disgusting things? Did *she* get them for you? Who is she? Are you mad, Father? Give them to me here this instant.'

'I'll do no such thing, Kate Musgrove. And a person can't rob their very own alcohol and cigars. They were given me in the first place in good faith, for me to drink and smoke as I liked, not to be hidden away by a woman for whom pleasure is an insult.' The priest's face had gone red. He tucked the bottle behind him and held the cigars against his chest. 'Get out of me house. You're sacked. Don't ask for a reference, 'cos you're not getting one. Emma here's looking after me from now on. She's a qualified nurse, which is more than you are. If Emma ses I can drink and smoke, then it's all right. Isn't it, Nurse Harrison?'

'I'm . . .'

The woman turned back to Emma. 'Is he really dying tonight? Oh, is he really?' She began to weep bitterly, clearly distraught with grief or some other strong emotion. Emma wondered if she should make herself scarce, but the situation was too fascinating to miss. 'I couldn't stand it if the eejit died,' the woman wailed. 'I don't know what I'll do without him.'

'You'll soon find someone else to bugger about and make another life a misery,' Father McKeown remarked tartly.

The woman removed her scarf and mack, and for some reason threw them on the floor. She had violent red hair and was wearing a pinny over a shabby blouse and skirt. 'Don't say that, Jack. I haven't truly made you miserable, have I?'

'You made a pretty good job of it most of the time,' the Father said uncompromisingly. 'For nearly a year, I've been confined to me bed and you've denied me everything most precious. You wouldn't even allow me a telly in me room, case the excitement made me heart explode to pieces. There's a UEFA cup match on tonight and I'm missing all them mad Englishmen rioting on the streets of Brussels.'

'But you're sick, Jack. Doctor O'Leary said . . .'

'Doctor O'Leary said there was no hope. A man standing in front of a firing squad isn't going to worry he'll get cancer from his final cigarette.'

'Don't talk like that!'

'I'll talk any way I want. My own personal firing squad is about to take aim and I'll do as I like until they pull the trigger.'

The woman uttered a deep, wretched sigh. For a reason known only to herself, she made the Sign of the Cross, then said, 'I've brought someone to see you.'

'Then tell them to go away. I don't want to see anyone except me new friend, Emma.' He blew an expert smoke ring and watched intently as it floated towards the ceiling, getting larger and thinner until it disappeared.

'He's waiting downstairs, Jack.'

'He? If it's that eejit Monsignor friend of yours, he's not welcome. If it's someone come to give me the Last Rites, then I've already given them to meself – the long version, not the disgraceful scanty one they inflict on the dying nowadays.'

'Shall I fetch him up?'

'No.'

'I won't be a minute.' She left the room.

Father Jack glanced at Emma and rolled his eyes. 'Do you get the distinct impression she doesn't take a blind bit of notice of what I say? She's always been that way. If I say I want stew for me tea, she'll make an omelette. If I ask for an omelette, I get sausage and chips.'

'How long has she been with you? I take it she's your housekeeper?'

'Too long,' he said gloomily. 'Thirty-five suffering years.'

'She's obviously very fond of you. She's only doing what she thinks is best.'

'Don't make excuses, Nurse. The woman's a pain.'

Mrs Musgrove returned with a young man of about Emma's age. He was neither tall nor short, but solidly built, with thick, corn-coloured hair and wide-apart, guileless blue eyes. He wore jeans, trainers, and a black sweatshirt. Emma found him unexpectedly appealing.

'This is little Jack,' said Mrs Musgrove.

'Is he a priest?'

'No, he is not a priest. This is me sister's lad. He's your son.'

For the first time since Emma had met him, Father Jack looked taken aback. He choked on the whiskey and it dribbled down his pink chin. Mrs Musgrove wiped it with the corner of her pinnie, but he irritably pushed her away. There was silence in the room for several seconds. Emma sat frozen to the bed. Mrs Musgrove glared challengingly at Father McKeown. Little Jack folded his arms and looked amused.

'I think I'd better make meself scarce,' Emma muttered.

'No!' The housekeeper laid a claw-like hand on her shoulder. 'I'd like a witness to this.'

'A witness to what?' growled the priest, still shaken. 'To the fact that you just made me waste a mouthful of good whiskey? What desperate nonsense is that to come out with! I concede I am forgetful, but if I search the furthest reaches of me memory, I cannot recall having had carnal knowledge of your sister. In fact, I don't even remember having met the woman. Is she as loathsome and peculiar as you?'

'You fathered the boy, I bore him, Netta raised him on the farm.'

'How neat.' Father Jack's face had collapsed. His eyes were watery. He suddenly appeared very old.

'I think you should both leave for the moment,' Emma said firmly, her nursing training coming to the fore. The patient was obviously very upset.

'I'll not be leaving,' Mrs Musgrove said aggressively, but little Jack spoke for the first time.

'Come on, Ma.' He put a hand on his mother's arm. 'She's right. Let's go down and make ourselves a cup of tea. You just dropped a bombshell. The Father needs time to get used to the news.'

'He's not *the* father, he's *your* father.' Nevertheless, Kate allowed herself to be led away.

Emma listened until they'd gone downstairs and the ancient plumbing squealed as water was poured into the kettle. She straightened the bed, plumped the pillows, and hoisted the old man up a few inches. Elizabeth peeped out from beneath the eiderdown.

'Are you all right?'

'Are you talking to me or the cat?'

'You.'

'How would you feel if you discovered you had a son the night before your eightieth birthday?'

'Not as surprised as you, obviously. The fact wouldn't have passed me by as it clearly did you. Is it true? I mean, is it possible?'

'I took a vow of celibacy,' he grumbled. 'I consider it an impertinence to ask a Catholic priest whether or not he's had sex.'

'Oh, come off it! I've just seen the living proof. I was only being polite, asking if it was true. It's clearly true. He's a nice lad,' she said encouragingly.

He brightened. 'Do you think so?'

'Seeing as we're being truthful with each other, I think he's drop-down-dead gorgeous.'

'Drop-down-dead gorgeous! What a strange phrase.' He sighed. 'So was Kate when she first came. Only sixteen, a country girl, with roses in her cheeks and fire in her hair. It was even redder in those days. I was in me forties and as innocent as a newborn babe. She seduced me on the spot. It only happened the once.'

'Liar.'

'I beg your pardon!'

'You're a liar. Girls of sixteen don't seduce priests, particularly not then, and not in Ireland. I wouldn't dream of trying to seduce a priest even now. In fact, I can hardly believe I'm in a priest's bedroom, talking to you the way I am. And Kate was well past sixteen when she had little Jack and you must have been well into your fifties. He only looks about twenty-five.'

'Who do you think you are,' he enquired testily. 'Inspector Morse?'

'I don't like being lied to.'

'Tough.' He was beginning to look better. 'I suppose I'd better speak to the lad. T'would be cruel not to.'

'Shall I fetch him up?'

'In a sec. Pour us another shot of the demon drink before you go. Me hands are shaking all over the place.' His voice became querulous. 'It's not fair, springing a surprise like this on a dying man.'

'You're right.' Emma made a face. 'She should have told you before.'

There were four people sitting round the kitchen table when Emma went in. Kate and little Jack had been joined by an elderly couple who had apparently heard that Father McKeown was on his last legs, as the woman put it, and had come to pay their respects with a few prayers.

'We'll say them in the parlour,' the woman announced.

'He'd like to see you,' Emma said to little Jack when the couple had gone.

'I'm going too.' Kate pushed herself forward.

'No, Ma. It'd be best if I went alone.'

Emma went with the young man to the door. 'How long have you known, about him being your father, like?'

'All me life,' he said, grinning. 'An awful lot of people know, or at least they've guessed. The nuns at school treated me with kid gloves, knowing I was the son of a priest.' He frowned. 'He won't get maudlin, will he? I'd hate it if he started crying and slobbering over me.'

'I doubt it very much. He's probably worried you'll get maudlin and slobber over him.'

The door closed. Kate was leaning on the sink, arms outstretched. She glanced darkly at Emma. 'I had the baby during the months when Jack was in Rome. I debated whether to tell him, but decided not. I suppose you think it's all desperately shocking.'

'I'm not shocked in the least.'

'I loved him. I still do. And he loves me. We've loved each other for thirty-five years. Nowadays, priests go off with women all the time. They get married, have families. There was a case in the paper only the other day. Of course, they'd had to move to England. I'd have gone anywhere in the world with Jack McKeown. It wouldn't have bothered me.' She burst into tears. 'Oh, I say that now, but it bothered me then. He wanted us to go away, but I refused. Next minute, I'd want to go, but it would be him having the doubts. We never seemed to want the same thing at the same time. He signed a petition the other week, Jack did, addressed to His Holiness, the Pope. It said that men who join the priesthood shouldn't have to be celibate. I wish that had been the case forty years ago.'

Emma didn't know what to say. She went over and poured herself tea out of a big iron pot.

'Where did you come from?' Kate asked. 'How did you get in?'

'Through the back door. I was passing the church and heard Elizabeth miaowing. She had something wrong with her paw. Father heard and invited me in. Somehow, I found meself upstairs, though it's not normally the sort of thing I'd do. I feel as if I'm under a spell or something. Perhaps it's a magic, Irish spell. I didn't have it until I came to Dublin, and it's rather nice, though a bit dangerous. If someone suggested I swim back to Liverpool, I'd set off like a shot. I know it'd be dead silly, yet I'd still have a go.'

'I'm glad you were here, that the quare feller upstairs wasn't by himself for long.' Kate came and sat beside her. Close up, calmer, she looked quite pretty, with grey-green eyes and still the suggestion of roses in her thin cheeks. 'You're very nice, very kind, and you're very pretty too. I always wanted blonde hair when I was a girl. There's not many young women these days who'd sit with a silly old priest and put up with his nonsense. You're a real old-fashioned girl.' She patted Emma's hand. 'Me now, I flew off in a blazing temper when he kept insisting tonight he was going to die. Then I decided to fetch little Jack, just in case the eejit was right. A man should know he has a son before he closes his eyes for the last, final time.'

'Does he really have second sight?'

Kate smiled. 'So he ses. Mind you, he's done it before, predicted the future. That's why I believed him about tonight.'

There was a knock on the kitchen door and it opened to admit about a dozen women of assorted ages.

'Hello, Kate,' said one. 'We heard Father Jack was on his way out, and thought he'd appreciate a few rosaries.'

'You'll have to say them in the parlour,' Kate said brusquely. 'There isn't the room in here.'

'That's the Legion of Mary,' she said when the women had shuffled out, their rosary beads already threaded through their fingers, already muttering Hail Marys. 'Jack'll hate that. He's not very religious for a priest. Oh, listen, there's a fire. Can you hear the engines? It doesn't sound too far away.'

44

'Does little Jack work on your sister's farm?' Emma enquired.

'Lord, no. He belongs to a folk group, the Castaways, they call themselves. He plays the guitar. He should have been at one of them gig things tonight.'

'Is he married?'

'Engaged.' Kate pursed her lips disapprovingly. 'He's getting married next year. What about you?'

'I'm getting married next week.'

'Nice feller?'

'I wouldn't be marrying him if he weren't.'

There was another knock on the door and this time a crowd of teenagers came in. 'We heard about Father Jack on the way to the disco. We've come to say some prayers,' announced one.

'You'll have to find somewhere else to pray. But not in the bedroom, he needs his peace and quiet.'

'Did you know the Bartons' house along the road has gone up in flames, Mrs Musgrove?' the same youngster said. 'The whole place was ablaze when we went past. There's hardly a brick of it left standing.'

Kate crossed herself. 'I know they're Protestants, but I wouldn't wish a fire not even on an atheist. Is there anyone dead?'

'I don't know, Mrs Musgrove. We didn't wait to ask, but the ambulance men were carrying some poor woman out on a stretcher.'

'God rest the poor woman's soul.'

Little Jack came in. 'Where's the phone, Kate? I'm going to ring the lads. Father said he'd like to hear them play a couple of numbers. I only left them in that pub along the way, Maloney's.'

'What did you talk about?' Kate asked eagerly.

'Music, films, books. Oh, and football.'

'Did you not talk about God, about forgiveness? Did he not bless you, ask if you went regularly to Mass? Did you not tell him you'd been an altar boy until you were sixteen, that you'd come top in the catechism when you were at school, that you'd won a prize in the bible study class? Did you not talk about anything spiritual in all that time?'

'No, much to my relief.' Little Jack winked at Emma. 'Is the phone in the hall or the parlour?'

'The parlour, but you'll have to step over the congregation to get near it.'

'There's already piles of kids on the stairs.'

The strains of 'Faith of our Fathers', came from outside. 'That sounds like the choir,' said Kate. 'They were singing in the cathedral tonight. They must have heard about Jack. There'll be a hot dog stand along any minute.'

'He must be very popular, Jack.'

'Everyone likes him, which is odd, because he's not very nice for a priest. He makes jokes at all the wrong times, particularly when people are saying their confession. It can be very hurtful. He's got a reputation for the bottle and an eye for the girls. He swears like a trooper. His sermons are a scream, but not everyone is inclined to laugh, not in church.' Her grey-green eyes moistened. 'Even so, I love him. I kept meself single for him all these years, just in case – I'm not Mrs Musgrove, but Miss. You know,' she went on thoughtfully, 'before tonight, I've never told all this to a soul except Jack himself, yet I'm telling you, a complete stranger. Why do you think that is?'

'Because you're upset. You're not thinking straight. You'll probably regret it tomorrow.'

Kate shook her head. 'I don't think so. Tomorrow, I might not care any more what people think.'

The choir had started to sing 'Queen of the May'. Little Jack came in. 'The lads are on their way, and the Knights of St Columba have arrived. They want to say a personal ta-ra to the good Father.'

'Tell them that they can't. He's not to be disturbed.'

'He might prefer to be disturbed,' Emma said.

'Not by that lot. Jack claims they're too unctuous. Would he be wanting to see me? What d'you think, son?'

'As long as you don't nag.'

'When have I ever nagged, I'd like to know.' Kate left, indignant.

Little Jack grinned. 'Well, 'tis a right ould farcical situation you've landed yourself in, Emma Harrison.'

'I'm enjoying it. I know I shouldn't if someone's dying, but nevertheless I am. I feel different tonight than I've ever felt before, more alive, as if me brain's been sharpened like a pencil.'

'We all feel more alive when we're faced with death,' he said sagely. 'It makes us realise how lucky we are to have breath to breathe and a heart to beat, that we have a future.' He sat beside her and Emma was conscious of his arm touching hers. 'Father Jack's quite taken with you. He said you're getting married next week to someone called Matthew.'

'Kate said you're getting married next year, but she didn't say who to.'

'Her name's Veronica. She wears skirts up to her arse and has a stud in her nose. Mam strongly disapproves. She sometimes sings along with me and the lads, Veronica that is, not me Mam.'

'Do you love her? Veronica that is, not your Mam.'

He pretended to look outraged. 'That's a cheeky question to ask someone you've only just met. Do you love Matthew?'

'I asked first.'

'Why do you want to know?'

'I'm not sure. I don't know why I asked. You're right, it's a cheek.'

'I do love her.' He stared moodily at the table. 'Least, I think I do.'

Emma sighed. 'I love Matthew, I'm pretty sure I do. Almost sure.'

' 'Tis a terrible decision to make, getting married,' he said soberly. 'You worry if you should go ahead when you have the least little doubt.'

'I know. If you really loved each other there should be no doubts at all.' Emma's pretty face screwed earnestly. 'You know what Matthew said three weeks ago? He said, "If we should ever get divorced." I nearly did me nut. I wondered if I should go ahead with the wedding to a man who could already see the possibility of us splitting up. I'm a terrible Catholic, but we'd be married in the eyes of God and that means for always, for all eternity, until one of us dies.'

'Did you not think of cancelling it, the wedding?'

'I did, but only for a minute.' She sighed again. 'You see, me mother has gone to this awful expense with the arrangements. Least me poor dad has. He was forced to. Mum gave him no choice. He claims to be almost bankrupt. Not only that, me and Matthew have put a deposit down on a house.'

There was shouting outside. 'Queen of the May' was being submerged by a raucous rendering of 'Amazing Grace'.

48

'The Knights of St Columba are trying to drown out the choir,' remarked little Jack. 'They've never got on.'

A young man with a ponytail wearing jeans and a T-shirt bearing the intriguing slogan, MADONNA FOR POPE, came into the kitchen by the back door. 'We had the divil of a job getting here. There's fire engines along the way and they wouldn't let us through until we explained about the Father's imminent demise. Is there electricity in this hovel, Jack, so we can plug in the amplifiers? I've got the long lead with me.'

'I'll see if there's a socket in the hall. Sean, this is Emma. Emma, Sean, he plays the fiddle for The Castaways.'

'Hi.'

'Hi.'

Emma was left alone, but not for long. A few seconds later, Kate appeared, her eyes as red as her hair. 'Jack would like to say goodbye,' she whispered. 'He hasn't got long to go.'

'To me?'

'Of course, to you. Who did you think I meant, the teapot?'

There were people kneeling in the hall and on the stairs. On the bottom stair, two young lads were playing cards. A buzz of Hail Marys came from the parlour. Hands reached out and grabbed the hem of Kate's skirt.

'Is he gone yet?'

'Is he shortly going?'

The front door was wide open. Emma saw the churchyard was crowded. Candles flickered. The choir and the Knights of St Columba had stopped singing and were involved in a fist fight, tipping each other over gravestones and stamping on the bodies. She could have

49

sworn she could see an ice-cream van on the road and it was playing the first two lines of '*Tantum Ergo*'.

Then everything was drowned out by The Castaways' rendition of 'The Red Rover'. The house shook, the floorboards shivered, the ceiling threatened to fall.

'That's a grand sound,' said Father Jack when Emma and Kate went in. 'That's the sort of music I like. I wish I had the energy to join in.' He was smiling, but his face looked creased and old and his voice was sleepy. Kate had removed some of the pillows so that he was lying flat which made his chin sink into his chest. Nevertheless, his eyes danced at Emma. 'Give us a goodbye kiss, Nurse Harrison. Not one of them French ones, mind, else the thrill might kill me. And I hope you don't want blessing, I'm not in the mood.'

'I don't want blessing, Father.' She kissed his cheek.

'I understand you've been having a little chat with my drop-down-dead gorgeous son?'

'Just a little one.'

'He thinks you're gorgeous too.'

'For goodness sake, Jack,' Kate interjected.

'Oh, be quiet, woman. I'm talking to Emma, not you.' His voice was becoming slurred. He reached for Emma's hand. 'About next week's wedding, I didn't like the way you sighed when you told me you were marrying Matthew. You need to do some hard thinking before you say, "I do".'

'I promise to think hard, Father.'

Father Jack's eyes were blinking tiredly. He uttered a deep, heart-rending sigh. 'I'd like to go to sleep now,' he said in a high-pitched voice, like a child's.

Kate gasped and threw herself on to her knees beside the bed. 'No, Jack, no! Don't leave me. Please don't leave me, Jack.'

'We'll meet again, my love,' he whispered, and his bright blue eyes slowly began to close.

Emma slipped unnoticed out of the room, closing the door quietly behind her. The Castaways were playing 'Mollie Malone', and people had stopped praying and joined in. Crates of ale were being hauled through the front door. The scene had all the elements of a wild old party and Emma hoped it would be like this when *she* died.

She sat on the top stair, head spinning and thumping at the same time. She felt completely detached from the life she'd always known: Liverpool, the hospital, her family. And Matthew. Why, she could hardly remember what he looked like. Yet in seven days' time they would be married and on their way to the Canary Islands for the honeymoon. She thought about little Jack, whom she hardly knew, but felt very close to.

The door behind opened and Kate came out. 'He's gone,' she said numbly.

'He's gone!' The words were repeated by those nearest and carried down the stairs, through the hall, into the parlour, out into the churchyard.

'He's gone.'

'Father Jack's gone.'

'The good Father's snuffed it.'

'God bless him.'

'God bless Father Jack.'

People began to cry, and Kate said irritably. 'I didn't say he was dead, did I? He's gone to sleep, that's all.'

'He's only asleep.'

'Father's not gone after all.'

'He's just having forty winks.'

'He's still with us, Father Jack.'

'Thank the Lord. We don't have to go home yet.'

Chapter Four

———————◆———————

The foyer of the tiny theatre was empty when Tracey looked through the doors. She shook them, but they wouldn't budge. The clock inside showed five past seven. The notice outside announced the play wouldn't start until eight o'clock.

'Damn!' she muttered mildly, surprising herself, for her language was inclined to be overripe when she was annoyed, which admittedly was rare. Life for Tracey had been a struggle, with an unstable mother deserted by a rat-bag father to support as well as two useless brothers who had made a career out of being unemployed. She had grown up an admirably self-possessed young woman, with a sensitivity few people witnessed apart from her patients and her mother, and with a healthy contempt for men in general and the ones in her own family in particular.

'I need to sit down before I fall down.' For some reason, she felt extraordinarily calm and relaxed. All her worries, and there were many, seemed very far away. In fact, she could hardly remember what they were. Glancing down the road, she saw Pauline march briskly out of sight around a bend.

'Damn!' she said, mildly again, rattling the doors a second time. If someone came, she'd ask if she could buy a ticket and sit in the theatre till the play started. It might even be possible to have a cup of tea. She gave the doors a final half-hearted rattle but they stayed closed.

'Ah, you're here!' A man had appeared from nowhere and was regarding her with unconcealed pleasure. He was an extremely handsome man, young, not very tall, with long silky brown hair and huge blue eyes. His nose and mouth were perfectly chiselled as if from snow-white marble. He wore a floppy white shirt and tight black velvet trousers that gave him a dashing, Byronic charm. 'I can't tell you how pleased I am to see you. Our Lady Agatha went down late this afternoon with one of those frightful bugs, as Peter no doubt told you. It's such a tiny part, we didn't have an understudy, and our spare actresses are all too old.' He put a delicate white hand to his smooth marble brow and pretended to swoon. 'It was panic stations all round, I can tell you, until Peter said he knew someone he could ask to step in. How lovely of you to come at such short notice. I really appreciate it. The stage door is round this way.'

The words made no sense. Tracey graciously allowed her elbow to be taken, though under different circum-stances, i.e., had she been feeling more her normal herself, she would have shoved the elbow into the offending male's ribs with the earnest hope of breaking one. She didn't like men treating women as if they were witless invalids, unable to walk a few yards without the support of a hairy male arm, incapable of opening a door for themselves or carrying their own luggage.

Had Tracey been built differently, such independence would have been allowed to flourish. But Tracey was beautiful, breathtakingly beautiful, with chestnut hair and chestnut eyes, a nose to die for, and an eminently kissable mouth. Her voluptuous figure had been compared to that of Venus di Milo, once an icon for women, but now considered fat and overweight, except by men, who rushed in droves to open doors for the shapely Tracey. They fell over themselves to help her upstairs and down again, offered to carry things when Tracey was perfectly capable, if not more – she was a strong girl – of carrying them herself. They gave up their seats on buses and trains and Tracey would offer the seat to a woman older and plainer than herself who'd been ignored, male chivalry being distinctly choosy.

Lord Byron led her down a path at the side of the theatre and through a dilapidated door into the rear. Inside, he mysteriously shook her hand. 'I'm Mark Costello, the director. Tonight is a very special performance. Did Peter tell you?'

'No.' Tracey couldn't recall having met anyone called Peter, but the night's events were rather vague. Well, more than vague. She remembered arriving at Maloney's over an hour ago to meet Eileen O'Brien, but from that moment on, except for marching down the hill with Pauline, her mind was a blank. Peter must have been in the pub. Perhaps that's why she'd instinctively stopped outside the theatre. She'd agreed to do something, obviously, and wondered what it was. Sell programmes, perhaps. Sell programmes dressed as Lady Agatha, who-ever she may be.

'Well,' Mark Costello gushed, 'we've been running since Tuesday and tonight is our final performance. There's all sorts of dignitaries coming; two members of the Dáil and their families, a bishop, various celebrities from the theatre and media, plus, most importantly of all, a gentleman on the board of the Abbey Theatre.' He giggled nervously. 'I've been more than a year setting this up. The costumes cost a fortune to hire, and some of the cast are professionals and have to be paid.' He crossed his arms over his chest and emitted a breathy, fragrant sigh. 'It's always been my dream to direct at the Abbey, so world famous, as you know.'

'Oh, yes,' agreed Tracey, who'd never heard of it.

'I'm rather hoping to be talent spotted, as it were. Well, more than hoping. I'm desperate.' He giggled again. 'Desperately desperate. Until now, I've only directed amateurs. Tonight is my big chance.'

'Where did the money come from for everything?' Tracey enquired. She couldn't understand why he was telling her all this, but it seemed polite to show interest.

'I've used all my life savings,' he said simply. 'I wanted to do something grand, a classic, not some dull two-hander with minimal scenery that would depress the audience to death – if they came, that is. Oscar Wilde is my favourite playwright. Have you been in any of his plays before?'

'No,' Tracey said cautiously. Surely she hadn't agreed to be in one now! 'I saw *The Importance of Being Earnest* once on television. Look, what exactly is it you want me to do? Peter wasn't very clear about it.'

'Naughty Peter.' He rolled his big blue eyes. 'I want you to play Lady Agatha Carlisle, don't I?' The blue eyes stopped rolling, narrowing slightly. 'You've acted before, haven't you?'

'Well, yes. But what about the lines? I don't know them.' Tracey experienced several moments of panic but, as has been said before, she was an admirable young woman who made a point of never letting people down. If she'd promised this mysterious Peter to take a part in *Lady Windermere's Fan*, then she'd do it, no matter what hazards might lie ahead.

Mark wagged a pretty, doll-like finger. 'I'll be having words with Peter when I see him – he'll be here for the party afterwards. He should have told you, all Lady Agatha does is say, 'Yes, Mamma,' on thirteen separate occasions. You'll get the cue from your mother, the Duchess of Berwick. She asks a question and you reply demurely, 'Yes, Mamma.' You can do that, can't you?' He was beginning to look a trifle worried.

'Of course. But couldn't you have got someone else to take such a tiny role?'

'Not someone with stage experience, I couldn't,' he sniffed. 'You've no idea how awkward and self-conscious people look if they've never been on a stage before. Anyway, there was no need to get someone else. Peter offered to get you. He rang earlier and said you'd agreed and would be at the theatre by seven, which reminds me, it's a quarter past and the curtain goes up at eight. I'll show you to the dressing room. If you need help with make-up, ask Sarah – she's Lady Windermere. Had a part in *Emmerdale* last year, did Sarah,' he finished proudly.

The sound of Beethoven's Fifth tinkled from the back pocket of his velvet pants and he plucked out a dinky yellow mobile phone. 'Should I answer it?' He chewed his pretty lips.

'I wouldn't if I were you. It's almost certainly bad news.' She'd never had good news via her mobile since she'd got it.

'You're probably right. The cast are all here, which is all that matters. What a wise Lady Agatha you are!'

He switched the phone off and returned it to his pocket.

The dressing room was small and packed to the gills with women in massively bustled dresses. She was introduced as, 'Our replacement Lady Agatha,' and Mark Costello fluttered away.

The women regarded Tracey with somewhat alarming expressions of dismay. 'What size are you?' enquired one who was dressed in a plum-coloured brocade suit and a giant hat covered with ostrich feathers, who Tracey was later to discover was her mother, the Duchess of Berwick.

'Fourteen or sixteen, it depends on the fit,' she replied, with a feeling that something was terribly wrong.

'Lady Agatha's costumes are only size ten. They'll never go near you.'

'Trust a man to forget we wanted a little Lady Agatha, not some thumping great outsizer,' snapped a tall, waspish woman who turned out to be Sarah who'd appeared in *Emmerdale*. Offended, Tracey vowed never to watch it again.

'They'll *have* to fit. We'll *make* them,' cried a woman in a pink ballgown. 'Take your clothes off, dear, and we'll all have a go.'

Tracey was pulled and pummelled, pushed and pinched, into a long grey afternoon dress. Mounds of flesh were scooped up and squeezed inside the tight material and her pneumatic breasts became two cushiony pancakes as several pairs of hands tried to fasten the hooks and eyes at the back. She was told to breathe in and not breathe out again just in case embarrassing bits of her popped out and distracted the audience. A shawl was found that would hide the gaps at the back where the hooks and eyes refused to meet.

'Are you nervous, dear?' enquired the pink ballgown.

'Not a bit,' Tracey said serenely in a hushed voice, her lung power having been considerably diminished by the tightness of her costume. 'I'm quite looking forward to it.' It was entirely different to how she usually spent Saturday nights – either on duty or studying. The occasional outings to the cinema or the pub were always ruined because she felt guilty if she enjoyed herself. But now, she felt a bubble of excitement rise in her throat. She was about to appear in a play by Oscar Wilde, something she hadn't remotely considered possible when the evening had begun. It was a pity about the costume – she felt like a pilchard in a sardine tin – but she'd cope. Somehow, Tracey always managed to cope.

Mark Costello opened the door. He looked very pale and was visibly shaking. 'I'd like Lady Agatha to see the set, familiarise herself with it before the curtain goes up,' he said shakily.

'Calm down, Mark,' Lady Windermere ordered. 'It's gone well all week. By now, the cast have worked up a head of steam and tonight will be even better.'

'So much depends on it.' He looked close to tears.

'We're all aware of that, darling. Now, go away, else you'll give us all the jitters.'

Tracey got stiffly to her feet. She could hardly breathe, hardly move, and walking proved even harder. Everything hurt, including the grey satin shoes which were neither long enough or wide enough. She felt as if her entire body was being strangled by an over-enthusiastic ape.

She managed to limp as far as the stage with Mark Costello trembling at her side. The set was impressive: cream satin walls, silky rugs, a white sofa with a curled end

and gold legs and two tiny matching armchairs, an elegant
bureau, a few equally elegant half-round tables against the
walls each with a vase of real flowers, gold-framed
pictures, an elaborate mirror, and a massive crystal chan-
delier suspended centre stage. Floor-length windows
opened on to a stone terrace with flowering shrubs.

'It's fantastic,' Tracey whispered encouragingly.

'This is the Windermeres' morning room. I designed
the set myself. The furniture is genuine antique, all
borrowed from a local dealer. That wallpaper cost twelve
pounds a roll. What's happened to your voice?'

'I've lost half of it. Me lungs are being squashed
something awful.'

'Oh, my God! You can't whisper like that! The
audience won't hear you.'

The murmur of voices came from the other side of the
dusty curtain, the rustle of sweet papers, the occasional
cough. By now, the audience would be assembled.

'Every time I say, "Yes, Mamma," I'll nod emphatically just in case I can't be heard,' Tracey promised in a
husky whisper.

A man in a frock coat came on to the stage. 'Curtain
up in five minutes, Mark.'

'I think I'm going to die!' He grabbed Tracey's arm, a
dangerous thing to do, because the stitching of her frock
tensed audibly.

'Don't die till after the performance, there's a good
chap,' the man in the frock coat urged.

'I need a drink.'

'Then you shall have a drink. Come along.'

Lady Windermere appeared and casually draped herself along the white settee. A woman in turquoise wool
sat on one of the chairs.

'Sod off, Mark,' Lady Windermere said impatiently. 'The audience won't want to see you having a panic attack when the curtain goes up.'

Tracey went to wait in the wings with the Duchess of Berwick. They would be on in fifteen minutes, she was told.

The gist of the play seemed to be that Lord Windermere was two-timing Lady Windermere with an older woman, and the caddish Lord Darlington, with an eye on the main chance, was trying to persuade Lady Windermere to two-time Lord Windermere with *him*.

The Duchess of Berwick and her daughter, Lady Agatha, arrived on stage during the attempted seduction. Lady Agatha stood dutifully behind her mother's chair, keenly aware of the inherent danger present in attempting to sit down.

The two older women conducted an extended conversation, and Lady Agatha felt super-conscious of retaining an upright position while not saying a word. She felt inordinantly huge and prominent stuck behind the little white satin chair.

Her mother spoke to her at last. 'Agatha, darling!'

'Yes, Mamma,' Lady Agatha croaked, nodding furiously.

'Will you go and look over the photograph album I see over there?'

'Yes, Mamma.' She nodded furiously again, and hoped it wasn't titters she could hear from the audience, particularly when it took some time to locate the whereabouts of the photograph album.

A minute later. 'Agatha, darling!'

'Yes, Mamma.'

'Will you go out on the terrace and look at the sunset?'

'Yes, Mamma.'

Lady Agatha exited gratefully through the windows at the rear of the stage.

'*Stay there, within view of the audience!*' Mark Costello whispered frantically when she was about to step off the terrace and take refuge in the darkness of the wings, having lost all interest in Lady Windemere and being an actress, and wishing she'd never met Peter whatever-his-name-was and agreed to appear in such a silly play. This was turning out to be one of the rare situations when she wasn't able to cope, because in order to cope it was also necessary to inhale a certain amount of oxygen which she wasn't currently managing to do.

Mark Costello looked as if he might have been tearing his hair out. 'You have to go back on shortly. Sit on the terrace wall, look casual.'

'I can't bend and I feel the opposite of casual,' Lady Agatha murmured, and she spent the next five minutes attempting to look soulful while watching a beautiful sunset when in reality she was slowly choking to death.

'Agatha, darling!' her mother cried when Lady Agatha felt as if she was about to bust a gut.

'Yes, Mamma.'

'Come and bid good bye to Lady Windermere and thank her for your charming visit.'

Lady Agatha smiled weakly at Lady Windermere, before exiting left with her mother.

'Christ Almighty!' Tracey gasped, stumbling into the dressing room and tearing off her costume. Hooks and eyes flew dangerously across the room. 'Is that it?' she demanded of her stage mother.

'I'm afraid not, dear. The next act is the ballroom scene. I have a horrid feeling your ballgown is a tighter fit than the frock you're now wearing.'

'I'm not sure if I can stand it. I keep getting the urge to vomit.' Mark should have got bigger costumes or a smaller actress. Or at least, Peter should.

Mark Costello came into the dressing room accompanied by a petite young woman who was weeping copiously. Tracey, sitting in front of the mirror, covered her recently and thankfully released breasts with a towel. Her eyes met the hot eyes of the producer in the mirror.

'You bitch!' he snapped.

'I beg your pardon!'

'What the hell do you think you're playing at? *This* is Lady Agatha.' He pointed to the tearful girl. '*This* is the person Peter asked to play the part tonight. Why didn't you say something? Why did you let me think it was *you* Peter had asked?'

'Because I thought I was,' Tracey said lamely. 'Anyroad,' she nodded at the girl, '*she* was late.'

'There was a fire in one of those big houses on the hill,' the girl sobbed. 'There were fire engines and an ambulance blocking the road and I couldn't get through.' She turned to Mark. 'I tried to call on my mobile, but yours was switched off. I still couldn't contact you when I was only a few minutes from the theatre to tell you I was on my way. There would have been time to change into my costume before I was due to go on, but when I arrived you'd already started and you already had a Lady Agatha. I was so looking forward to playing her again. I've done the part twice before in rep. I felt so upset, I just went into the Ladies and cried and cried and cried.'

'You shall go on in the second act,' Mark announced, beaming rays of hate at Tracey through the mirror. 'This woman is utterly hopeless.'

'Don't be so bloody stupid, Mark,' the Duchess of Berwick said cuttingly. 'Have you lost your reason or something? Do you think the audience won't notice that Lady Agatha has lost four stone and shrunk six inches between one act and the next? *And* changed the colour of her hair!'

The ballgown was white satin with gold lace trimming and a tiny bustle. It had miniature puff sleeves and a low-cut bosom, and took the efforts of the entire female cast, including the genuine Lady Agatha, to encase Tracey within its narrow satin confines. The urge to vomit returned with a vengeance.

At the commencement of Act Two, the Duchess and her daughter were the first guests to arrive at the ball. They were received by Lady Windermere.

'You have kept those five dances for Mr Hopper, Agatha?' enquired the Duchess.

'Yes, Mamma.' She wasn't up to dancing and neither was her gown. To her relief, music was coming from off stage where the mythical ballroom apparently was. Mr Hopper entered shortly afterwards, a callow, yellow youth, wearing a too big collar into which his negligible chin popped in and out.

Lady Agatha felt resentful at being forced to dance with such an unprepossessing creature. 'Yes, Mamma,' she said sulkily when they were ordered into the ballroom by her mother.

Mr Hopper couldn't take his eyes off his partner's yawning cleavage while they waited in the wings to go back on stage. 'Will you marry me?' he whispered through large, broken teeth.

'No, I bloody won't!'

'I didn't mean it.' He looked hurt. 'I was just trying to be realistic. I'm supposed to take you on to the terrace and propose. I want you to come with me to Australia. Did you know that?'

'No, I bloody didn't.'

'There's no need to get snotty. It's only a play.'

It didn't feel like a play to Tracey. By now, it felt eerily real and horribly confusing. She had positively no intention of going all the way to Australia with the objectionable Mr Hopper. Who did he think he was? The place was full of criminals who'd been deported from England in boats – she remembered learning about it in school. Another thing, Oscar Wilde was supposed to be gay. You'd have thought he would have had the sensitivity to create female characters who weren't just objects, there purely for the convenience of men. She was a *nurse*, for God's sake. She had a responsible job, whereas Mr Hopper looked as if he collected trolleys at Sainsbury's.

'Agatha, darling!' The Duchess beckoned her on stage.

'Yes, Mamma.'

'Did Mr Hopper propose?'

'Yes, Mamma.'

'And what answer did you give him, dear child?'

'No, Mamma.'

A strangled cry came from the wings and Mark Costello could be glimpsed frantically waving his neat little arms. The prompt whispered something audibly unintelligible.

The Duchess looked momentarily taken aback. 'Surely you mean "yes", my dear one.'

'*No*, Mamma,' Lady Agatha said firmly.

'You don't mind my taking Agatha off to Australia, then, Duchess?' Mr Hopper clearly hadn't been listening.

'Did you say that, Agatha?' enquired the Duchess, wincing slightly as she waited for her daughter's reply.'

'No, Mamma.' Lady Agatha tossed her head indignantly and the sudden movement caused both breasts to pop out of her white satin gown. The audience giggled.

'You are probably right,' her mother said smoothly. 'There are lots of vulgar people in London, but at least there are no horrid kangaroos leaping about. Well, good night, Lady Windermere. Agatha and I have enjoyed ourselves enormously. As for Mr Hopper, he must answer for himself. Oh!' She gave an impromptu and unconvincing chuckle. 'It would seem my dear little girl is urgently in need of a dose of laudanum.'

Lady Agatha had rushed on to the terrace and was being violently sick on one of the potted plants.

The audience were shrieking with laughter when Tracey felt her arm being seized and she was dragged off the terrace, through the wings, out of the theatre, and pushed into a car. She felt too wretched to protest. She couldn't remember having felt so thoroughly sick before. It must be food poisoning. Urgent treatment was necessary. Her body needed flushing out.

'Are you taking me to hospital?' she asked weakly of the driver, of whose identity she was so far ignorant because she could hardly see.

'No, I'm fucking not,' said Mark Costello, for it was he. Rage must have blessed him with the strength of ten men for him to have dragged someone as large as Tracey as far as he had. 'I'm taking you somewhere very far away, where there'll be no one else around. Then I'm going to kill you.'

'Why?' Tracey asked weakly.

'*Why!*' he screeched. '*WHY!*' Because you've ruined everything: my play, my reputation, my dream of making it in the theatre. You've made a laughing stock of me. I couldn't bring myself to direct another amateur production, presuming anyone would want me to. I won't be able to hold my head up in Dublin from this night on. Oh, and my fucking life savings have gone up in smoke. Is that enough to explain why?'

'I was only trying to help.'

'Fortunately, you won't be in a position to help anyone after tonight,' he sneered, 'Because you'll be dead.'

'Don't forget, it was you who approached me outside the theatre,' Tracey said reasonably. Perhaps it was self-preservation, the thought that Mark Costello might possibly cause her serious harm, that made her feel a trifle better. He genuinely did seem mad enough to kill her, or at least try. The car was veering crazily along roads that were getting darker and the houses fewer. 'I just went along with things. I thought I was doing you a favour.'

'A favour! Some favour! All you had to do was say I had the wrong person. Going along with things is what caused this fucking disaster. Did you do it on purpose?' He frowned suspiciously. 'Was this all a set-up? Whose idea was it? Was it Peter's? He's always been jealous of me. Do you *know* Peter?'

'I'm not sure.'

'You're not sure!' he screamed and the car nearly skidded off the road, narrowly missing an elderly couple walking a dog. 'How can you not be sure if you know a person? You either know them or you don't.'

'I had a blackout earlier.' Tracey explained chummily in the hope of calming him down, 'Between six and seven o'clock. I thought I might have met Peter then.'

'Do you have blackouts often?' he asked sarcastically. 'Did you have one during my play? For example, the time you decided to change the plot rather than follow the one that Oscar Wilde had so brilliantly written? And the time you were nauseatingly sick in full view of the audience? Oh, and don't forget the partial striptease. Oh, God!' he sobbed. 'Those poor actors! There were two more acts to go. How on earth are they managing? I shouldn't have deserted them. Once an audience gets in a certain mood, they'll laugh at fucking anything.'

'Perhaps it would be best if we went back.'

'We? Oh, no, *I'll* go back. I'll go back when I've killed you. Besides, if you showed your face in that theatre again, the cast would lynch you. I'm not the only person whose life you've ruined tonight.' He gasped. 'Oh, Lord in heaven!'

'What's the matter?'

'I've just remembered, Mr Hopper's girlfriend was videoing the whole thing. I must make sure the tape is destroyed.'

'I wouldn't if I were you,' Tracey said sensibly. 'You never know, one of these days you might like to watch it. In a few months' time, you'll find yourself laughing over what happened tonight.'

Which was just about the worse advice she could have offered at such a sensitive time. The car turned into a narrow lane with tall, tangled bushes either side and screeched to a halt.

'I've just remembered,' Mark Costello remarked coldly. 'You said the same thing earlier when I was about to answer my mobile. "I wouldn't if I were you." It would have been Lady Agatha to say she was on her way.'

'I was only trying to help. I thought it might be bad news.'

'Your trying to help was been the cause of the entire fucking tragedy. Are you cold?'

'Yes.' Tracey was shivering.

'Then take my scarf. It's pure silk. Here, let me put it round your neck.'

Before she knew what was happening, a silk scarf was thrown around her neck and Mark Costello began to pull, though by now the strength of ten men had dissipated somewhat, and the strength of a dimunitive theatrical director was puny when compared to that of Tracey, who had been forced to defend her honour on more occasions than Mark Costello had had hot dinners. Surprisingly for such a desirable young woman, at twenty-three, her virtue still remained intact.

A blow to his stomach followed by a powerful punch to his little round jaw, was enough to make him release the scarf and collapse back in the seat, gasping for breath.

Tracey tried the passenger door and was relieved to find it unlocked. She tumbled out of the car, into the bushes, behind which was hidden a ditch full of slimy, rotting leaves and other unspeakable things she preferred not to think about just then. She lay there shivering, this time with fear, because she hadn't seriously thought Mark had meant to kill her. The door slammed and she assumed he was closing the passenger's side and was about to return to Dublin. Instead, when she raised her head, she saw he was rooting around inside the boot.

He was looking for something to kill her with!

Stumbling up the other side of the ditch, she found herself in an open field. In the black distance, an occasional light pinpointed the occasional farm. She began to run, not across the field, but alongside the ditch. About fifty yards on, she dived back in and lay completely still, hardly flinching when something bit her leg. Minutes later, she heard footsteps on the road. She had thought Mark would come on to the field after her, but perhaps he'd been too stunned to notice where she'd gone. She shrank into the dank leaves, hardly breathing, as the footsteps came nearer.

'Lady Agatha! Lady Agatha! I was only trying to frighten you. Come out, come out, wherever you are, there's a darling, and we'll go back to Dublin.'

He might have been speaking the truth, but Tracey wasn't prepared to risk it. She'd sooner make her own way back, even if it meant walking all the way.

'Lady Agatha! I don't know your real name, do I? I never thought to ask. Don't be frightened. I won't harm you. I was only pretending. I had no intention of killing you.'

The footsteps faded as he walked back to the car. 'Lady Agatha! Lady Agatha!' The words sounded mournful in the still night air. 'Lady Agatha!' Then, 'Oh, fuck it.' A door slammed, an engine roared, and the car backed full pelt out of the lane.

Tracey got to her feet and watched through the bushes until the headlights disappeared. She waited still until the sound of the engine faded completely and she could hear nothing at all, before climbing out of the ditch and limping painfully down the lane towards Dublin.

Her feet hurt in the too small shoes and the gown

pinched in the places where it was still attached to her body. She seemed to be carrying with her a revolting smell from the ditch and the bite on her leg had begun to throb. She was also carrying the scarf with which Mark had tried to throttle her, or had pretended to, she wasn't sure. She tied it around her bust where the dress no longer reached.

Tracey was a stalwart, not given much to complaining, but now she felt exceptionally sorry for herself. She'd come to Ireland for a hen party, had had a blackout, fucked up a performance of *Lady Windermere's Fan*, and had nearly been murdered.

And the night was still only young. She wondered what else it might have in store?

Chapter Five

There was a tree by the bus stop, bare and spindly. It curved over a bench on which it had scattered its crisp golden leaves. Pauline pushed the leaves away and sat down. She stared at the navy-blue sky through a cobweb of branches, pleasantly tired, and looking forward to the comfort and privacy of her Donna-less hotel room where she could examine in detail how she felt. She had the exhilarating sensation that her head was a balloon and the only thoughts it contained were light, airy, nothing thoughts.

It was a sensation she would have liked to maintain for the rest of her life, but she knew that, as sure as eggs were eggs, her current happiness would eventually fade, her problems would return, and her thoughts would once again be dark and heavy: her lousy marriage to Dennis, for instance, her stressful job.

She was glad she'd come to Dublin. Though to be frank, at the moment, she could have been almost anywhere in the world, apart from somewhere exotic, such as in the middle of a desert or up a mountain. The bus stop was situated in a well-lit, relatively busy residential road of semi-detached houses. A few cars were parked nearby, including a big, black Mercedes, the sort her husband, Dennis, lusted after with the same enthusiasm he'd lusted after Pauline during the first years of their marriage. She could hear people's televisions. There was that lovely, Saturday-night feeling in the air, electric, that she remembered from her teenage years when weekends used to be special. These days, Saturday and Sunday merged into the other days and meant nothing at all.

The relative tranquility was briefly and noisily disturbed when two fire engines went hurtling past, away from the city, sirens blaring.

Pauline sighed contentedly when the clamour faded, and suddenly became aware she had two handbags; her own smart black patent leather and a shabby brown suede shoulder bag with a fringe that she recognised as Donna's. It meant Donna was stranded somewhere without money and her credit cards – and her poisonous ciggies. So mellow was Pauline's mood she actually felt sorry for the long, worm-like woman whom she normally couldn't abide. Emma had told her that Donna's ex-husband was a truly revolting guy. Well, Pauline knew all about truly revolting guys, having been married to the king for nearly fifteen years. Next time she saw Donna, she'd be more friendly. After all, they had something significant in common.

One of the first things she'd do was persuade her to stop smoking. It would show how much she truly cared – Pauline cared about all sorts of things tonight that normally she wouldn't have given a damn about because she had more than enough cares of her own. Her father had died ten years ago of lung cancer. While he was dying, he'd cautioned his children never to smoke. 'I wish someone had stopped me!' he'd said more than once.

74

Well, *she* would stop Donna. What's more, she'd make a start right now. She opened the suede bag, removed a packet of Marlboros, and threw it into the rubbish bin attached to the bus stop.

There!

Pauline felt smugly pleased with herself, but after a while it crossed her mind that chucking away the most important contents of Donna's handbag might not provide the basis for a long and lasting friendship. Indeed, it might even cause the very opposite. At some time tonight, Donna would turn up urgently in need of an injection of nicotine and she would be cross when she found her bag had been raided. Better to put the ciggies back and start the process of stopping Donna smoking in a more leisurely way, with gentle little lectures from time to time.

The rubbish bin was only half-full, but the Marlboros had dropped to the bottom. Pauline was rooting through, trying to find them, when she touched something that felt very much like yet another handbag. Frowning slightly, she pulled out a sensible leather satchel with buckles and straps, the sort she'd carried to school herself a million years ago, but you didn't see much of these days, youngsters preferring garish nylon things with fluffy animals attached or football slogans.

She was about to open it, expecting to find school books and possibly an uneaten sandwich lunch, when one of the cars parked quietly along the road, suddenly roared into life and screeched to a halt in front of her. Two men leaped out, and Pauline was roughly dragged across the pavement and bundled into the back, along with her three bags. One of the men, the biggest, fell in beside her and the suspension creaked in protest. The other man got in the driver's seat and the car sped away.

'Where is it?' the big man snarled, seizing Pauline's wrist and squeezing hard. The streetlights made it possible for her to see he was a most unpleasant looking individual, with a square, red face screwed in a scowl. The lack of hair on his head was probably due to all the in-built fertilising agent required to produce hair having concentrated itself on a pair of eyebrows that grew like miniature forests, shading his eyes.

Pauline gave the meaty hand clutching her wrist a sharp slap. 'You're hurting me,' she snapped. 'How dare you!'

Surprised, the man let go. 'Where is it?' he repeated aggressively.

'Where is what?'

'The kid. Where's the bloody kid?'

'A child? Is that how you refer to a child, as 'it'? Are we talking about a boy or a girl here?'

'You know bloody well it's a boy.'

'I know no such thing, and in future, refer to the child as 'he' or 'him', not 'it'. I find that most offensive.'

'Look, lady,' the man put his face in hers. 'I'll refer to the kid any way I like, see. I don't give a shit if you find it offensive. I won't ask again, *where is it?*'

'I won't answer till you ask properly. And I'd prefer it if you didn't swear.'

'Ask properly and don't swear, Seamus.' The driver spoke for the first time. He sounded more reasonable than his companion, quite polite.

'Where is *he* then?' Seamus asked sulkily.

'I haven't the faintest notion what you're talking about.' Pauline had been enjoying waiting for the bus, experiencing nice thoughts for a change. These people were raining on her parade and she felt annoyed rather than scared.

'Listen, lady,' the big man began threateningly, but Pauline interrupted. 'You've seen too many films. No-body says things like, "Listen, lady," in real life.'

The driver spoke again, 'Why did you take the money?'

'What money?'

'The money in the bag.'

'What bag?'

'The bag you took out the bin.'

'Oh, *this* bag.' Pauline held up the satchel. 'I didn't know it had money in, did I? I was looking for cigarettes when I found it.'

The driver laughed. 'Come off it! You don't look the sort who scrabbles for cigarettes in bins.'

'I was looking for the cigarettes I'd just thrown in the bin, if you must know,' Pauline said indignantly. 'I had second thoughts and decided to take them back.'

'You must be chronically short of willpower if you only gave up smoking for half a second.'

'I don't smoke. They're someone else's ciggies.' Which reminded Pauline she hadn't found them. Donna would do her nut when she got her bag back.

'This is a mad woman we've got here, Ralph,' the big man complained. 'She's more than a wee touched if you ask me.'

The car slowed down and turned into the drive of a large, old house which had lights on in every window. None of the curtains had been closed. The driver hooted, the door opened, and a woman came rushing out as if she'd been waiting on the other side for the car to return.

'You were quick! Have you got him! Where is he? Where's my baby?' She opened the rear door and burst into tears when she saw only Pauline and the man with the overdeveloped eyebrows. 'Who's this?' she sobbed. 'Where's Harry?'

The driver got out and took the weeping woman in his arms. 'Everything went wrong, Nicky, darling. We'll have to start all over again.'

'Didn't someone turn up for the money?' the woman cried.

'Yes. *She* did.' The man nodded at Pauline as she climbed out of the car. 'But I'm inclined to believe she's got nothing to do with it. She's just a crazy woman, a bag lady of some sort, who was rooting through the bin and found the satchel.'

'Here, do you mind!' Pauline drew herself to her full five feet, four inches. 'I happen to be the assistant headteacher of a junior and infant school. *You're* the ones who are mad. I was merely waiting for a bus. Next minute, I was thrown into a car and accused of doing something mysterious. I'm still not sure what it is.' She sniffed and tossed her head. 'So far, no one's done me the courtesy of explaining exactly what it is I'm supposed to have done.'

'Torture her, Ralph,' the woman said tersely. 'Tear her hair out, her fingernails, pluck out her eyes. Make her tell where my Harry is.'

Pauline laughed. 'Don't be stupid.' She went towards the open front door. 'Is there any chance of a cup of tea while someone tells me what's going on? My name's Pauline Gallagher, by the way.'

'I told you she was mad, didn't I?' said Ralph. 'Any sane person would have run for their lives the minute they got out the car, whether they were involved in the kidnapping or not.'

Pauline had taken charge. 'So, your little boy was kid- napped,' she said over a cup of tea in the large comfor- table kitchen, the sort with lots of repatriated pine that made it look a hundred years old, yet had every con- ceivable modern device. She was sitting on one side of a long pine table and her three new acquaintances were on the other, as if she were conducting a class in school. 'When did it happen?'

'Yesterday afternoon, when he came out of school,' Nicky said tearfully. She was a tall, dramatic woman in her mid-twenties, with enviable cheek bones and long, untidy black hair. Her brown eyes were bloodshot with weeping. Just now, she looked more than a little un- hinged. Ralph was slightly older, a lanky, drooping man, with a placid, kindly face and a weak chin. The recent shenanigans must have been an effort for someone so blatantly gentle. Neither were Irish and spoke with a middle-class Home Counties accent. Seamus the Eye- brows was Ralph's friend who'd just come out the Army.

'I usually pick Harry up from school,' Nicky said, 'even though it's only just round the corner. Yesterday, I was a few minutes late. I waited for ages, but he didn't appear. I should have been more careful, I know, even though Harry's five and a half and very sensible. I thought he knew better than to go off with a stranger. I've had no contact with Tony for over six years. Anyway, I'd never told him about Harry. He didn't know he had a son.'

'Who's Tony?' Pauline enquired.

'Harry's father. I met him in the States. I used to work for the United Nations in New York.'

'Were you married?'

'No.'

'What business is that of yours?' Seamus said pugnaciously.

'I'd like to get the whole picture straight, that's why,' Pauline replied in kind. 'I'm part of this now, aren't I? Don't forget, I was recently kidnapped meself by your goodselves. I could call the police if I had a mind.'

'Oh, *please* don't!' Nicky said frantically. She reached out and put her hand on Pauline's arm. 'We haven't involved the Gardai. I'd sooner we sorted this out ourselves.'

'I wouldn't dream of it,' Pauline assured her. 'I was just pointing out the obvious to this big ape.' She made a face at Seamus. 'Are you saying it was Harry's father who kidnapped him?'

'We know it is,' Ralph said quietly. 'He called Nicky last night to say he had the boy. He pointed out Harry was born in the States and is therefore an American citizen. He wants regular access – or ten grand which we were to leave in the bin by the bus stop by eight o'clock tonight. Once he had the cash he promised to leave us alone.'

'Why has he suddenly appeared on the scene now, after all this time?' Pauline wanted to know.

Nicky began to cry. 'Somehow, he must have found out about Harry. He was terribly cross. He said I should have told him.'

'Why didn't you?'

'Because, Pauline, I didn't want him to know. Tony Bianco is a crook, a member of some New York Mafia family. I dumped him the minute I found out. When I discovered I was expecting a baby, I moved to another part of the States. I had medical insurance and some good friends over there. Once Harry was born, I found another job, but when it came time for him to go to school, I decided to come home. In London, I met Ralph, we got married almost straight away, and me and Harry moved to Ireland where he works. I never expected to see Tony Bianco again.'

'It must be some dead piffling Mafia family he belongs to if he's come all the way to Ireland for a measly ten thousand pounds,' Pauline remarked.

'Oh, Tony could buy and sell Dublin if he wanted to. It's just his way of torturing me. He's good at torturing people.'

Pauline remembered the things Nicky had suggested Ralph do to her and thought she didn't sound so bad at it herself. 'And the ten thousand pounds was in the bag in the rubbish bin by the bus stop?'

'Not bloody likely,' growled Seamus. 'There's a newspaper in the bag. The money won't be handed over except as a direct return for the kid. There's a note in there telling Tony as much. If he'd turned up, me and Ralph intended to follow him and get the kid back. We thought it was you who'd come to collect the bag on Tony's behalf, so we decided to grab you and make you tell us where he and Harry were holed up.'

'Do I look like a gangster's moll?'

'Not really,' Ralph conceded. Seamus and Nicky shook their heads.

Pauline, the epitome of respectability in her neat, navy blue suit and white blouse, lightly permed brown hair, with merely a faint suggestion of powder and lipstick on her earnest, unremarkable face, could not possibly have looked more different to the impression usually given of a gangster's moll.

'Well, what are we going to do now?' she asked. The problem, like disruptive children and school budgets, had become her own. She had a feeling in her bones that Harry wouldn't come to any harm, but felt guilty for having disrupted the 'drop' as it was called in films. What distressed her most was knowing the agony Nicky was going through while she worried over her lost child, for Pauline, too, had lost a child, a little boy called Jamie, though in her case it had been final. It had happened thirteen years ago and she and Dennis hadn't made love since. She sighed. She would do everything in her limited power to get Harry back if only to ease another woman's pain. Her own pain would never go away.

'I suppose we'll just have to wait for Tony to ring again,' said Ralph, making a face. Nicky uttered a tiny scream. Seamus scowled.

Pauline had an idea. 'He mightn't have been to the bus stop yet to collect the bag.' She looked at her watch. 'It's only a few minutes past eight.'

'So what!' Seamus grunted.

'So why don't I take the bag back, sit with it on me knee, like, and see what happens.'

'What d'you think's likely to happen?' Seamus again.

'I've absolutely no idea,' Pauline confessed. 'Possibly nothing at all. If he's been, you'll just have to wait till he rings again, as Ralph said. If he hasn't, if he turns up, then we'll take it from there – I mean, I will.' She pursed her lips. 'I'll give him a piece of my mind if I get the opportunity, Mafia, or no Mafia. Fancy kidnapping your own child!'

82

'That could be dangerous.' Ralph looked concerned. 'Tony's a pretty dodgy character.'

'I don't mind,' Pauline said stoutly.

'You're very brave.' Nicky squeezed her hand.

'No, I'm not. I'm very drunk, if the truth be known. Another night, and I'd've run a mile from all this, but someone bought us a drink in a pub earlier tonight, and I haven't felt the same since, though it was only supposed to be Irish lemonade. The friends I came with are scattered to the winds.' She wondered where they were, Emma, Donna and Tracey – and Rosemary, left in the Ladies' lavatory in Maloney's. She hoped they were coping without her.

'If you're going to go, then shouldn't you go now?' Seamus said pointedly. 'The sooner the better.'

'You're right.' Pauline gulped the remainder of the tea. 'What a pity I haven't got my mobile. I could have kept in touch if necessary.'

'Take mine,' Nicky said instantly. 'Just press auto and 1, and you'll get through to the house.'

'Ta.'

A quietly confident Pauline was dropped off at the bus stop she'd been snatched from a mere half-hour ago.

'We'll wait further down the road, see what happens,' Ralph assured her. Nicky had stayed at home in case Tony called.

Pauline returned to the seat, clutching the satchel prominently on her knee. She didn't feel quite so carefree as she'd done when she'd been at the bus stop earlier. Her head felt more like a football than a balloon, just as empty, but heavier and as if it had been kicked around a bit. She twiddled her thumbs, stopping mid-twiddle when a tiny Fiat Punto drew up behind the black Mercedes that had been there before, and a slight, undernourished man with a straggly moustache got out and came towards her.

'Are you waiting for someone?' he enquired. It clearly wasn't Tony Bianco because he had an Irish accent, and looked too insipid to be any sort of gangster. She could smell the alcohol on him when he was still several feet away.

'I might be,' Pauline replied enigmatically.

'It could be me.'

'It could well be.'

He sat down on the bench, unnecessarily close, she thought. 'I haven't seen you around these parts before.'

'That's because I haven't been around these parts before. Does it matter?'

'It doesn't matter a tinker's cuss to me, sweetheart.' He winked. 'I like your image. Very demure.'

Pauline gave him a curious glance. 'My image is irrelevant. I'm just an intermediary.'

'Is that what they call it nowadays!'

'You probably weren't expecting me to be here.'

'Not at this bus stop, no. It's a pleasant surprise.'

'That's strange.' Pauline frowned. 'It's the place Tony said to use.'

'It's a good place, very convenient.' He nudged her playfully in the ribs with his elbow. 'You don't look as if you do this very often, sweetheart.'

'How often is a person called upon to be an intermediary?'

'Are you doing it for a bet, like? Or are you just short of a few bob to pay the electricity?'

'I'm not doing it for money,' Pauline said stiffly. 'I'm doing it because it's my duty as a citizen.'

The man started to shake for some reason. 'There should be more women around like you,' he said huskily. 'Shall we go? How long have you got?'

'I'd like to get it over with as quickly as possible.'

'In that case, let's do it in the back of me wee car.'

'Do what?'

He sniggered. 'Intermediate, if that's the word.'

It dawned on Pauline that wires had somehow been crossed. She wasn't quite sure what the man wanted, but suspected he had nothing to do with the kidnapping. 'Look, did Tony Bianco send you?'

'No, my little sweetheart. Nature sent me. In other words, I'm desperate for a shag.' He took her arm with the intention of leading her across the road towards the Punto. Pauline was about to inform him angrily that his intention was a vain one, when the engine of the Mercedes sprang into life. Two men leapt out, grabbed Pauline, and for the second time that night she was thrown into the back of a strange car.

'This is getting rather boring,' she said with a yawn.

'Shut yer bleedin' cakehole,' snarled the man sitting next to her in the back, leaving her in no doubt as to his nationality.

'Where are we going?'

'I said shut up and give us that bag.'

'If you insist,' she said, hurt, closing her mouth and handing him the satchel.

The men wore hoods with slits for the eyes and mouth. They were altogether a more sinister pair than Ralph and Seamus, who were pussy cats in comparison. Pauline, however, was determined to remain calm, though she couldn't help but feel slightly scared. What had she let herself in for? She wished it was the money, not an old newspaper, in the satchel. Her fists clenched until the nails bit painfully into her palms, remembering the two lost little boys, Jamie and Harry. At least she would play a part in getting one of them back.

The car was driving away from the city, deep into the countryside, much too fast. They passed a figure, a strange woman dressed in a long, tattered white frock, like a ghost, limping along the road. For some reason, Pauline thought she looked familiar, but she couldn't possibly be. Some miles afterwards, they turned into a narrow earth path with a sign indicating it led to a place called Orchard Farm. The tyres bumped and veered over the uneven ground. A curve of moon had appeared, stars twinkled in the sky, there was a slight breeze.

They drew up outside a large, single-storey building, presumably Orchard Farm, which appeared to be in darkness.

'Out!' commanded the man on the back seat. He opened the door.

'Thank you,' Pauline said sarcastically, but it was wasted.

The driver knocked three times on the front door of the building, waited a few seconds, then unlocked it and went in. Pauline was pushed in behind.

She blinked at the scene of cheerful domestic bliss that met them. The room was large and low-ceilinged, obviously a converted farmhouse, with a massive brick fireplace in which a log fire crackled, spitting sparks. The fitted carpet was cherry red, matching exactly the thick, velvet curtains. A cream upholstered settee that looked big enough to accommodate an entire football team stretched in front of the fire, with an accompanying armchair either side for the manager and the referee.

Pink shaded wall-lights cast a rosy glow on to the ceiling. In the corner, a television was on without the sound and, in the centre of the room, two people were laughing and joshing each other as they played snooker on a full-size table: a man of about forty, the handsomest, most charismatic man Pauline had ever seen, at least six foot tall, with dark, crinkly hair and olive skin, wearing jeans and a white sweatshirt with the sleeves pushed up, and a smiling, slender boy of about five, also dark and olive-skinned, quite obviously his son. The child could barely see over the edge of the table and stood on tiptoe to wield the cue.

'I think I've got you, Pops,' the boy said.

The man looked up and saw Pauline and her most recent kidnappers standing by the door. He threw the cue on to the table. 'You beat me again, kiddo. Look, I've got a little business to discuss. Watch TV in your room, for a while. Hey, kiddo?'

'Okay, Pops.' The child pretended to punch his father in the stomach. 'Can I have a can of Coke?'

'Help yourself, kiddo. It's in the kitchen.'

This, presumably, was Tony Bianco and Harry, and Pauline found it incredible that the two had developed such a rapport within the space of little more than twenty-four hours. According to Nicky, Tony had only recently discovered he had a son. They'd never seen each other before yesterday afternoon.

'You look puzzled,' Tony Bianco said when the boy had gone.

'I am,' Pauline confirmed.

'Sit down.' He nodded towards the cream settee, then turned to the men by the door. 'Have you looked in the bag, Sydney?'

'It's just an old newspaper, boss.'

Both men had removed their hoods, revealing the driver to be a blonde young man with a sneering, aristocratic expression. He wore an expensive, well-cut suit. His companion, Sydney, had a sour, bitter face that appeared to have been chipped out of decayed stone. Pauline couldn't imagine him ever smiling. The most astonishing thing about him was his hair; long, thinning at the front, and secured in a bun at the nape of his neck.

'I thought as much.' Tony Bianco's handsome face was grim, thin lips stern. 'Any followers on the way?'

'Yeah, but we got rid of 'em. A Mercedes can outrun a crappy Probe any day.'

'Thanks a million. Why don't you and Roxy help yourselves to something from the kitchen?'

Sydney took the hint. 'Give us a call if you need us.'

'I will. Oh, and guys, stay off the booze. I want you both stone cold sober over the next few hours.'

'Sure thing, boss.' The door closed on the two men, and Tony Bianco sat beside Pauline on the cream settee. Pauline had lost all interest in men years ago, but felt a surprising twist in her heart and an unexpected turbulence in her guts, at the sight of the dark, brooding profile and the long, strong hands clasped elegantly around the jean-clad knees. Her thoughts, usually so practical, rather trite, unimaginative, common or garden thoughts, took a wildly erotic turn, and she found herself hoping – nay, *praying* – that Tony Bianco would push her down on to the settee, drag off her clothes, and make love to her in front of the crackling fire. Her disappointment was intense when he did no such thing.

'Are you a friend of Nicky's?' he asked.

She shook her head. 'No. I was just waiting for a bus

and somehow got involved. I've to give you a message. You're not getting the ten thousand pounds except as a direct return for Harry.'

'I don't want ten thousand pounds.'

'You don't! Oh, dear, I find this all very confusing.' She looked at him earnestly and remembered she had promised to give him a stern ticking off for having kidnapped his child. 'I can imagine how wonderful it must be to have found Harry,' she said understandingly, 'but Nicky is suffering terribly. You probably don't realise how cruel you're being. I think you should let her have him back immediately.'

Tony didn't answer straight away. 'What's your name?' he asked eventually.

'Pauline Gallagher.'

'Can I call you Pauline?'

'Please.' It gave her a little thrill, just hearing him pronounce her name.

'Would you like a drink, Pauline?'

'I wouldn't mind an orange juice.'

He went over to a door, opened it and said something. A minute later, Sydney came in with a glass of orange. Tony had opened a cupboard and was helping himself to something short. Before sitting down again, he threw another log on the fire and Pauline could smell the dampness of the wood.

'Cheers!' He touched her glass with his and, for a moment, Pauline worried that she was being softened up, consorting with the enemy. She remembered Nicky's haggard face and pulled herself together. This was a man who had kidnapped a poor, desperate woman's child. It might well be his child, too, but he'd known nothing about Harry until recently.

'Nicky isn't Harry's mother,' Tony said softly. 'I'm telling you this because you seem a nice lady. I don't want you thinking bad of me, and I don't want Nicky fooling you no longer.'

Pauline almost dropped her glass. 'What!'

'Nicky has never had a baby, at least, not to my knowledge, not since I've known her. I took her on as a nursemaid for Harry when he was only a few months old. My wife had just died.'

'But she said she worked for the United Nations in New York!'

'She worked in New York, but for me.' He sipped his drink and stared thoughtfully into the glass. 'She was a great nursemaid. I couldn't have found better. We got on well. She loved Harry. Sometimes, I worried she loved him just a bit too much, but I guess I thought that could only be a good thing. A year ago I put Harry's name down for grade school. Nicky wouldn't be needed no more once he started. I knew she'd be gutted, leaving, so I found her a job with some friends of mine who were expecting another kid. She seemed pleased. As a favour, I agreed for her to stay on a few months until Harry had settled in school.' His face grew dark and Pauline gritted her hands for some reason. 'Then Harry started getting stomach cramps. I thought he was nervous about going to school, though he didn't mention it, until one day I came home and found Nicky sprinkling washing soda on his ice cream.'

'Oh, my God. Is it poisonous?'

'Not in small quantities, but it didn't exactly make healthy eating for a young kid. I let Nicky go on the spot. She hit the roof. Christ, that woman!' His voice was full of awe. 'I've never seen anyone so mad. She completely flipped her lid. She said if she couldn't have Harry, no one would. I told her to leave on the spot and took Harry to a movie while she packed. She was gone when we came back. I breathed a sigh of relief and put Harry to bed and thought the whole crazy business was over and done with.'

'But next day,' Pauline breathed, 'Nicky went into school and said Harry had a dentist's appointment and the teacher saw nothing wrong about it and let him go.'

Tony looked at her in astonishment. 'Did Nicky tell you that?'

'No, it just seemed the obvious thing to do.'

'I wish it had seemed obvious to me at the time,' he said drily. 'It was the paediatrician she said he had to see, not the dentist, otherwise you got it in one, Pauline.' He smiled. 'You've got a clever head on those cute little shoulders.'

Pauline had never blushed so thoroughly before. Warmth spread like a flame from the top of her head to the soles of her size four, sensibly clad feet. Was it possible he was attracted to her as she was to him!

'I was in a state and about to contact the cops,' Tony went on, 'but had second thoughts, remembering the things Nicky had said. I didn't trust her not to do something totally irrational if she saw herself on TV or in the papers.'

'Such as?'

'Such as killing Harry,' Tony said simply. 'She was flaky enough. Then I checked on his passport and found it had gone, and so had every other piece of paper that was precious to me: marriage and birth certificates, letters and little mementoes my wife had kept all her life, photos a century old, snaps of Harry since he was a baby, the deeds of the house and other legal stuff it would be difficult to duplicate. I cared most about the photos and my wife's things.'

He went over to the cupboard and poured himself another drink, glancing at Pauline's glass, still half full. 'I've been looking for Nicky ever since. England seemed the obvious place, so I hired Sydney to dig around, but he got nowhere. Months later, Sydney came to Dublin to do another job for me. First day here, he spots Nicky taking Harry home from school. I flew over straight away. I didn't want a stranger snatching back my kid. I preferred to do it myself, and do it quietly, without Nicky around, so there wouldn't be a scene. The poor kid's already confused enough. I rented this place and bided my time until yesterday, when I picked up my boy outside his school, then rang Nicky and offered her ten grand for the papers.'

'Isn't it a bit crude to have suggested she leave it in a rubbish bin by the bus stop?' Pauline said primly.

'The garbage bin was Nicky's idea. I told her it was stupid, what was wrong with a straight swop, but she insisted. Mind you, that's Nicky all over. She's always been over-dramatic.'

'She said you'd asked *her* for the money. She seemed terribly sincere.' Pauline wrinkled her nose. 'I can hardly believe she wasn't telling the truth.'

'Perhaps she thinks she is. Perhaps she's convinced herself by now she's Harry's mom, that he's genuinely been kidnapped. Sydney said she's married. What's the poor guy like?' he asked curiously.

'Very nice. His name's Ralph. *He* believes her, and so does his friend, Seamus. They're both determined to get Harry back.'

Tony laughed, but there was a threat in his voice. 'There's not much chance of that.'

'I feel sorry for Nicky,' Pauline said. 'And it will be a terrible shock for Ralph when he finds out the truth.'

Her hand was taken and warmly squeezed and she felt as if every bone in her body had turned to jelly. 'You're a nice lady, Pauline, like I said before.'

There was a funny thickness in her throat, and she seriously considered kissing him, making the first move. Women did that sort of thing nowadays, propositioned men, asked them out. She leaned slightly forward, took a deep breath, then moved quickly away when a door at the back of the room opened and a woman came in, a pretty woman with short blonde hair and a pixie face, wearing a white towelling robe with a hood. She had laughing eyes and a wide, full mouth.

'We've got visitors! Why didn't you wake me, Tony?' She smiled at Pauline. 'Hi, I'm Lucy, Tony's wife.'

'But I thought . . .'

'Lucy and I only got married a few weeks ago,' Tony explained. 'She's another reason why we didn't need Nicky no more. Honey, this is Pauline. Nicky spun her a tale and she thought she was helping out. I've just put her straight.'

Pauline got to her feet, feeling sick. She'd just avoided making a perfect fool of herself. As if someone as gorgeous as Tony would be interested in *her*, when there were millions of women like Lucy in the world.

'I'm just about to make myself a cup of coffee,' Lucy said brightly. 'Would you like one, Pauline?'

'No, I was just leaving. Will you ask one of the men to take me back, please?' she said when Lucy had gone.

'Sure thing. Before you go, I'd like to ask if you'll do something for me.'

93

'What's that?' she asked dully.

'Get those papers and I'll give *you* the ten grand.'

She flushed. 'I don't want your money.' What sort of person did he think she was! 'I said I felt sorry for Nicky.'

Tony's eyes went cold. 'I felt sorry for myself when she took my son. I felt even sorrier for Harry, without a dad for six whole months. You know, she told him Lucy didn't want to be his mom and as I preferred Lucy to him, he was being taken away with my blessing. Those letters and photos mean a lot to me. It sticks in my craw to think of that woman touching them, reading my wife's mail, having Harry's passport, even if I've got him another. Those things are a part of my family and I want them back. I won't feel the nightmare's over till I've got them.' He went towards the kitchen. 'I'll tell Roxy you want a ride back to Dublin.'

'Just a minute. I'll try and get your papers – and I'll take the money too, if I'm successful. There's a lot of things my school could do with ten thousand pounds.' She wanted to please him, he was that sort of man.

'You're a teacher?'

'Yes.' She also wanted him to know that she was *somebody*. 'But how will I recognise your things? Are they in a box or something? I can't turn the house upside down looking through every piece of paper. Nicky will be there. I won't have much time, even if I find the opportunity.'

'All the stuff was in an orange plastic folder with a zipper. I see no reason for her putting them in anything else. If you don't find them Pauline, I'll just have to get them back some other way.' He gave a lovely, warm smile and put a hand on her knee. 'But I just know that you'll do your best, though be careful. As I said before, Nicky's a pretty flaky lady.'

'I'll be careful, don't worry.'

'And I don't need to remind you that the contents of that folder are highly personal.'

'I'm not in the habit of reading other people's correspondence,' Pauline said stiffly. 'Can I make a phone call? I need to get Ralph and Seamus well out the way.'

'How will you do that?'

'Where abouts is this house situated?'

'Just outside Bray, on the coast.'

'I'll ring Nicky and say I'm somewhere else and to tell Ralph and Seamus to go there immediately.' She shrugged. 'But where? I don't know this part of the world.'

'This morning I took Harry to a place miles away called Marlay Park. He had a ride on a model steam engine,' Tony said helpfully.

'Right.' Pauline took Nicky's mobile from her bag and dialled auto followed by one. An hysterical voice answered. Ralph and Seamus hadn't come home, but they had mobiles, she could get in touch. 'Tell them to go to Marlay Park, outside the gates. I'll meet them there.' She rang off before Nicky had a chance to ask questions.

'Very smart,' Tony said admiringly. 'I could do with more people like you in my organisation.'

She looked at him under lowered lashes. 'What sort of organisation is that?' Nicky had claimed he was in the Mafia.

He grinned. 'Don't ask! Where can we meet so you can give me the stuff?'

'If I've got it,' she reminded him. 'My hotel, tomorrow morning, about nine. It's called the Arcadia.' She'd remembered the name. The effect of that mindblowing drink was wearing off, she thought sadly, and wondered if she would ever feel so happy again.

'Suits me fine. I'd planned on flying back to the States in the morning if everything works out.'

Roxy took her back. 'Where abouts do you come from?' Pauline asked in friendly fashion as they bumped over the rutted track.

'Shut the fuck up,' the young man growled, somewhat discouragingly, in a cultured voice that reminded her of Prince Charles.

'Oh, well, if that's how you feel,' she sniffed. What an unpleasant young man! His manners were appalling. She turned to look out of the window, at the dark, narrow country lanes edged with thick, tangled bushes and unfriendly trees, prepared to spend the journey in silence.

'Mind out,' she shrieked, minutes later. The Mercedes was driving straight for a white-clad woman stumbling along in front. There was no pavement, nothing for pedestrians to walk on. Roxy swore and swerved at the same time.

'Stop!' Pauline shrieked again. It was the same woman they'd passed on the way to Tony's and once again was struck by the fact she looked familiar.

Roxy swore again. He had no intention of stopping until Pauline rapped smartly on his skull with her knuckles. She'd box his ears if he didn't obey.

The Mercedes drew to a reluctant halt and Pauline opened the door. The white figure limped unsteadily towards them.

'Tracey! Is that you?'

'Oh, Pauly!' Tracey cried. She began to run in an

uneven, lopsided manner. 'I've never been so pleased to see anyone in me life.'

'Come along, dear, get in the back,' Pauline said fussily. 'Look at you! Where on earth did you get those clothes?' She was wearing only half a dress. A scarf was tied around her bust and she smelt disgusting. 'Oh, look at your poor feet, filthy, and full of cuts and scratches. And your arms. What happened to your shoes?'

'I threw them away. I have to get to a hospital straight away, Pauly. I urgently need a tetanus jab.'

Pauline helped the girl on to the back seat. Roxy had miraculously come to life and produced a tartan rug from the boot. Even more surprisingly, he climbed into the back and began to tuck the rug carefully around Tracey's body, showing particular attention to her bottom, something Pauline noticed, though Tracey didn't. Had she not been so upset, she would have floored him.

'However did you get in such a state, dear?' the older woman enquired.

Tracey rolled her chestnut eyes. 'Don't ask!' she said darkly. 'Anyroad, what are you doing being driven around the Irish countryside in such a dead posh car?'

'Don't ask!' said Pauline, making a face. 'It's turned out to be a pretty weird hen party.'

'You can say that again.'

In the presence of the beautiful Tracey, Roxy had found his voice, as well as his manners, and began to chat amicably. On reaching Dublin, he followed the hospital signs and eventually drew up outside the Accident and Emergency department, where Tracey got out. After she'd gone, Roxy didn't speak again, not even to say goodbye when he stopped outside Nicky's house and Pauline got out.

The lights of the house were on, the curtains were open, and inside there was an unbalanced young woman, possibly crazy, who had stolen a dead woman's child.

Chapter Six

Back at Maloney's, the burly barmaid announced gruffly to her customers, 'I'm off to take a wee piss.'

The customers, predominently male, didn't blink an eyelid at this bald statement. In public, their own wives would have said, 'I'm going to the Ladies,' or something about powdering their noses, but the burly barmaid was a coarse woman, without finesse, who had no truck with disguising her lavatorial needs behind flowery verbal niceties.

The barmaid, whose name was Trish, made her way out of the bar and along the dingy corridor to the Ladies' lavatory. She opened the door. The smell of urine didn't bother her for she was the most indelicate of creatures. The sign on the lock of the single cubicle showed, 'occupied', or at least some of the letters did, others having faded with age, making the sign read 'cupid', an inappropriate word in such unlovely, rather seedy surroundings. Trish waited, somewhat surprised, as Maloney's was generally considered a man's bar. Women customers were few. Only mutinous, awkward wives and girlfriends were willing to accompany their menfolk to a bar that discouraged members of the female sex. These occasional creatures were merely showing their disapproval of the mysogyny of Irish men. At the same time, they wished the seats were more comfortable, that there was a carpet, not sawdust on the floor, and that they didn't have to bring their own paper if they wanted to use the disgusting lavvy.

Trish, who kept a careful eye on the customers, could have sworn there were only three of these bothersome women there that night, and that all were present when she'd abandoned her duties for a pee. Had a woman sneaked in and managed to escape her baleful, fearsome, unwelcoming glare? She banged on the door.

'Who's there?' she grunted.

No reply.

She banged on the door again. 'Who the fuck's in there?' Spittle flew out of her mouth and ran down the chipped wood. She wiped it off with her sleeve, along with several flakes of blue paint.

Trish dragged over the chair with only three good legs to the door, climbed on it, and peered over the top. A woman was sitting on the bowl, her head leaning against the partially tiled wall, eyes closed, very still. The wall had once been fully tiled, but Trish had spent a year, from March 1999 to February 2000, prizing off a tile a month so that her da could make a surround for her ma's kitchen sink. She told the landlord it was being done by one of the women customers. He had taken to logging the time their few female regulars spent in the lavatory, but it had, not surprisingly, got him nowhere.

The woman was one of them five miserable English bitches who'd been in earlier and had been given a pint of Paddy's Brew. Trish could have sworn they'd all left

together in the vain hope of hailing a taxi. But apparently
not. She felt a prickle of alarm. She got off the chair,
applied her sturdy shoulder to the door, and shoved. The
door flew open, banging the women's knees, causing her
head to slowly sink forward until she unbalanced, top-
pling off the bowl on to the unwashed floor.

'Fuck!' She felt the woman's pulse. Nothing. The
white face was tinged with blue and felt cold to the touch.

The woman was dead!

Trish's armpits were suddenly puddles of sweat, and
the wool of her sweater, already thick, became even
thicker. She was about to call for the Gardai and an
ambulance, but hesitated. Say if it was Paddy's Brew that
had contributed towards the woman's death. Say if it had
caused it. She might have had a weak heart, or some other
medical condition, and wasn't supposed to drink alcohol,
most particularly alcohol that was inclined to play tricks
on the brain. A man who'd once drunk Paddy's Brew had
gone home, climbed on to the roof, and dismantled his
chimney, brick by brick, for no other reason than the idea
appealed to him. He had started taking his garage to
pieces before he was stopped.

Maloney's would get into desperate trouble if was
discovered Paddy's Brew had been served to five
innocent women under the guise of lemonade. It
had all been Rory McLaughlin's idea, but Trish would
be blamed, she being the one who had poured it into
the glasses, knowing how potent it was. She might
even be charged with manslaughter. Her sluggish
imagination ran riot. There could be four other women lying dead around Dublin that night. Perhaps they
all had medical conditions. Perhaps that's why they
were friends.

What was she to do? Trish's little-used brain cells swung into action.

She would have to get rid of the body.

How?

By moving it somewhere else.

Where?

Somewhere far away from Maloney's.

And how was she supposed to do that?

Trish was trying to think of an answer when she heard a car drive into the car park. Someone got out and went into the Gents' lavatory outside.

Bastard!

People were always stopping to use the Gents without coming into the bar and buying a drink in appreciation of a free pee.

She crept along the passage, peeked out the back door, and saw a large, luxurious grey car crookedly parked. The someone must have been desperate, because the driver's door had been left wide open and the light inside was on, revealing fine leather seats and a thick grey carpet. Keys dangled from the dashboard.

With one stride, Trish pulled out the keys. There were only two and one opened the boot which was empty. She returned the keys to the ignition, and with two strides, was back in the Ladies, where she hoisted the woman's body over her shoulder, picked up her handbag, and ran outside – she was a hefty girl, with the build of a heavyweight boxer – and threw the corpse and the bag into the boot. As she closed it, the corpse gave a tiny sigh. Trish's heart did a double somersault, but it was too late now. There were footsteps in the Gents. She shot inside, closed the door, and listened as the car drove away, the engine sounding as smooth as if it was shredding velvet.

THE HEN PARTY

Phew!

There was a slight feeling of unease at having consigned a corpse that wasn't dead to the boot of an unknown car, but the driver could cope with the consequences. Serve him right for availing himself of a lavatory that was there for the convenience of the patrons of Maloney's, not any flashy, passing salesman who happened to be caught short.

Monsignor Aloysius Innocent (after the Pope) McGillivray drove out of Maloney's car park and turned right in the direction of the R119 which led to Dun Laoghaire where he was booked on board the Stenalink car ferry sailing at midnight for Holyhead. The impressive black briefcase on the passenger seat beside him contained a highly secret document, too important to be trusted to the post.

The Monsignor gave a sigh of relief when Maloney's disappeared from sight in the rear-view mirror. People might have found it surprising that such an illustrious man of the cloth was acquainted with a Gents' lavatory situated at the rear of such a desperately unsavoury establishment.

(It's not what you think.)

The third of twelve children born to a devoutly religious mother and a farmhand father, the good father had been raised in the immediate area, and had frequented Maloney's most nights of his life between the age of fourteen and eighteen. In those days he was known as Ally. In those days, he had no wish, no intention, not even the faintest inkling of desire, to become a priest. He liked girls too much. He adored girls. He thought about

103

them all the time, and whenever he had the opportunity, he kissed and cuddled them, made love to them if they'd let him – about half did – said a prayer every night, thanking God for girls and for not having been born the eldest son of Mr and Mrs Gillivray, a burden that would automatically have led to the priesthood and thus denied him access to a never-ending supply of girls. At the time, his elder brother, Francis, had been in a seminary in North Wales merely to satisfy the fanatical desire of their mother to have a priest in the family. No mother could die more contentedly, Mary McGillivray stated frequently and dramatically, than one who was given the Last Sacraments by her very own son.

Poor Francis had died at twenty-one, supposedly of peritonitis, but Aloysius suspected it was downright misery that sent him to his grave. He no more wanted to become a priest than any other male member of the large McGillivray family. He'd always wanted to drive a train when he grew up, an innocent, useful, and noble calling, but had been leant on by Mary to join the church.

With Francis gone and the next to eldest child a girl, it became Aloysius's turn to take up the priesthood in order to please his devout ma. It started off with gentle coaxing, but gentleness turned to violence when he refused, to screaming and shouting, pleading and crying, threats, scoldings, thrashings, refusal to cook his meals, do his washing, the promise of eternal damnation, descriptions of hell, of the devil himself, as if Ould Nick was a close acquaintance of Mary McGillivray and had told her precisely what tortures would be perpetrated on her son, Aloysius, if he didn't take Francis's place in the seminary in North Wales.

Months passed, and Aloysius couldn't have felt more

feeble and debilitated had he been building the bridge over the River Kwai.

In the end, he gave in. He had no choice. His family were suffering, all due to him sending his ma into flaming hysterics day after day, week after week. His da had taken to drink – well, drinking more than usual – his siblings were losing weight, having nightmares, doing badly at school, stealing strange things, like buttons from the haberdashers, corn plasters from the chemist, not because they needed them, but they were grossly disturbed. The brother next in line, Xavier, was threatening to cut his own throat if Aloysius continued to hold out, knowing that his mother's holy attentions would be heaped upon him.

It was the thought of her death that had kept Mary going. She was in her seventies now, hearty and healthy, showing no signs of kicking the bucket, yet Aloysius had been a sodding priest for twenty-five sodding years just so she could have a bit of a thrill on her deathbed.

He shook himself. He was losing his temper, something he was apt to do whenever he thought about his ould ma. Sometimes, he considered arranging to have her killed in her sleep, just for spite, so she'd be denied the satisfaction of having the Last Rites administered by anyone, let alone her son.

Father McGillivray had become an excellent servant of God and the church. He'd even been notched up a bit, become a monsignor. He looked like a priest and behaved like a priest. He had the appropriate gravitas. But he didn't think like a priest. Inside his head, he was still the young man who'd haunted Maloney's and picked up girls. In fact, he still picked up girls occasionally, but that's another story. The reason why he hadn't gone into the pub after he'd used the lavvy, was because some of his old mates would be there, middle-aged now, married with families. They knew what he'd become and would have fawned over him and bowed their heads respectfully, which he couldn't have stood. They would have envied him, yet he couldn't tell them how much he envied *them*. He badly wanted a wife, nay, he urgently *needed* a wife. What's more, he knew the wife he wanted, one of his parishioners, a pretty, dark-eyed widow in her thirties called Estelle. They'd talked so far of mundane things, but had exchanged glances that said everything. Estelle was as much in love with him as he with her. He wanted to marry her. He wanted children.

Which is what the important document in his brief-case was about. It was a petition, signed by more than fifty of his colleagues in Ireland and the six counties still attached to Britain, urging the Pope to drop the vow of celibacy for the priesthood. It was ludicrous that men were born with natural desires and the means to satisfy them, yet were denied this simple pleasure if they wished to serve God – or had no wish to serve anyone, as was the case with the monsignor.

He wasn't the only priest who wanted what ordinary men had, witness the fifty signatures on the petition. Tomorrow, he would deliver the petition to a friend, a priest in Liverpool, who would circulate it among other like-minded men of the cloth. Then it would be passed on to Manchester, Birmingham, London, and every other city in the British Isles. When completed it would be delivered to His Holiness in Rome, along with similar petitions from countries all over the world. There would be thousands of signatures, hundreds of thousands. The monsignor had hopes for a million.

In the meantime, secrecy was vital. If the media got hold of the story they'd make fun of it. Parish priests would be contacted and asked if they'd signed, would they sign, why wouldn't they sign? Some who would have signed would get cold feet. A witch hunt would be instigated by those on high. The Vatican would crank up its spin machine.

An hour later, Monsignor McGillivray drove on to the ferry bound for Holyhead, parked the car on the lower deck, and went up with his briefcase to find a drink.

His passenger in the boot, Rosemary, who'd gone to Dublin for a hen party, was curled up in such a deep, peaceful, dreamless sleep that her heart rate had dropped considerably. She hadn't slept so well since she was a baby. She'd been exhausted for years, what with working extra hours, working night shifts, double shifts, lifting patients, running here, running there, fetching this and fetching that until her feet swelled and her back ached and her head throbbed with tiredness. Yet she went to bed and slept only fitfully, waking, anxious and alert, at the slightest noise or if her husband of six months merely turned over.

Now there was a lovely buoyant, floaty motion, which only added to the fullness of her delicious slumber.

Rosemary slept on,

And on,

And on . . .

Chapter Seven

The waiting area in Accident and Emergency resembled a scene from the Crimean War; rows of bloody, broken bodies with temporarily bandaged parts, huddled figures nursing their pain. All that was missing was the horses.

A few men who'd thought they were dying, perked back to life when the Rubenesque Tracey entered; barefoot, bare shouldered, resembling a shapely tube of toothpaste in her skintight ballgown. They longed to snatch away the scarf tied mysteriously around her bountiful breasts.

'I need a tetanus jab,' Tracey explained to the nurse in Reception, a stout, fiftyish woman with cynical eyes and a world weary expression, who looked as if she'd seen everything and had come to the decision that it stank. 'You're obviously busy, so I can give it meself, save wasting your time like. I'm a nurse.'

'Are ye now!' the woman said sarcastically.

'I've been involved in an accident. I've got scratches all over me body from a variety of sources. I've no idea what most of them were. I might even have been bitten by a rat.'

'A rat!'

'Something bit me leg and it wasn't human.'

'And where did this happen pray?'

'In a ditch somewhere. I was hiding from this guy who was trying to murder me.'

'And I'm supposed to believe that?'

'I don't care if you believe it or not,' Tracey snapped. 'I've had an accident and I'm an emergency. I've got the scratches and the bite to prove it. I need a jab and I need it urgently. Are you going to give it me or not?'

'There's no need to get yer knickers in a twist, Miss – what's yer name?'

'Tracey Rogers.'

'Age?'

'Twenty-five.'

'Address?'

'4 Somerfield Avenue, Liverpool. Occupation – staff nurse at Liverpool General Hospital.'

'Ye really are a nurse?' said the nurse incredulously.

'Is that so hard to credit?'

'Frankly, yes. Ye look more like a pro who's had an argument with her pimp.'

'Is this how you usually talk to the patients?'

'Only when they claim they've been hiding in a ditch because someone was trying to murder them.'

'Okay, so I lied. The truth is, I was walking innocently along this country lane when a ditch leapt up and attacked me. Will that do?'

'Sounds more believable than the other explanation. See that row of cubicles over there? The next to end one is empty. Wait there and I'll get someone to give ye a jab. Ye'll be between an attempted suicide and a saint.'

'A saint?'

'The media have dubbed her, "The saint with no name". No one knows who she is. Did ye not notice the scrum outside trying to get in?'

'I assumed they were either accidents or emergencies, that this was just a normal Saturday night in Dublin, though I wondered why the hospital staff were being so rough with them.'

That's the media. They want to film her, take her photey, interview her, though they'll be lucky. The poor woman's still unconscious.'

'Did she work a miracle or something?' Tracey asked curiously.

'In a way. She appeared from nowhere and rescued three children from a terrible fire. We're desperately trying to find a private room so we can move her out the way.'

'Well, I won't disturb her.'

'Ye'd better not.'

Tracey entered the cubicle and pulled the curtain to. She'd hoped to exchange Lady Agatha's costume for a hospital gown, but there were none. She sat on the edge of the trolley, imagined the various poisons seeping into her body, and waited for her limbs to seize up.

A groan came from the next cubicle which held the attempted suicide. It sounded like a man and the professional in Tracey wondered what method he'd used. She slipped off the bed and peeped through the curtain. The clearly restless patient was lying on a trolley wearing a dinky pair of buttercup yellow Y-fronts and nothing else. His wrists were unslashed and his neck unmarked, so he hadn't tried two of the most popular methods. It might have been an overdose and his stomach had been pumped, which would account for why his clothes had been removed – a pair of black velvet trousers and a dazzling white satin shirt were hanging on a hook on the wall.

She was about to close the curtain when it occurred to her that the clothes looked familiar. Earlier that night, she'd met someone who'd worn an outfit very similar.

Mark Costello!

Had she actually driven the poor man to attempt suicide! She crept inside and examined the patient's twitching face. It was indeed Mark Costello, fast asleep, possibly drugged, a somnolent nervous wreck.

'I was only trying to help, you know,' Tracey whispered soothingly, stroking the boyish brow. 'I never intended any harm. I've acted before and I would have been fine if the costumes hadn't been too small. In a way, it was partially your own fault. You should have realised I was the wrong size. Anyroad, I didn't think of this before, but you could have done the part yourself. You must only be about a size ten, and you'd have made a grand Lady Agatha in a wig.'

Mark Costello slowly opened his blue eyes and they glazed in terror when he saw the gorgeous Tracy bending over him. A fearful, horripilant, hair-raising scream emerged from his rosebud mouth, and two men in the waiting area immediately went home and an elderly lady fainted.

Tracey smartly nipped back to her own space when she heard footsteps approaching. 'What on earth's the matter? Ye nearly frightened us all to death,' demanded a voice in the next cubicle. It sounded like the nurse with the cynical eyes.

'I saw an apparition,' Mark Costello croaked. 'I think I must be going mad.'

'Ye'll send us all as mad as heathens if ye scream like that again, young man.'

'It was my Nemesis.'

'I don't care if it was your mother. Yer quite safe here. In fact, ye can go home soon. Isn't there someone on their way to collect ye?'

'My friend Peter.'

'Close yer eyes, there's a good boy, and have a nice rest till Peter comes.'

'Yes, Nurse,' Mark said obediently.

The nurse left. Tracey looked through the curtain. Mark had his eyes closed, though his face was twitching more than ever. She badly wanted to help, but it seemed sensible not to approach him again. She twiddled her thumbs and thought about the saint on her other side.

What did a saint look like? She'd never seen one in the flesh before. Moving the other curtain slightly, she saw a woman on a trolley wearing a blue towelling dressing-gown, lying unnaturally still, arms folded over her breast. Unusually for a saint, the long fingers of her right hand were badly stained with nicotine.

Just like Donna's.

Donna!

'Donna?' Tracey gasped.

The saint didn't move.

'Since when have you been a saint, you lousy hypocrite. I thought you were an atheist. I doubt if you've ever been near a church.'

'Is that you, Tracey?' Donna whispered hoarsely without opening her eyes. 'Are you alone?'

'It's me, and I'm alone.'

'Oh, Trace! I daren't move an inch. You've got to

help get me out of here. I'm in a terrible pickle. They think I rescued three children from a fire.'

'Didn't you?'

'Well, yes, but it was me who started the fire in the first place. No one knows yet, except this kid whose bound to have guessed the truth. He, or it might be she, is sure to tell someone, and I'll be thrown into prison. I'm sure arson's a crime. I'll never be able to nurse again.'

Which wouldn't be such a bad thing, Tracey thought, but this wasn't the time to debate Donna's dodgy nursing skills. 'The media's outside, desperate to see you.'

'I know, a reporter followed the ambulance. Once me photey's in the paper or on telly, Trace, I'm lost. The house was gutted and it belonged to some top copper in the Gardai. I'll be wanted all over the sodden world.'

'Doesn't anyone know who you are?'

'I haven't said a word so far. I'm pretending to be unconscious – they've fitted a bloody catheter, case I pee in the bed. But I can't stay unconscious for ever, Trace. For one thing, I'm longing for a fag. I don't suppose you've got any on you?' she said hopefully.

'So you can set the hospital on fire too!' Tracey guffawed. 'You know I don't smoke. Anyroad, I've lost me bag.'

'So've I,' Donna said miserably. 'I think I left it in that pub.'

'Mine's in the theatre.'

'You've been to the theatre?'

'Sort of.'

'Where is everyone?'

'I've no idea. Pauline's being carted round Dublin in a chauffeur-driven Mercedes. Emma and Rosemary have disappeared.'

Suddenly, Donna's curtains were whisked aside and a female doctor entered accompanied by a nurse. Tracey watched with half an eye.

'So this is her!' the doctor said in a low voice. 'The saint with no name.'

'She was terribly brave,' murmured the nurse. 'Commander Barton has just been on the television news – it was his children she saved from the fire. He says he'll be recommending her for a medal and they're saying Mass in the Cathedral tomorrow to pray for her full recovery.'

'The poor dear has singed her hair. What are these marks on her hands?'

'We wondered if they might be stigmata,' the nurse said in an awed voice. 'They're on her ankles too.'

'I doubt it. There's nothing supernatural about them. I'll just check her pulse. You say they've found her a room?'

'It's on the fourth floor, nice and quiet. Two nuns have arrived from St Theresa's. They've brought some clothes, her own were ruined, and they'll sit with the good woman so she won't wonder where she is when she comes to. We couldn't possibly have spared the staff.'

'Well, her pulse seems quite steady. I don't think she's come to any real harm. She's in a state of shock, that's all. I suggest we find a porter and have her moved immediately.'

'I'll see to it, Doctor.'

'Shit, Donna, I think I'm going to be sick,' Tracey said when the two women had gone. She pretended to retch. '*Stigmata!*'

'Shurrup. I'm coming in there.' Donna climbed off the trolley, flung back the curtains, and almost fell into Tracey's cubicle, dragging the catheter behind her. 'What am I going to do, Trace?' Her eyes wild with terror, not a bit like a saint's.

'I'd do a bunk, if I were you, while there's time,' Tracey said sensibly, unhooking the catheter.

'In a dressing-gown? I'd be spotted straight away. Oh, I know it's asking a lot, but give us your clothes, Trace. I'll be grateful for the rest of me life.'

'Haven't you noticed what I'm wearing? Half a dress and someone's scarf on top.'

Donna groaned. 'I'm going to be hung, drawn and quartered. Do they still execute people in Ireland?'

Tracey had an idea. 'Half a mo!' She snaked her arm through the curtain into Mark Costello's cubicle and took the black velvet trousers and white satin shirt off their hook. 'These should fit, though the trousers will be too short. They'll look like matador pants which are all the rage.'

'Ta, Trace,' Donna said breathlessly, already struggling into the trousers. 'There's things in the pockets.'

'It doesn't matter about that now.'

'Is there any shoes?'

'There's bound to be.' Tracey crawled across the floor of the doomed theatrical producer's cubicle and returned with a pair of bisexual brogues with cuban heels from under his trolley. 'They're a seven.'

'I take eights, but they'll do. What about me hair, it's all singed at the front? Is there a hat in there?'

'We're in an ozzie, Donna, not Dorothy Perkins. Sit down and I'll tie me scarf around your head in a turban.'

'How do I look?' Donna enquired when the trousers were zipped, the shirt buttoned, and the turban tied in an artistic bow.

'Unrecognisable and a touch bizarre. A bit like a

model,' Tracey said truthfully. 'You should wear clothes
like that more often.' The tight trousers emphasised the
narrowness of her minimal hips, and the turban gave her
an exotic, unconventional air. For the first time since
Tracey had known her, Donna actually looked quite
attractive.

'What are you doing here, Trace? I was in too much
of a state to ask before.' It must have dawned on Donna
that, while she'd just been helped out of a very deep hole,
she was leaving her half-naked helper in another, possibly
not so deep, but a hole all the same.

'I came for a jab, but I don't think I'll bother. I'd
sooner not be around when the guy in the next cubicle
finds his clothes have gone.' She'd already given him
enough reason to want to kill her. Peter could arrive to
collect him any minute. She'd wait and have the jab in
Liverpool, and just hoped she wouldn't catch anything
unspeakable in the meantime and die.

'But you can't find your way back to the hotel like
that!'

'Give us your dressing-gown.'

'That won't help. They won't let you out the door if
they think you're a patient.'

'It's all right,' Tracey said stoically. 'I'll manage somehow. You'd better go.'

'But I don't like leaving you in such a state! Now
we've found each other, we should stick together.'

Suddenly, there was a yell. 'Jaysus, Mary and Joseph!
The saint's only gone and bloody disappeared!'

Donna slid through the curtain and Tracey was left
alone.

Within minutes, there was mayhem outside, as hundreds – or so it sounded – of shocked and mystified

hospital staff had arrived to exclaim on the fact the saint was no longer there.

Had she been abducted?

If so, was it aliens or the divil himself who'd taken her?

Perhaps the woman had never been there in the first place, not *really* there, if you know what I mean.

Perhaps God had sent her to save those sweet, little children, and now she was back in heaven, sitting by His side, where she belonged.

In other words, she was an angel in disguise.

'Has anyone looked *under* the trolley?'

'It was the first place, Doctor.'

'Maybe she's gone to the lavvy?'

'She had a catheter, idiot.'

'How dare you call me an idiot!'

'Where *is* the catheter?'

'Maybe it's gone up to heaven with her.'

Tracey grabbed the catheter and sat on it, rather fortuitously, as her curtain was suddenly whisked aside.

'Have ye seen her?' demanded the nurse with the cynical eyes.

'Who?'

'Oh, never mind.' The curtain closed.

'Oh, *shit*! Here's the media. Who let them in?'

'Hi, there, Mark, me ould mate,' said a loud, cheerful voice on Tracey's other side. 'It's Peter. How many tablets did you take this time? Two? Three? You know, it's becoming rather boring, collecting you after yet another failed suicide attempt – or perhaps I should say "faked". Have you got your own red telephone straight through to the Samaritans?'

'I really meant it this time, Peter,' Mark Costello said weakly.

'I take it the play didn't go down too well?'

'It went down *awfully*. The most desperately terrible thing happened. It's been the most miserable night of my life.'

'Wasn't the girl I found for Lady Agatha any good?'

'I wouldn't know. Some other girl . . . Oh, never mind.' Mark's voice shuddered. 'I'll tell you all about it another time, otherwise I'll want to kill myself again.'

'What you need is a drink. Come on, mate, and we'll go to a club.'

'But I should go back to the theatre. We were having a party after the show – you promised to come, remember? I've let the cast down badly. I just buggered off and left them to it when I should have stayed and seen them through the last two acts.'

'In that case, we'll take a taxi to the theatre first, then go to the club, but you'd better get your clothes on first.'

It was time Tracey did her own disappearing act. She put on the dressing-gown and plunged into the fray outside.

What was she to do, wondered Tracey with a remarkable lack of resentment for a person in somewhat of a pickle of their own, not knowing where she was (other than in an ozzie), where the hotel was, what the name of the hotel was, and dressed as she was, as if for bed, with not even a pair of slippers to her name? She also had no money and didn't know where the theatre was, or what it was called, where she'd left her bag and her clothes.

She went into a lavatory for a think and a drink of water and emerged refreshed, having remembered where a set of women's clothes could be had, thus solving the most important of her immediate problems.

The fourth floor was pleasantly quiet except for the gentle hum of a generator, the long corridor empty. Behind the windows of the small wards accommodating only three or four, the patients, mainly elderly, watched television or slept. All the doors were closed, apart from one at the end of the corridor towards which Tracey sped, her bare feet making not a sound on the wooden floor.

The room was small, containing only one bed which was empty, as Tracey had expected. Two nuns in full habit were seated, one each side of the vacant bed, their united gaze fixed intently on the naked pillow, as if practising for their role as watchers over the shortly expected saint. They looked up, smiling sweetly, when Tracey entered.

'Did ye bring the clothing, sisters?' Tracey enquired politely, for some reason adopting an Irish accent.

'We did indeed, child,' replied one. 'Are you wanting it already?'

'That I am, sisters, if y'don't mind like.'

'We don't mind, not at all, child,' said the other. 'Here it is, in a nice, new plastic bag from Marks & Spencers. Sister Dominic took it by mistake.'

'Thank you kindly, sisters.' Tracey bowed and curtsied, and a feeling of guilt swept over her. It was like taking sweets from the hands of innocent babes. She'd never realised nuns could be so *nice*, or so very gullible.

'They're a bit on the large side, the clothes,' the first sister remarked, 'but we thought it wiser to bring them too big rather than too small. Mind you, I'm sure the good woman downstairs would look beautiful whatever she wore.'

'Will she be long arriving?' enquired the second. They both crossed themselves.

120

'I wouldn'na know, sisters,' Tracey responded humbly, crossing herself back. 'I've merely been sent up for the clothes for a reason known only to the person who sent me.'

'God bless you, child.'

'And God bless you too, sisters.' She backed respectfully out of the room, then ran like a maniac towards the stairs.

She could have used the frock as a tent and lived inside quite comfortably. It was made of brown silky stuff patterned with roses, and the shoulders hung as far as her elbows, the sleeves down to her knees, and the hem swept the floor. Tracey didn't care. At least she'd be able to breathe, though felt a louse when she dumped the hammock sized bra, the elephantine bloomers, and the crocheted Angora beret with a double pom-pom, in the bin in the women's lavatory, along with the ballgown that had cost Mark Costello so much to hire. But, rooting through her memory, she couldn't recall the events of the night being any of her fault. It was a situation she'd been landed in due to an entirely innocent wish to help.

The sisters had brought a pair of size 9 black gym pumps which she was able to keep securely on by tying the laces as tight as they would go. There was also a blue Crimplene cardy which she wrapped around her middle. She rolled up her sleeves, washed her face, then looked in the mirror and removed the leaves and twigs from her hair.

Now, all she had to do was find the theatre, collect her bag, and change into her own clothes. After a night like tonight, any sensible person would have then gone straight to bed, but Tracey was no longer the sensible young woman who'd left Liverpool the day before. Her brain felt as if it had been notched up a gear or two. It might even be in fifth. Peter had mentioned a club. *She* would find a club, because she was determined to get some enjoyment out of the weekend in Dublin.

Downstairs in Accident and Emergency, the excited crowd had grown and now included several armed policemen. Tracey lowered her head and pushed her way through to the exit, arriving in the open behind two men; one a stranger, the other by now ominously familiar. It was a distraught Mark Costello, wearing a set of green operating scrubs and weeping copiously.

'But you shouldn't have *stolen* them, Peter,' he sobbed.

'Had no alternative, mate. After all, someone stole yours. We'd have been there forever if you'd reported they'd vanished at the same time as that fucking saint.'

'I feel like a criminal.'

'You look like a prat.'

'My money and my mobile were in those trousers.'

'For Chrissakes, stop complaining and keep your eyes peeled for a taxi.'

Tracey remembered they were going to the theatre. She followed. If she got close enough when a taxi came, she might be able to hear Peter's direction to the driver.

'Trace!' hissed a voice, and the strangely elegant figure of Donna appeared at her side. 'I've been hiding. I thought I'd wait for you.'

'Ta, Donna.' Tracey gratefully squeezed her friend's hand. 'You'd better keep out the way a bit. See that chap in front in the green? It's his clothes you're wearing and he's already in a state.'

'Then let's go the opposite way.'

'They're looking for a taxi,' Tracey explained with extraordinary patience. 'If I catch the address of the theatre, I can collect me bag and clothes. I hope it's not far because I'll have to walk. I've no money for a taxi of me own.'

'I've got *loads* of money, Trace. A whole wallet full. It was in the pocket of me trousers. Oh, and I've also got a mobey. I've been invited to a party.'

'A what?'

'A party. The mobey went off. At first, I thought it was me bottom playing a tune, it does sometimes, but it was some girl asking me to a party. Well,' Donna nodded towards the sadly stooped green clad figure in front, 'asking *him* to a party, but she said it was open house. It's in a club, the Green Lizard, which is over a pub in Lower Baggot Street, wherever that is. Shall we go?'

'I wouldn't mind, once I've got me clothes back.'

The night was looking up for a change.

Chapter Eight

Meanwhile, back at the priest's house, the crowd was becoming restless. They prayed dear Father Jack would live, naturally, but the feller was nigh on eighty and had been out of sorts for months. If he was going to pop his clogs, it would be more convenient if he did it sooner rather than later, before it got too cold or started to rain again. In less than an hour, the pubs would close and what was a wake without a crate or two of Guinness? True, they could come back tomorrow or whenever the good Lord decided to take the good father, but they were in the perfect mood for a death right now, all tanked up and ready to cry their hearts out.

In the parlour, the Legion of Mary had stopped saying the rosary and were engaged in a pow-wow.

'So, it's true, after all. I guessed it long ago. Kate Musgrove's been at it with the father, the slut.'

'I've never felt able to trust a woman with red hair.'

'Is that not a wee bit unfair?' queried a woman with red hair.

'I wonder when they started doing it? She's been with him now for over thirty years.'

'Within the first few weeks, I reckon, knowing Kate Musgrove.'

'I wonder when they *stopped* doing it? The father's not a young man. My ould feller couldn't get his small parts together once he turned fifty-nine.'

'I wonder how many *times* they did it? I mean, it only takes the once to put a bun in a woman's oven.'

'Ha, Ha, Ha. Only the once! More like every day, I reckon, before Mass and after Mass and twice on Sundays. She's sex mad, Kate Musgrove. I can tell.'

'How can you tell?' enquired the woman with red hair.

'She has a look in her eye, as if she'd do it with the whole flaming parish if she could find the time.'

'I wonder *where* they did it?'

'Ooh, er!'

There was a throbbing pause.

'Oh, in bed upstairs, his bed or hers, we'll never know. They'd have never done it anywhere sacred.'

'Like in church?'

'Oh, no, no. No, no, no. Neither would've have done it in church, not even Kate Musgrove, though I'd like to bet it was *her* who came up first with the idea of doing the you-know-what, wherever it was done, counting out the church. Doing something so disgusting would never have entered the good father's saintly wee head on its own.'

'It might have entered his saintly wee trousers,' suggested the red-haired woman, but the suggestion went ignored.

'She probably walked around the house half-dressed.'

'Jezebel!'

'Flaunting her desperately skinny body at the poor, ould feller.'

'Making eyes.'

'Egging him on.'

'Titillating him.'

'Not wearing a brassière.'

'Or any knickers.'

'Phew! It's getting hot in here. Can someone open a window?'

'Mind you, and I'm saying this because I want to be fair, Kate Musgrove or no Kate Musgrove. He's a fine-looking lad, the son. His name's Jack an' all.'

'Didn't think much of that music he played though.'

'Me, neither. Give me Val Doonigan any day.'

'He wore lovely jumpers.'

'Me sister, Biddy, she knitted him a jumper once and sent it to the BBC in England. She got a nice letter back, but she never saw him wear it.'

'Wasn't he on some other channel? That's probably why.'

At ten o'clock, the ice-cream van drove away to the tinkling strains of '*Tantum Ergo*', having done a satisfactory amount of unexpected business. The candles were burning low. A goodly portion of the crowd went home, preferring their warm beds to spending the night in a graveyard, waiting for a priest to die who might not die at all. The Castaways, minus little Jack, went off to do their gig – after all, they'd been booked and didn't want to let people down. The youngsters were chased home by Kate, who was entirely unaware that in another part of the house her reputation was being torn into a million disgusting pieces, not that tonight she would have cared.

'Shoo, the lot of yis,' she cried, gesturing with her

hands as if the children were a plague of bothersome flies. 'Get back to your mammies and daddies, otherwise they'll come looking for yis any minute.'

'Who'll be saying Mass tomorrer, Mrs Musgrove?'

'The same as whose been saying it for the last few months, Father Evans from the Holy Name.'

'I don't like him, Mrs Musgrove. His nose is full of snot.'

'You little divil, Barry Mulligan,' Kate screeched, 'saying a thing like that about a priest! I'll be telling your mammy of yis the next time I see her.'

'It was me mammy who said it first, Mrs Musgrove.'

Emma and Jack went upstairs to see the old man who was sleeping soundly, looking frail but very much alive. Elizabeth the cat was curled on his feet.

'He's probably in a drunken stupor.' Emma noticed the whiskey bottle was barely half full.

'I wouldn't mind dying in the same condition,' said Jack. He sat on the bed.

Emma sat beside him. 'I hope that'll be a long time off.'

'Why?'

'Well, I wouldn't want to wish an early death on anyone,' she said gravely.

'So, it wasn't meant specifically for me? I mean, it's the sort of thing you'd say to any-old-one who was twenty-five?'

'I suppose so, except . . .' She paused.

'Except what?' He raised his eyebrows and smiled in a way that Emma found extremely endearing.

'I'd be particularly upset if I heard *you'd* died,' she said with a gulp.

'But when I do, die, that is, you're not likely to hear

about it, are you? By this time tomorrer you'll be back in Liverpool. As from next Saturday, you'll be Mrs some-thing-or-other. We'll never hear from each other or see each other again.'

'We could write!' Emma said in a small voice.

'Wouldn't – I've forgotten his name – your new husband mind?'

Emma had forgotten too, and it took a worrying few seconds before she could remember what her husband-to-be was called. 'It's Matthew and yes, he'd mind very much. What about Veronica?'

'She'd hate it.' He made a desperate face, something else Emma found endearing. 'I'd never hear the end of it if she found I was writing to another woman.'

'It's understandable.' Emma nodded, sympathising with Veronica. 'It's a disloyal, despicable thing to do. You shouldn't marry someone if you intend to carry on with someone else behind their back, even if it's only by letter.'

'It was your idea,' Jack said.

'I know.' It was Emma's turn to make a face. 'And what does that say about me?'

'I think, I'm not sure, it ses you're not very certain about marrying this Matthew guy.'

'But how certain should a person be?' Emma cried.

'A hundred per cent?'

'Oh, but I'm not, I'm not. How about you with Veronica?'

'In my case,' Jack said in a slow, meaningful voice, 'the reading's slowly dropping towards the negative.'

There was silence and they stared at the floor. Father Jack uttered a loud, angry snore and his breathing stopped. Emma held her own breath when she turned to look at him, willing him to start again. The breath, when it came, emerged in a long, shuddering sigh and she smiled with relief.

The two young people faced each other. He had a strong face, the priest's son, Emma thought, open and sensitive, with honest, straightforward eyes, and a dependable brow, a wide mouth. She tried not to compare him with Matthew because she could no longer see Matthew clearly. Her memory must be playing tricks, because she felt sure his eyes weren't really quite so close together and that they didn't squint, or that his mouth was as thin and mean as on the face she could only vaguely see in her mind's eye.

Then Jack put his finger under her chin and tipped her face towards his. He bent and their lips had almost touched, when a hair-raising scream came from downstairs.

Jack jumped to his feet. 'There's only one person who can scream like that and it's Kate doing her Lady Macbeth act.' He smiled ruefully, held out his hand, and pulled Emma to her feet. 'We'd best go down and see what's happened.'

The atmosphere in the kitchen had sunk to North Pole proportions. Kate's face was frozen in an expression of horror and two icy tears gleamed on her cheeks.

A man and a woman were sitting at the table whom Emma hadn't seen before. The woman was attractive, sixtyish, with short, iron-grey curly hair. Expertly made up, she wore an expensive fur coat and, from the smell, had recently overdosed on equally expensive perfume.

The man was considerably younger, about forty, fair-haired, and quite good-looking. He reminded Emma of someone, though she couldn't think who.

'Who's this, Mam?' enquired little Jack.

Kate unfroze. 'Ask *her* who she is,' she shrieked.

'I'm Grace O'Reilly, the woman announced haughtily, 'and this is my son, Jack.'

'Jack!' exclaimed Jack.

'And who are you?' Grace O'Reilly snapped.

'He's *my* son,' wept Kate.

'I'm Jack an' all,' said Jack.

'Jack!' gasped Grace.

Jack nodded.

'Don't tell me . . .' A look of horrified realisation swept over the carefully preserved face. 'You're Father Jack's son!'

'I am indeed,' confirmed Jack.

'But *my* Jack is Father Jack's son!'

'A man can have two sons. It's been known before,' Jack said simply, sitting down and looking stunned, as any man would when he'd discovered at the age of twenty-five that he had a half brother with the same name as himself.

'What's the matter with *your* Jack?' Kate sneered. 'Was he born mute or something?'

'No,' the new Jack said pleasantly. 'I was waiting for an opening to introduce myself, but it's already been done.'

'How do you do?' Little Jack reached across the table and shook hands.

'Very well, thank you, Jack. How's yourself?'

'I'm altogether fine, Jack. It's nice of you to ask.'

'The bugger swore I was his first woman,' Kate wept. She glared at Grace O'Reilly. 'Why are you here? What have you come for?'

'My sister Biddy rang. She lives not far from here. Me,

131

I live just across the border in County Wicklow. Biddy had heard Father Jack was due to pass on by twelve o'clock tonight and thought he might like to know what a fine, good-looking son he had before he left this world for the next. It was fortunate Jack happened to be staying with me, he normally lives in England. We came racing over like lunatics in the car.'

'*My* Jack lives in Dublin,' Kate said boastfully.

Grace O'Reilly showed no sign of having heard. She seemed to have shrunk inside her fur coat. Her face was pale and tight, a mixture of sadness and anger. 'He told me I was the only woman he would ever love,' she whispered. 'We adored each other. I was worried it would break his heart for ever when I left. I've thought about him many, many times over the years.'

'Left? Left where?'

'Here,' said Grace O'Reilly. 'I was his housekeeper.'

Kate screamed again. Emma went upstairs for the whiskey and fetched glasses from the sideboard in the parlour. The Legion of Mary had gone and the house was almost empty, apart from Father Jack, two more Jacks and their mothers, herself, four men playing pontoon on the landing, and a man fast asleep in the hall who looked like a tramp and she didn't like to disturb.

She glanced through the window. A few candles still flickered in the darkness of the churchyard where a dozen or so stragglers remained propped up against the grave-stones. She could hear the clink of bottles and the sound of a mournful voice singing 'Danny Boy'.

'I came in 1956 when I was nineteen,' Grace O'Reilly was saying when Emma returned to the kitchen. 'Jack was born three years later. I left for England as soon as I found myself expecting. Father Jack never knew. Not long afterwards, I got married. I only came back to Ireland when my husband died.'

'*I* didn't leave,' Kate said pugnaciously. '*I* stuck by him.'

'And what happened to your boy?'

'He went to live with me sister on her farm, but he's always known I was his mammy.'

'*I* put my child first.' Grace proudly tossed her iron-grey head. '*I* wasn't going to farm him out with some relative and pretend to the world he'd never been born. Anyway, you don't "stick by" a man who's made you pregnant. It's his job to stick by you.'

'But I . . . but . . .' Kate scowled and looked flummoxed.

Little Jack put his hand over hers. 'It's all right, Mam.'

'You've been happy, haven't you, son?' She sniffed tearfully.

'I have indeed.'

'Look, is there any need for this?' enquired the other Jack. 'You both did your best according to the circumstances at the time. *I've* been happy, *he's* been happy. Isn't that what matters? If blame is to be apportioned, I reckon it's Father Jack himself who deserves the main share. The man's supposed to be a priest, Goddammit, yet no woman seems to have been safe under his roof.'

'Don't say things like that, son,' protested Grace. 'I take it we're not too late?' she said to Kate. 'That the father is still in the land of the living?'

'He's upstairs, fast asleep.'

'Shouldn't someone be with him?' Grace said pointedly.

'Someone was – till you came,' Kate said pointedly back.

'I'm sorry I let you talk me into this, Mother,' the other Jack said sulkily. 'I don't know what good it will do either me or him.'

'Why don't you go upstairs and take a peek at him now?' suggested little Jack. 'I'll show you the way.'

'That's the only reason we came.' Grace swept out of the room followed by the two Jacks.

Emma glanced at the clock; nearly quarter past eleven. If Father Jack's prediction was to be proved right, he only had another three quarters of an hour left. 'Would you like some whiskey?' she asked Kate.

'I wouldn't mind the whole, flaming bottle.' Kate gave a sigh that might have been a snort. 'Did you hear that? He called her "Mother". Oh, and did'ya see her coat! Was that mink? I wouldn't know. And she was plastered with enough make-up for three women. His Holiness upstairs never liked make-up much, particularly that mascara stuff. That's why I never wore it. She lost her Irish accent in England, but found a husband instead.' She buried her head in her arms and began to cry. 'I wasted me life on the bugger, that I did. I stayed because I thought he loved me, but if I'd left, like *she* did, there'd probably be another Jack around from whoever came after me, and another and another if there'd been more than one.'

'I don't think so.' Emma put her arms around the distraught woman. 'I'd bet a million pounds that he truly loves you.'

'Would you really?' Kate gave her a pathetic look. 'She seemed quite nice, that Grace woman. Under different circumstances, I'd've quite liked her.'

'You can still like her. She probably feels dead hurt that you took the place in his heart that she thought would always belong to her.'

'I did, didn't I?' Kate said smugly. 'You're a very wise young woman, Emma Harrison. Why are you still here?'

Emma blinked. 'Would you like me to go?'

'Absolutely not.' Kate shook her head violently. 'I'd like you to stay for ever, but you didn't come all the way from Liverpool to Dublin to mend a cat's paw and spend the night with a dying priest and a crazy woman like me.'

'I know. I came for an entirely different reason, but I wouldn't leave for anything. I'd far sooner be here with Father Jack and you.' And little Jack, Emma added, but she was the only one who heard. Her head had cleared. She knew who she was and why she was there – her own hen party – but preferred not to be reminded she was getting married in seven days' time.

It was ten to twelve and all five of them were standing awkwardly around the bed on which Father Jack and his faithful pussy cat lay. The priest was on his side, sleeping peacefully and snoring softly, looking nowhere close to death.

The minutes ticked by.

'I feel an idiot,' commented the other Jack.

'I feel in the way,' Emma muttered.

'Who exactly *are* you?' asked Grace.

'Just someone who happened to be passing earlier. Me name's Emma.'

Five to twelve.

'I've got cramp in me foot,' Kate muttered. Little Jack tittered and she nudged him sharply in the ribs with her elbow. 'I'll have none of that nonsense in here. Show some respect for your ould da.'

Four minutes to twelve.

'Is his breath slowing down?'

'No, it's getting faster.'

'Is that a bad sign or a good one?'

'He's probably humping some woman in a dream,' the other Jack said cynically.

Three minutes.

'Couldn't you have found some smarter pyjamas for him to die in?' Grace complained. 'I seem to remember that pair from when I was here.'

'Was it you who darned the knee?' Kate sneered. 'I've never seen such a knobbly darn in all me life before.'

'Be quiet, Mother.'

'Keep your gob shut, Mam.'

Two minutes.

Father Jack turned over with a flounce and lay on his back. Everyone gasped and an annoyed Elizabeth curled herself between his knees.

One minute.

Kate knelt beside the bed and spread her scrawny arms over the old man's body. 'Don't leave me, Jack,' she moaned. 'If you die, I'll die too. I can't live without yis.'

Grace O'Reilly looked pityingly at the woman sprawled over the body of the dying priest, and the other Jack put his arm around his mother's shoulders.

Little Jack took Emma's hand.

A clock somewhere chimed midnight and on the last stroke Father Jack opened his watery blue eyes which widened in surprise when he saw the assembled company. 'Well, if it isn't racy Gracie!' he said with a grin. 'What are you doing here? You've aged, Grace. I hardly recognised you.'

'It's been forty years, Jack. I'm not Sleeping Beauty, and you're not exactly Prince Charming yourself.'

Kate burst into the inevitable tears. 'It's tomorrer, Jack, and you're still alive! Happy birthday.'

'What's the crowd for?' Father Jack struggled to a sitting position. 'Are you waiting to do an autopsy on me poor, dead body? Who are you?' he asked the other Jack.

'An unwilling bystander.'

'He's your son,' Grace said bluntly. 'His name's Jack.'

The old man groaned and rolled his eyes. 'Not another one!'

'Next time you think you're going to die, Jack,' Grace continued, 'I'd keep quiet about it if I were you, otherwise the chickens are given plenty of time to come home to roost.'

'Don't talk to him like that,' Kate cried.

'I'll talk to him any way I want.'

'Stoppit!' Emma stamped her foot. 'He may have done all sorts of disgusting things, but he's very old and very ill. If you're going to row, then do it downstairs.'

'Who are you to give us orders?' Grace snapped.

'She's me nurse,' said Father Jack.

'I thought she was just someone who happened to be passing earlier?'

'Yes, but now she's on the payroll as me nurse.'

'I think Emma's right,' the other Jack put in. 'If you don't mind, I'd like a quiet word with my father. Jack can stay.'

'Which Jack?' queried his mother.

'This Jack.' The other Jack put his hand on little Jack's arm.

Emma raised her eyebrows. 'A *nice* quiet word?'

'There's no need to worry. I'm quite pleased to meet him after all this time.'

'At least someone likes me,' grumbled Father Jack.

'Everyone likes you,' Emma said in her brisk, nurse's voice as she straightened his bedclothes. 'Though I can't think why. You've got a nasty habit of scattering your seed all over the place. It's very irresponsible.'

Father Jack winked. 'It tells you to do that in the bible.'

'Would you like some whiskey?' Emma asked Grace when the three women were back in the kitchen.

'I wouldn't say no. My nerves are in tatters.'

'And mine are in shreds,' put in Kate, determined not to be outdone in the nerves stakes.

'I'm sure you've both had a terrible shock,' Emma soothed, 'but there's no need for you to be enemies. Looked at one way, you should be friends. After all, you've shared the same experience in that when you were innocent young girls, you were taken advantage of by the same much older man.'

'I wasn't *entirely* innocent,' said Grace.

'Nor me,' said Kate. 'Not *totally*.'

'*Almost* innocent then. Will that do?'

'More or less.'

'I suppose so.'

'Both your Jacks are very nice,' Emma said encouragingly.

Grace nodded at Kate. 'Your Jack is a very fine-looking young man.'

'So's yours. Is he married?'

'Yes, he has a wife back in England, Fiona, and three bonny children. How does your Jack stand?'

'He's engaged, but . . .'

'But what?

Kate pursed her lips, unsure if she wanted to confess everything wasn't perfect with *her* Jack. 'I'm not all that keen on the girl. Her name's Veronica, and she's not good enough for him. I'd prefer . . .' She glanced at Emma. 'I'd prefer he married someone else.'

'I'm still not all that impressed with Fiona after all this time. I find it hard to keep my tongue still when I go to stay. The house is a tip and I doubt if the girl knows what a duster looks like.'

Kate tut-tutted. 'Veronica has the same non-relationship with a face flannel.'

'Young people today! They take no pride in their home or in themselves.' Grace glanced around the kitchen. 'I see this place hasn't changed a jot since I was here. The same old sink, the same old units. I expect you've missed having a place of your own to tinker round with?'

'I have indeed.' Kate sighed. 'I should have left when I was expecting Jack, like you did. I'd've found a husband, same as you, and ended up with a mink coat an' all.'

'It's only beaver coney.'

'Still, it looks nice.'

'Thank you, Kate,' Grace said graciously. 'I hope you don't mind my saying, but I love your hair. It's a nice, tasteful red.'

'Why, ta!' Kate blushed. 'It used to be even redder. What colour was yours?'

'Though I say it myself, it was quite a nice brown.'

'Your skin's still lovely and clear.'

'And you've still got the figure of a young girl. But then I suppose you're on the go the whole day long; looking after Jack, keeping the place clean, dealing with the endless parishioners. I used to think half only came for a free cup of tea and a home-made scone.'

'I've often wondered the same meself. Actually, Grace,' Kate leaned forward and said with a worried, confiding air, 'I've had a thought that I find just a wee bit troublesome.'

'And what would that be, Kate?'

'When you came in 1956, Jack would've been touching forty. Did he have a housekeeper before you?'

Grace patted her hand. 'I know what you're thinking, but there's no need to worry. I only met her the once, the day I started. Her name was Beattie and she was older than him with a face like a horse and a voice similar to two saws grating against each other. The quare feller upstairs wouldn't have touched her with a barge pole.'

The two Jacks came in. 'He'd like to talk to you, Mother,' said the other one.

Little Jack glanced warily at Kate and looked relieved when it appeared she didn't seem to mind. 'I think Emma and me should go out,' he announced.

'Out where?' demanded a surprised Emma.

'To the same place as the Castaways, a party. It's about time you and I had a little light relief. Himself upstairs looks in no danger of dying in the relatively near future. What do you say?'

'Yes!' Emma said promptly.

'Then I'll ring for a taxi.'

'Do you mind if I say goodbye to Father Jack first?' Emma said to Grace who was just about to leave the room. 'We're flying back to Liverpool in the morning and I might not see him again.'

'Go right ahead. Tell him I'll be up in a minute.'

'Do you realise what a fright you gave everyone?' Emma said sternly when she entered the priest's bedroom. 'Second sight, me foot.'

'I'm not eighty yet. According to me ould ma, I arrived in the world at around half past three in the morning, same time as the milk – people were up early in those days. I've still got a few hours to go.'

'Don't start that again!'

'I'm just warning you not to get too complacent.' He grinned complacently.

'You're an evil old man. You just like everyone fussing over you.'

'I do an' all,' he agreed.

'Anyroad, I'm off. Me and little Jack are going to a party. I've come to say tara.'

'Tara then, Miss Emma Harrison. Look after yourself for the rest of your life. And *don't* marry that miserable Matthew feller.'

'I'll marry who I like, Father,' Emma said primly.

'So you will.' He sighed. 'I don't suppose you could sneak us back that whiskey? Some bugger took it when I was sleeping the sleep of the just.'

'You only got the whiskey because I thought you were dying. I've no intention of letting you have it back. I'm a nurse, remember?'

'Oh, well, Nurse. Give us one last kiss before you go.'

'I've already given you one last kiss, but here's another.' She kissed his cheek and ruffled his white hair. 'Bye, Father Jack.'

'Bye, Emma.'

After another emotional farewell to Kate and a promise made on her heart to come and see her again, Emma left, rubbing away a stray tear as she went down the path towards the waiting taxi, and Jack, who was holding open the door.

She was about to get in, when another taxi screeched

to a halt behind and an old woman got out who, even the kind-hearted Emma couldn't deny, bore a strong resemblance to a horse, and whose name was almost certainly Beattie.

'Is it true that bastard Jack McKeown is about to kick the bucket?' she asked in a raw, grating voice.

'It was true. It isn't any longer. He's very much alive.'

'Well, I'm not coming all this way again when he decides to take his final departure. I've got a surprise for him and he can see it now, or not at all. Come on, girls, get out.'

Two grey-haired women alighted from the taxi, identical twins wearing identical clothes. 'Is this it, Mam?' enquired one.

'Aye, this is it. Now, get inside the pair of you. There's someone I want you to meet.'

Emma hurriedly shoved Jack into their own taxi. 'What d'you think that lot wanted?' he asked as they drove away.

'I've no idea.' She had a strong suspicion, but would sooner not be there when the suspicion was confirmed.

More than a hundred people were crammed into the room over a pub somewhere in the very heart of Dublin. Emma wondered if the floor was strong enough to stand up to the exuberantly stamping, dancing feet and if the walls themselves mightn't collapse outwards in protest at the horrendous racket. She watched, awestruck from the door. The Castaways were playing a crazy jig, increasing the sound and the tempo, so that the dancers stamped harder and harder and twirled their partners around faster and faster. The scene resembled an out-of-control merry-go-round that was about to fling its maniacal passengers into the middle of kingdom come.

'Come on!' Jack seized her waist and they joined in.

Emma let herself go. She danced with the enthusiasm of someone who'd had too much responsibility for far too long, wildly and with utter abandon. She threw her arms in the air, flung back her head, and thumped the floor with her feet.

'Enjoying yourself?' Jack panted.

'Oh, *yes*,' she said breathlessly.

The music ended, suddenly, abruptly, taking everyone by surprise. They laughed and sank to the floor, exhausted. Little Jack grabbed Emma and began to kiss her passionately.

Emma was kissing him back, matching his passion with her own, when she became conscious that someone was calling her name, and that the someone sounded very annoyed. She reluctantly opened her eyes and saw a strange woman waving to her from across the room.

'Emma!' The woman began to climb over the bodies on the floor. 'Where on earth have you been? And where are the others, I'd like to know? This party was arranged especially for you, and not one of you has bothered to turn up till now, when the bloody thing's half over.'

'Eileen!' It was Eileen O'Brien, her friend from the hospital, who had no right to be annoyed given that it was her who'd let them down in the first place. 'We waited for ages in that pub,' Emma said indignantly.

'You did no such thing. *I* waited for ages in the pub, but you didn't come.'

'But we did, Eileen,' Emma protested. 'It was such a grotty pub too. We were there at least an hour.'

'Mahoney's isn't grotty. It's only just downstairs and it's very nice, as it happens.'

'Mahoney's! But we went to a place miles away called Maloney's,' wailed Emma.

'You set of idiots! Where are the others?'

'I have absolutely no idea.'

'What a fucking cock-up this has been!'

'Never mind,' Jack said comfortably. 'If they'd gone to Mahoney's, then me and Emma would never have met.'

'And who are you when you're at home?'

'I'm Jack Musgrove, her fiancé.'

'I thought she was marrying someone called Matthew.'

'I was . . . I mean, I am. Oh, I'm all confused.'

'It strikes me, Emma, that in more ways than one, your hen party has turned out a total fucking failure.'

'Oh, I don't know,' said Jack.

Chapter Nine

———◆———

Hours before Emma was to meet Eileen O'Brien at the party that had been arranged especially for the five Liverpool women, and several miles away, in a quieter part of Dublin, the disagreeable Roxy dropped Pauline off in front of Nicky's house.

Nicky must have been watching. She came running out to meet her and grabbed her by the arms. 'What's happened?' she cried frantically. 'Ralph and Seamus are on their way to Marlay Park to meet you. They should be there by now.'

'Unfortunately, Tony heard me call them,' Pauline lied. 'We were getting on okay till then, despite him having found the bag contained only newspaper. After the phone call, I'm afraid he got quite violent and shut me in a bedroom, but I managed to escape and catch a taxi back.'

Nicky stamped her foot. 'Why didn't you call and let me know, you idiot?'

'Because Tony took the mobile off me. Kindly don't call me an idiot, Nicky. I did the best I could. Now, if you don't mind I'd like to go inside and I'll tell you what happened over a cup of tea.'

'Tell me if you found my Harry first.'

'I did.'

'And where is he?' The words came out in an anguished wail.

'In a house by Marlay Park, an old cottage with a thatched roof.'

'I'll ring Ralph and tell him.' She ran into the hall and picked up the phone. 'Has the cottage got a name?'

'If it has, I didn't manage to see it. It's got a red front door.' Pauline squirmed when she heard her fictitious description being relayed over the telephone by the poor, suffering woman with the haggard face and tormented eyes. She hated telling lies, but hoped that by the time Ralph and Seamus had given up and driven home, she'd have found the orange folder and be back at the hotel, out of things, apart from collecting the ten thousand pounds off Tony in the morning.

'I'm sorry I called you an idiot,' Nicky said when she put down the phone. 'I'm in such a state I'm not myself at the moment. I'll put the kettle on. Did you manage to see Harry?'

'Yes. He seemed fine.'

'Fine?' By now they were in the kitchen. Nicky turned away to put the kettle on, but Pauline knew it was an attempt to avoid meeting her eyes.

'Yes, fine,' she said. 'It was extraordinary really. They were playing snooker and you'd never dream they'd only just met. It was was if Harry had known his father all his life.'

'In a way, I'm not surprised,' Nicky said unconvincingly. 'Tony manages to do that to people. He makes each individual feel as if they're his best friend in the world. They'll do anything for him. I bet he tried to butter you up.'

Pauline laughed. 'He tried, but he didn't succeed.'

'Are you sure?'

'How could I not be sure?' This time it was Pauline who dropped her eyes away from the woman's intense gaze. She was undoubtedly crazy, but it didn't prevent Pauline from feeling desperately sorry for someone who'd become so attached to a child she'd begun to think of it as her own. Still, no matter how heart-rending the situation was, Nicky couldn't be allowed to take Harry away from his father.

The tea was made. Pauline picked up her mug and the two women sat at the table, facing each other.

'Have you got any children, Pauline?' Nicky asked.

'No.'

'You don't know what you're missing.'

'Yes, I do,' Pauline said bleakly. 'I had a little boy. His name was Jamie, but he died when he was nine months old. It was a cot death.'

'I'm so sorry.'

'So am I. Life's never been the same since.'

'Life would never be the same for me without Harry.'

Pauline didn't answer. She sighed and finished her tea. If only things could be changed back to the way they'd once been! 'Where's your toilet?'

'It's the door facing at the top of the stairs.' Nicky seemed calmer now. She stood at the same time as Pauline. 'I can't thank you enough for what you've done, but I think I can understand why you did it.'

Upstairs was as nice as down. Pauline did a quick tour in the hope of seeing a place where the orange file might be hidden. She peeped through the open doors of the big, high-ceilinged rooms; pine doors and pine furniture everywhere, a cherry-red carpet on the stairs and landing, a duvet with a patchwork cover on the double bed in the main bedroom, white cotton curtains, creamy walls. Harry's room was painted sky blue and covered with Star Wars posters. Pauline winced when she saw a pair of tiny pyjamas with the same motif folded neatly on the blue pillow. A baby lamp shaped like a rabbit had been left switched on, as if the room's occupant was expected home any minute.

It was a pity the girl couldn't be content with what she had – a beautiful house, a nice husband who obviously thought the world of her and who seemed to have plenty of money. There was plenty of time for her to have children of her own. What had happened to send her over the edge and lay claim to someone else's child?

Pauline had just entered the bathroom, when the mobile in her bag rang. She fumbled with the bag's zip, switched off the phone, and prayed Nicky hadn't heard.

What was she supposed to do now, ransack every upstairs drawer looking for a file that might, possibly, be secreted under the clothes? No way, not with Nicky in the house. Perhaps there was a way of getting Nicky *out* of the house, but if so, Pauline couldn't think of one. She wondered if there was a study or an office downstairs which held a filing cabinet, the obvious place to keep a file.

She crept downstairs. Nicky was still in the kitchen. There were two doors in the hall. The first opened on to a lounge, the second a dining-room. Pauline bit her lip. She didn't like to do it, but it looked as if she'd have to let Tony down.

But she hated letting people down. She crept further along the hall, around a corner, and found another door,

smaller than the others. Turning the knob, she found
herself in a tiny office with a computer on a grey enamel
desk and a matching filing cabinet in the corner. Pauline
crossed swiftly towards it.

The top drawer contained several neatly arranged
beige folders which there wasn't time to examine in case
the contents of the orange one had been transferred.

She had just opened the drawer beneath, when
Nicky said from the doorway, 'If you're looking for
Tony's stuff, it's in a safety deposit box in a bank in
London.'

'I was just admiring your house,' Pauline stammered,
conscious that the explanation was wholly inadequate,
and wanting the ground to open up and swallow her
when she saw the look of contempt on the woman's
haggard face. She also felt not a little scared. Nicky wasn't
exactly sane. She was also bigger than she was, younger.
Tony had warned her to be careful.

'Including the contents of Ralph's filing cabinet?
Come off it, Pauline. Tony wrapped you round his little
finger, didn't he? I had my suspicions straight away. That
wasn't a taxi you came back in. It was a Mercedes. Ralph
phoned earlier and said you'd been taken from the bus
stop in the same sort of car. Then you couldn't meet my
eyes when I asked if Tony had got to you. But you
seemed so nice, so straightforward, I couldn't believe you
were two-timing me. To make sure, I called my mobile,
the one you said had been taken off you, and I heard it
ring upstairs.' She smiled pityingly. 'You're not the sort of
person I thought would be taken in by Tony's big, brown
eyes, the crooked smile. Or did he bribe you? Has he
offered you the ten thousand quid in return for the
papers? Or did he do both?'

It occurred to Pauline that she wasn't exactly in the wrong here. She was helping Tony Bianco get back his private papers, including the love letters he had written to his wife, things that Nicky had no right to have.

'You've got no room to criticise,' she said coldly. 'Wasn't it enough that you stole his child? Did you have to steal his precious letters too?'

'Oh, so's that the line he spun! Huh!' Nicky laughed sarcastically. '*I* stole *his* child! And precious letters my foot. You look too intelligent to be taken in by such a load of obvious crap.'

'One load of obvious crap I wasn't taken in by was your assertion that Tony had never seen Harry before,' Pauline retorted angrily. 'They were completely at ease with each other. Harry clearly felt quite at home.'

Nicky's face collapsed. 'Did he? Oh, did he? Did he not mention me once?'

'No,' Pauline said bluntly, regretting it immediately when Nicky burst into tears. 'Look,' she said, gently now, 'you've just got to accept the fact he's not your child. You've got a lovely home, a lovely husband. You can have children of your own.'

'I've already got a child of my own,' Nicky screamed. 'His name's Harry, and I've got to get him back before that crook takes him to America and I might never see him again.'

'But, Nicky . . .'

'Let me show you something.' Nicky spun around and ran into the kitchen. Pauline followed. Nicky had taken a brown envelope out of the dresser drawer. 'Look, here's Harry's birth certificate.' She shoved the document at the older woman. 'See what it says, "Mother's name: Nicola Sophie Warren." Here's a photo of me and Harry in the hospital when he was only a few days old. And here's one of him being baptised a few weeks later.'

'Tony's on this one as well as you.'

'Tony's Harry's father, that's why. I've never denied that fact.'

'What about the fact you *did* deny, that Tony knew nothing about Harry?'

'Holy Mary, Mother of God!' Nicky sat down at the table and buried her face in her hands. 'They say your sins will always find you out, don't they,' she said in a muffled voice.

'What did you do that was so wrong, Nicky?' Pauline sat down beside the stricken woman and put her arm around her shoulders. 'Shall I make more tea?'

'Please.'

Neither spoke while the tea was being made. When the mug was put in front of her, Nicky dried her eyes and composed herself.

'I knew Tony Bianco was a crook, right from the beginning,' she began in a steady voice. 'I went to America as an au pair, and I'd only been there a few months when we met in a club. He was almost twice my age and the most attractive man I'd ever known. I was only eighteen and then it seemed exciting that he was involved with the Mafia – he never tried to hide it. It wasn't long before I found myself pregnant. At first, Tony tried to persuade me to have an abortion.' She smiled wryly. 'I nearly did. I'd've done anything for him in those days.'

'You'd always have regretted it,' Pauline put in.

'I know that now, but I didn't then. Then Tony changed his mind and decided he'd quite like a child – a boy. So, I had a boy for him; Harry, and we lived together as man and wife for the next five years.'

'Why didn't you tell us this before?'

'Because I didn't want Ralph to know, that's why,' Nicky cried. 'He's the best thing that's ever happened to me, but he's very straitlaced. It's one thing taking on a woman and another man's baby, but another altogether if the man concerned was totally evil, yet she'd lived with him for years.'

'Why didn't you leave?' Pauline asked, puzzled.

'Because at first I was besotted with Tony. It took a good two years before I realised just how evil he was, by which time he loved Harry as much as any father would, good or bad. I knew he'd never let me go unless I was prepared to leave Harry behind, which I would never, never have done. I just gritted my teeth and tried to distance myself from the things that went on. That worked for another two years, then he met this woman, an actress called Lucy Minetto.

'I met Lucy. She's in Ireland with him.'

'I'm not surprised.' Nicky sighed. 'They're inseparable. He's as besotted with her as I used to be with him. They go everywhere together. It meant that suddenly I was in the way. Tony wanted me to go, but Harry to stay and for Lucy to move in. They got married and began to take him on holiday, to Disneyland and places. I was gradually being squeezed out of my son's life, no matter how much I protested. Can you imagine what that was like, Pauline?'

'Terrifying.' Pauline shuddered.

'Tony offered me money to leave, huge sums, but I refused. There was no way I was going to give up my child. Then he said he'd give me a million dollars and it was an offer I couldn't refuse. Do you know what that means?'

'I've seen *The Godfather*. He meant if you didn't take it, he'd have you killed.'

'Precisely.' Nicky nodded. 'I knew I didn't have much time. As soon as I could do so without Tony knowing, I bought two airline tickets to London for when I knew he and Lucy were going away – I was petrified he'd discover what I was up to. When the day came, I packed a few things and me and Harry caught a taxi to Kennedy airport and flew home. Of course, Harry missed his dad. He loved Tony. That's why they looked so at ease with each other when you saw them earlier, except Tony won't have told him he'll never see his mom again.' She winced painfully. 'Anyway, for six months, we buried ourselves in bedsit land in London while I wondered where we could go to escape from Tony's clutches for ever. Then I met Ralph and we came to live in Ireland where he works. I thought we'd be safe, but perhaps nowhere in the world is safe from Tony.'

'He'd had this chap called Sydney looking for you. He'd more or less given up, but when Sydney came to Dublin on some other business, he happened to see you. Tony flew over straight away.'

Nicky looked astounded. 'What on earth sort of business could Tony have in Ireland?'

'He didn't say. There's something happening tonight. He told Sydney and this other chap, the driver, to stay off the booze. He wanted them sober for the next few hours. Look, about the letters from his dead wife,' Pauline continued, wanting to get everything clear, but an irritable Nicky interrupted.

'He's never had a wife, apart from Lucy. It's not letters in the orange file, but tapes. He used to record all the meetings with some very important people who had no business knowing Tony Bianco, and would hate it to get out that they had. It was a form of insurance – and blackmail – but just as incriminating for Tony as everyone else. I took the file as insurance for myself. I knew he'd never try to kill me unless he got the file back first. That's why it's safely in a London bank, not that Tony knows that. I let him think the file was here so as to give myself more time.'

'I see.' Pauline wasn't all that sure if she did. She put her elbows on the table. 'What do we do now?'

'You do nothing,' Nicky said flatly. 'I don't know why you're in Dublin, but you didn't come to help me get back my kidnapped son. I suggest you return to your hotel or wherever you're staying and forget about me and my problems. Ralph and Seamus will be back soon and, you never know, they might have Harry with them.' She frowned. 'Though surely Ralph would have rung and let me know.'

The blood in Pauline's veins turned to ice. 'They won't have Harry,' she said in a frightened voice. 'I'd forgotten, I sent them on a wild-goose chase. The white cottage doesn't exist. Harry's in a place called Bray.'

They were on their way to Bray to retrieve Harry from his criminal father, haring along the dark country roads in the Ford Corsa that Ralph had bought Nicky for shopping. Pauline gritted her teeth and held on to the seat with both hands. Despite the seat belt, she felt as if she was about to be thrown through the windscreen. At any other time, Nicky might have been a good driver, Pauline wouldn't know, but now she drove like a total maniac.

'You won't be much good to Harry if you're dead,'

she shouted as the car went on two wheels around a corner. At least it felt like two wheels.

'Shut up,' Nicky snapped. 'I'm too mad at you to talk. I can't understand how you could have been so easily taken in, so much so, that you actually *conspired* with the bastard. If you hadn't lied for him, if you'd told the truth, Ralph might have found Harry by now.'

'*You* were taken in for two whole years.'

'I was only young. You're old enough to know better.'

'I'm not exactly ancient. And, unlike you, I'm not used to associating with criminals. Anyroad, if you'd told us the truth in the first place, I wouldn't have *been* taken in. What was all that guff about ten thousand pounds?'

'That was for Ralph's sake. I didn't want him knowing about the tapes. If the bloody things had been in Ireland, I'd've given them to Tony if I'd thought he'd let me have Harry back. Except I know he wouldn't. He wants the tapes *and* Harry.'

'If he gets away with Harry, you can threaten him with the tapes,' Pauline said reasonably. 'Tell him you'll send them to the police in America if he doesn't let you have Harry back.'

'You could do that with a normal person, but not with Tony Bianco.' Nicky's voice rose, becoming more and more hysterical. 'He'd have me followed. The minute I collected the tapes from the bank, I'd be shot. Either that, or he'd blow up the aircraft taking them to the States, or kill the mailman about to deliver them.'

'I think you're exaggerating a bit, Nicky.'

'How the fuck would you know?'

'Don't swear!' Pauline yelled. 'There's no need for it. And you're right, I wouldn't know. I don't know anything any more. I don't know what I'm doing here or why I'm being driven through the Irish countryside by a mad woman when I'm supposed to be in Dublin for a hen party. I've lost my friends, except for the one I found earlier wandering along this very road in an evening frock who's now in hospital and may have tetanus. I've lost my reason. I'm not sure if I'll be able to do my job any more.'

'Now who's exaggerating! We're nearly at Bray and approaching a crossroads. Which way should I turn?'

'Right, no left,' Pauline said sulkily. 'Then it's left again down an unmade road a few hundred yards further on. You're lucky I remembered.'

'No, *you're* lucky you remembered. I might have killed you if you hadn't.'

'Over my dead body,' Pauline replied, somewhat foolishly.

'We'd better stop here and walk if you don't want Tony to hear the sound of the engine,' she said a few minutes later when they were halfway along the dirt road. 'Hide the car, turn into this field.' The car turned into the field and stopped abruptly. Nicky went to open the door. 'Why not try and get in touch with Ralph again?' Nicky had tried before, but there'd been no reply.

'They're still not answering.' Nicky chucked the mobile on to the back seat. 'Either the battery's run down, or they're in a dip and out of range of the signal.' She uttered a short, barking laugh. 'And we know whose fault *that* is!'

'You can't hold me responsible for the contours of the Irish countryside.' They both got out of the car. Pauline's legs were shaking. 'Are you sure we should be doing this on our own?'

'Stay in the car if you like. I didn't ask you to come.'

'I know you didn't, but I thought Ralph and Seamus would be with us. What if Tony and both men are there?'

'Then we'll wait until the Mercedes leaves. You said there was something going on tonight. Tony might go with them and there'll only be Lucy left. Getting Harry back will be as easy as pie.'

'I hope so. I wish it wasn't so dark.'

'It's not too dark to see by. You'll soon get used to it.'

'Be ready to dodge out of sight if you hear a car. And walk quietly and don't talk. Footsteps and voices carry clearly in the countryside when there are no other sounds. I feel as if we're in the middle of nowhere.'

'Yes, miss.'

'Stop trying to be funny, Nicky.'

'I've never felt less funny in my life.'

Neither woman spoke again as they virtually tip-toed along the roughly surfaced lane. The silence was total until Nicky smothered a cry when she twisted her ankle in a rut.

'Are you all right?' Pauline whispered.

'Oh, I'm fine.'

'Sarcasm is the lowest form of wit and the highest form of ignorance.'

'Really!'

The farmhouse came into view, a squat, black building against the sombre, slate-coloured sky, its windows glinting blackly.

'That's the lounge at the front,' Pauline said in a low voice. 'I got the impression the bedrooms were at the back.'

'Then let's go round the back,' Nicky whispered.

'Skirt around the place a bit, don't go directly. See, through those trees on the left.' She was pleased to note the car wasn't there. Sydney and Roxy must have gone to do whatever Tony had planned later tonight.

Their feet made little sound on the leaf-strewn grass of what appeared to be an orchard. They reached the rear of the house and crouched behind the bushes at the foot of the long garden. By now, Pauline had got used to the dark and the windows of the building were clearly visible in the white walls.

'The second from the left could be Harry's room. The window's open. He doesn't like sleeping with the window closed.'

'What will you do, you and Harry, when you've got him back?'

Pauline felt the woman shrug beside her. 'What else can I do except drive straight to the airport and fly somewhere far away? I can't go back to the house, not now that Tony knows where we live.'

'What about Ralph?'

'He'll just have to get on with his life without me. And Harry.'

'That's not fair!'

'There's no need to tell *me* that. I know it isn't fair. But I haven't got much choice, have I?'

'I know where you can go, just for tonight. Our hotel. It's called the Arcadia. Ask for the key to room 58. There's no way Tony will know you're there. Get in touch with Ralph, talk to him, tell him the truth, let him decide if he wants to come with you. Don't just walk away. Give him a chance.' Pauline gasped. 'For goodness sake, Nicky, what are you doing?'

'Giving you a hug. You're the nicest person I've ever met. I'm sorry I've been so horrid. Now, I think it's about time I rescued my little boy from the Mafia.'

★   ★   ★

Harry was fast asleep in the bedroom with the open window, looking very small beneath the covers of a double bed.

'I'll have to climb in and wake him,' Nicky whispered, 'warn him to keep quiet, otherwise he'll alert Tony – if he's here.'

'It'd be wise to assume he is.'

Pauline gave her a hand through the window. She watched her bend over the bed, heard the child mutter a sleepy, 'Mommy! Pop said you were sick.'

'Shush, sweetheart. I'm not the least bit sick. Mommy's come to take you home.'

'Like home better than here.'

'I know, sweetheart. We're going to do something real exciting. We're going to climb out the window.'

'Okay, Mommy.' He lifted his arms and Nicky lifted him from the bed and brought him to the window. Pauline held out her own arms and took him while Nicky scrambled through and jumped on to the grass outside.

'I never dreamt it would be so easy.' She reached for Harry and her elbow caught the open window, loosened from its catch, and it slammed shut, echoing like a thunderclap in the silence of the night. The two women froze. Harry rubbed his eyes and yawned. 'Are we going home now, Mommy?'

'Tony,' a woman shouted. 'What was that?'

'I'll find out.'

'Run!' hissed Pauline. 'Go round the house the opposite way to how we came.

'What about you?'

'Forget about me. Run, quickly, run. Get away.'

Nicky began to run at the same time as Pauline ran towards the trees through which they'd just come. When she reached their shelter, she stopped and looked back at the house. She heard Tony yell — he must have discovered Harry had gone — and a few seconds later, the front door opened and he rushed out, stopped, and stared wildly around for his son and whoever had taken him.

Pauline began to thrash through the trees, swishing the branches, kicking the leaves, grunting. She came to a ladder and flung it to the ground. Tony ran towards the noise and Pauline stood as still as a statue, making no noise at all, while the man swore and stamped and thumped the trunks of the trees in rage, and Pauline's blood curdled when she thought of what he'd do if he found her. He tripped over the ladder and swore again.

'Harry! Are you there, son?' he called in a suddenly gentle, wheedling voice. 'Give Pop a shout if you are. If Mommy's got you, I told you she's sick. She needs help.'

'Tony!' Lucy called. 'Do you want a flashlight? There's one here.' The beam of a torch swept over the ground in front of the house.

'Coming.' Tony stamped towards the light. 'Whoever took Harry is somewhere in those fucking trees,' he said loudly. 'The kid's not answering. They must have stuck tape on his mouth. If it's Nicky, I'll kill the bitch, fuck the consequences. Anyone else, and I'll burn their fucking eyes out first. They'll die a very slow death.'

Pauline crossed herself and was in the middle of a heartfelt prayer, when the Mercedes swept up the drive. It stopped and Sydney and Roxy got out.

'What's up, boss?' Sydney asked in surprise when he saw the door wide open and Tony and Lucy standing outside. 'This food'll need warming up. We had to drive almost to Dublin before we found a take away.'

'Fuck the food, Harry's gone,' Tony roared. 'He's over here somewhere, in the trees.'

'We'll give you a hand, but we haven't got much time. They're expecting us at Guava Tech in just over an hour.'

'Be careful. I don't want Harry hurt.'

'Sure, boss.'

The three men descended on the orchard, and the flashlight shimmered madly, up and down the trees, in and out of the branches, disturbing the birds and the tiny creatures that lived under the leaves and slept in the soil.

Lucy was standing in the brightly lit doorway of the farmhouse, shivering in her white towelling robe. She turned, went inside, and closed the door. The driveway was thrown instantly into blackness, and as Pauline waited for the beam of the dancing light to come nearer, an idea came born by desperation, an instinct for survival she never knew she had. She took off a shoe and flung it high into the air, as far as it would go, and heard it land, well away from the house.

'Did you hear that!' Tony shouted. 'It was somewhere over there.'

As the men plunged towards where the shoe had landed, Pauline raced towards the far side of the Mercedes and checked to see if the keys had been left in the ignition.

They hadn't. But all was not lost. Not yet. She quietly opened the rear door and curled herself up on the floor between the seats. If all three men were going to Guava Tech, whatever and wherever that was, then she'd had it. She'd be discovered when one got in the back. But if it was just Sydney and Roxy, then she stood a chance.

The whole car seemed to be pounding in rhythm with

her heart and her chest felt as if it was about to explode. She had cramp in both feet and she'd cut the shoeless one on a stone.

In the far distance, she heard an engine start and recognised the Corsa. She prayed again that the men wouldn't hear the noise, but they were making too much themselves; thrashing about, swearing and shouting. In a few minutes Nicky and Harry would reach the main road and be safe.

Sighing with relief, she rested her throbbing head on the thick carpet. But seconds later, her heart began to pound even louder. She'd just remembered something.

She'd suggested to Nicky that she take Harry to the Arcadia. 'Tony won't know you're there,' she'd said. But Tony *knew* where she was staying. She told him herself so he would know where to come in case she'd found the orange folder and to give her the ten thousand pounds.

Tony was bound to connect Pauline with Harry's disappearance. She was probably the only person outside his inner circle who knew where Harry was.

Once he'd given up searching the orchard, once he'd calmed down and had had time to think, the Arcadia would be the first place he would look.

Chapter Ten

In the bar of the Stena Line ferry on its way to Holyhead, Monsignor Aloysius McGillivray sipped slowly and appreciatively on his glass of malt whiskey. He was enjoying the slow motion of the boat and the faint, comforting hum of the engine. It was nice to relax and forget he was a priest for a while. The bar was relatively empty, no one was looking at him respectfully, fawning over him, expecting to be blessed, or have their sins forgiven at the drop of a hat. He felt like an ordinary man for a change, able to think ordinary men's thoughts without the accompanying guilt that went with his job.

These unpriestly – though not unhappy – thoughts were directed towards the pretty widow, Estelle, and he wondered how long it would be before they could get married and he could satisfy his ordinary, unpriestly needs in the way the good Lord had intended – He wouldn't have equipped men with such a vitally important member then denied them its use. There was no restriction on other parts of his body; he had a mouth and was allowed to speak, he had ears, a nose, limbs, all of which he was at liberty to employ at will.

On the car deck below, where the good Monsignor's car was parked, there was no indication that, in the boot, a weary nurse was having the best sleep of her life apart from the softest and gentlest of snores and the occasional little satisfied grunts that no one could hear.

Rosemary was dreaming, lovely, peaceful dreams. She was a child again, sitting on her mother's knee being told her favourite story; playing on a golden beach while little frothy waves rippled over her feet; in bed with Gary, her husband, and they were having passionate, extremely satisfying sex – *and there was no need to hurry!*

A miracle had occurred and neither had to get up for work at their stressful jobs. There was time to do extravagent things like read books, cook interesting meals and eat them leisurely, go to the cinema and not fall asleep in the middle of the film, look out the window and actually *see* what was there.

The Monsignor ordered another whiskey, innocently unaware that within a few hours' time, the contents of his briefcase would be the lead story on the morning news and subsequently flashed around the world; that he would be accused of having abducted an innocent young nurse, an even more titillating titbit for the media.

But that was for the future. For now, the good Monsignor was content.

Chapter Eleven

———◆———

As is the way with these things, two taxis came careering along the road at the same time. Peter and Mark Costello hailed the first, and Donna and Tracey the second.

'Follow that cab!' Tracey said tersely when she got in. It meant there was no need to eavesdrop when Peter gave his driver the destination.

'Which cab?'

'How many bleedin' cabs are there?' Donna demanded, getting in behind. 'There's only the one in front.'

'There's no need to be rude.' The driver sounded hurt. 'I wanted to make sure I followed the right one. I've always hoped someone would ask me to do this and now you've gone and spoilt it.'

After a while, the route they were taking began to look familiar and Tracey recognised it as the way the first taxi had gone when it carried them from the cinema to Maloney's, only a matter of hours ago, though it felt more like a million years.

They passed, though they didn't know it, the bus stop from which their friend, Pauline, had twice been abducted, then turned into the dimly lit road that led to, (a) the theatre, (b) the priest's house where their other friend, Emma, was currently agonising over whether it was right to marry Matthew when she was so attracted to Jack, (c) the sad remains of the house belonging to a top member of the Gardai to which Donna had carelessly set light, and (d) Maloney's from where the supposed corpse of yet another friend, Rosemary, had been casually dumped in the boot of a car belonging to a madly frustrated priest, and where the customers by now were as drunk as pipers and had forgotten all about the five miserable English women who had been tricked into drinking a pint of Paddy's Brew.

The taxi in front drew up outside the unlit theatre. Tracey asked their driver to stop on the other side of the road and waited until Mark and Peter had disappeared before signalling to Donna to get out.

'You wait here,' she said as the taxi drove away. 'I shouldn't be long. I only want to collect me clothes and bag.'

'Why can't I come with you?'

'Because you're wearing the little guy's clothes. He'll only notice and get mad.'

'If you're not going to be long, we should have kept that bloody taxi. We'll need one to get to the Green Lizard.'

'I didn't think of that.'

'Hurry up then,' Donna said sulkily. 'I'm freezing.'

The side door was unlocked and Tracey could hear no sound of a party when she went in. The undermined cast mustn't have considered their final performance a cause for celebration and had abandoned the theatre with the same ruthless sense of preservation as rats abandon a sinking ship.

There was, however, an argument going on. Apparently, Peter wanted to leave immediately and Mark wanted to stay.

'What the hell for?' demanded an angry Peter.

'I'm not sure,' replied an anguished Mark. 'I'd just like to sit on the stage awhile, think about things.'

'That's a depressingly unhealthy thing to do.'

'I don't care. I'm not in the mood for a drink or a club. Anyway, I'm not dressed for it, am I? I just want to sit on the stage and ponder the meaning of life and stuff.'

'Why didn't you say so before?'

'I didn't realise I felt this way until I found the party had been cancelled. It brought home to me what a total balls-up the night has been.'

'Oh, well, please yourself,' Peter said carelessly. 'I'm off. You can sit and think on your own.'

'I'm sorry, Peter, for messing you about,' Mark said in a meek treble. 'Thank you for coming to the hospital to collect me and for bringing me here.'

'You're not going to try and kill yourself again?'

'No.'

'Sure?'

'Positive. Bye, Peter. Have a nice time.'

'When you've had enough of thinking, don't forget the party at the Green Lizard.'

'I won't.'

'And don't worry about the clothes. You look okay as you are.'

Tracey dodged into the ladies' dressing room when she heard Peter coming. The expensively hired costumes had been flung on to the floor, and the frills and flounces pointed at her accusingly. Tracey picked them up one by one and arranged them neatly on hangers. She tidied the shelf in front of the long mirror and wiped it clean, returned lids to the numerous jars of make-up, and put them in a tidy row. Then she changed into her own clothes, surprised they hadn't been torn to shreds by half a dozen actresses in an orgy of hate and bitterness directed towards their owner.

She felt herself again. She threw her handbag over her shoulder, opened the door, ready to creep out and forget the night had ever happened.

On the stage, Mark Costello was talking to himself.

'To be, or not to be, that is the question, Whether tis nobler in the mind to suffer the stings and arrows of outrageous fortune or to take arms against a sea of troubles . . .' There was a pause followed by a sob.

Was he all right?

Obviously not. Sane people didn't quote Shakespeare to themselves in a deserted theatre and cry.

Would he ever be all right again?

Who knows?

And if he wasn't, whose fault was it?

Tracey's, of course!

It hadn't been her intention to harm him. It was her job to make people better, not suicidal. She decided to have one more try at impressing on him that it had all been a giant mistake, that no ill will had been intended. If he tried to kill her again, she was perfectly capable of protecting herself.

She made her way towards the stage where Mark was sitting on the white satin sofa – Tracey drew in a sharp, panicky breath – *holding a dagger in both hands with the blade pointed at his breast.*

'No!' she screamed, just as Mark plunged the dagger straight into his heart.

She rushed on to the stage, ready to stem the bleeding, give mouth to mouth, but to her relief and astonishment, Mark turned towards her and said listlessly, 'Oh, it's you.'

'I thought you'd just stabbed yourself!' she gasped.

'In a way, I wish I had.' He pushed the dagger into the white satin sofa and the blade disappeared inside the handle. 'This is the dagger that Macbeth saw before him. We did the play a few years ago.'

'You gave me a terrible shock.'

'You deserve more than a shock for what you did to me,' he said in the same listless voice, as if all his anger had fled and he felt only despair.

'It wasn't deliberate. Have you ever been to a pub called Maloney's?' she asked, changing tack.

He pulled a face. 'The place that sells that vile Paddy's Brew? That stuff can change the course of your life. Personally, I wouldn't go near Maloney's if you paid me. Anyway, what's that got to do with anything?'

'I went there, earlier tonight, with my friends. We were supposed to meet someone who didn't turn up. They gave us a drink on the house, presumably Paddy's Brew. It tasted all right, but I haven't felt the same since. I had a blackout, I think I told you that before. It's why I genuinely thought I'd promised to be in *Lady Windermere*. I was only keeping my word.'

'So, Paddy's Brew has changed the course of my life and I didn't even drink the fucking stuff,' Mark said bleakly.

'I'm sorry, truly sorry. I've never been more sorry about anything before.' She went and sat beside him on the sofa, wanting to put him on her knee, pat him and comfort him, as a mother would have done an ailing child.

'Do you really mean that?' He looked at her, baby-blue eyes moist.

'Sincerely, with all my heart.'

He sighed. 'I suppose it makes it a tiny bit less painful, knowing it wasn't done on purpose.'

She patted his hand. 'I hope so.'

'To add insult to injury, some bastard stole my clothes, along with my wallet and my mobile. That's why I'm wearing this damn stupid outfit.'

'It suits you.' Tracey hoped he wouldn't notice her guilty blush.

'Perhaps I should have been a doctor,' he said gloomily. 'I've made a piss poor showing as a theatrical producer.'

'There's plenty more time to try again. You're only young.'

'I'm thirty-five, and I don't think I could bring myself to try again. I put everything I had into *Lady Windermere*.' He sighed again. 'What's it all about, eh?'

'What's what all about?'

'Life.'

'I dunno.' Tracey shrugged. It was something she'd never thought about. There never seemed to be the time. 'I just go from day to day and hope for the best.'

'So do I, but the best never seems to happen, at least not to me.'

'Have you got a job? I mean, an ordinary job?' He couldn't make a living working in amateur theatre.

'I work in an office, insurance. It's mind-numbingly boring.'

Tracey was trying to think of something else encouraging to say, when a voice called, 'Cooee! Is anyone at home?'

'We're here,' she called back when it became obvious Mark had neither the will nor the energy to do it himself. 'On the stage.'

A man appeared, fiftyish, very tall, very thin, wearing a plaid suit over a frilly pink shirt, gold hoop earrings and a jangly gold bracelet. His nose was as sharp as the dagger Mark still held in his hand and his dyed blond hair fell in cute little curls and ringlets on his shoulders.

'Am I addressing Mark Costello?' the man gushed.

'Yes,' Mark conceded reluctantly and his white brow crinkled in a worried frown, as if wondering what other dreadful thing was about to happen.

'Geoffrey Bannerman, Stellar Television.' He bowed obsequiously. 'I've just viewed your play, dear chap, and I must congratulate you. It was absolutely brilliant – farce of the very highest order.'

Mark's already pale face went even paler. 'You've just *viewed* my play!'

'A young lady brought the video into the station tonight, a friend of a friend of a producer who happens to be *my* friend. We decided to watch it for a laugh, and laugh we did, but quite genuinely, as was your intent.'

'What video? What station?' Mark enquired in a cracked voice. 'What are you talking about?'

'The video of *Lady Windermere's Fan*, dear boy. I'm so pleased I was there when it arrived. Perhaps I should explain, I'm in Dublin staying the weekend with my friend, Felix. He's a producer with Radio Telefis Eireann.'

'Mr Hopper's fucking girlfriend made the video!' Mark groaned. 'She was probably hoping to see it on *It'll Be All Right On The Night* or bloody Beadle.'

171

'Don't be silly, Mark.' Tracey squeezed his hand warningly. Geoffrey Bannerman seemed quite genuine. And he was from Stellar Television, which she'd never heard of, but it sounded very grand. 'Did you come to see Mark for a particular reason?' she asked.

'The best reason in the world, young lady.' The man beamed. 'I want him to work for us at Stellar Television. We make programmes, including drama, for all the main channels in the British Isles: BBC, ITV, Sky. I'm offering this young genius a job. It will mean moving house, moving countries in fact – we're based in Kent, twenty miles from London. Would that be a problem, Mark? Do you mind if I call you Mark?'

'He doesn't mind, and no, it wouldn't be a problem,' Tracey replied when it appeared that Mark had lost the ability to speak. 'Out of interest, did you watch the video through to the end?'

'It only contained the first two acts, but that was enough to delight my soul.' Geoffrey Bannerman's thin face adopted a dreamy expression. 'I immediately envisaged Oscar Wilde's entire repertoire reduced to farce, along with Ionesco, Ibsen, Shakespeare – can you imagine the blissful enjoyment of a slapstick, knockabout, laugh-a-minute version of *King Lear*?'

Mark groaned again and whispered, ' "reduced" being the operative word.' Tracey kicked him. 'He's a bit stunned,' she explained. 'He found tonight emotionally draining.'

Geoffrey Bannerman smiled understandingly. 'Why is he dressed as a doctor?'

'He's about to go to a fancy dress party. Out of interest, what salary does the job offer?'

'At least 100K.'

Tracey gulped. 'It'll probably seem more real to him when he's signed a contract.'

'I can get a contract to him tonight,' the man said eagerly. 'I'll call my secretary on the mobile – she has a computer at home and can email the contract to Felix, who'll be as mad as hell because he was hoping to get Mark for himself. How will I get it to you?'

'Come to the club called the Green Lizard later. There's a party and Mark and I will both be there.'

'The Green Lizard it is. Can I bring Felix?'

'Of course. If you'd like some privacy, you can talk to your secretary from one of the dressing rooms.'

'Ta very much. Won't be a mo.'

'What do you think?' Tracey asked when Geoffrey Bannerman had gone.

'Was he real?' asked Mark. He appeared totally stunned.

'He seemed real enough to me.'

'Did you *touch* him?'

'No, but I saw him clearly enough. I heard him say what he did.'

'Did he actually offer me a job?'

'He did.'

'As a producer?'

'Yes.'

'On television?

'On television.'

'Was the figure of 100K mentioned?'

'It was.'

'And a contract is in the offing?'

'It will be with you very soon.'

'Are *you* real?'

'Oh, don't act soft, Mark. Of course, I'm real.'

'If I take the job,' he said seriously, 'it will mean compromising my integrity.'

'Do you mind?'

'For 100K, I'd do Oscar Wilde backwards and Shakespeare upside down. Thank you, very much – you know, I don't know your name.'

'Tracey.'

'Thank you, Tracey. You did me proud. I'm not in a fit state to negotiate my way off this stage, let alone my future career.'

'It makes up a bit for what happened earlier. Oh!' She put a hand to her mouth. 'I'll have to go. I've just remembered I left me friend outside and I promised I wouldn't be long.'

'Perhaps I should come with you. Are you going straight to the Green Lizard?'

She remembered Donna was wearing his clothes. 'Yes, but don't forget Geoffrey Bannerman's still here.'

'How could I possibly have forgotten that!'

'We'll meet up later in the club. I can be your witness when you sign the contract.'

'Promise?'

'Promise. I won't let you down a second time.'

There was no sign of Donna outside. Tracey hung around for a while in case she appeared, then set off down the hill towards Dublin city centre. She wondered how events would have turned out if she'd done this earlier, ignored the theatre, walked right past, continued down the hill with Pauline? She didn't wonder for long because she was too practical to waste her time on obscure thoughts – what if *this* had happened, what if *that*? What had happened had happened and there was no going back. Her adventures in Dublin were over. She was on her way to the Green Lizard where no doubt she would meet up with Donna and have a great time.

At first, she didn't notice the long black car draw up beside her until the window rolled down and someone spoke. 'Hi. It's Tracey, isn't it? Remember we met before? I dropped you off at the hospital.'

It was the nice man who, along with Pauline, had picked her up ages ago on her trek along the country road. His name was Roxy. There was another man on the passenger seat beside him.

'Oh, hello,' she said cheerily.

'Where are you off to?'

'A club in town. It's a waste of time waiting for a taxi. I was going with a friend, but she seems to have disappeared.'

'Would you like a lift. We have to go somewhere first, but we won't be long, then we'll drop you off right outside the door.'

Tracey hesitated, only briefly. The guy must be all right, otherwise Pauline wouldn't have been with him. 'Okay,' she said.

'Hop in the back then. The door's open.'

'Ta.'

Tracey hesitated, only briefly, a second time, when she opened the door and saw Pauline crouched on the floor behind the two men, her finger held frantically to her lips, warning her to keep quiet. It wasn't too late to change her mind, refuse the lift, but Tracey wasn't prepared to leave her friend in what was obviously a highly precarious, possibly dangerous, position. She climbed inside, only narrowly missing Pauline's face with her foot.

Not only had she fucked up a performance of *Lady Windermere's Fan*, but she had brought a rather nice little man to the brink of suicide, stolen his clothes, rescued a saint, tricked two nuns out of the saint's clothes, yet *still* the night was fairly young.

She wondered what else it had in store?

Chapter Twelve

———————◆———————

While Donna appreciated having her saintly bacon saved by Tracey, she deeply resented being left outside the theatre to wait in the cold. Why hadn't the little guy been wearing a jacket? They could have pinched that an' all. She would have stamped her feet in an effort to keep warm, except the shoes were beginning to hurt.

'Come on, Trace,' she groaned aloud, sitting on a wall and flapping her arms, hugging herself.

She noticed a small figure tramping determinedly down the deserted hill and was surprised when it stopped in front of her and said, 'Hello.'

'Hello, yourself,' she replied curtly, not being in the mood for idle chit-chat with an unknown child.

'You don't remember me, do you?'

'No, I don't.'

'I remember you. You're the person who burnt our house down. There's hardly any of it left. The firemen are still trying to put out the flames.'

'Me!' Donna laughed incredulously, but inwardly felt worried. It was the child from the bedroom who'd directed her towards his or her daddy's cigarettes, which reminded her she couldn't half do with one now. The child wore jeans, a red felt bomber jacket, a baseball cap back to front, and carried a small haversack on its back. Moonlight glinted on its round, owlish spectacles. She briefly considered strangling it, but it would only get her into more trouble.

'Everyone ses you're a saint, but *I* know better,' the child said in a smarmy voice.

'I still rescued you, didn't I?' Donna snapped. It was no use pretending she wasn't who she was with this little know-all bugger. 'You wouldn't be here if it wasn't for me.'

'Our house would still be there if it wasn't for you, and there'd have been no need for anyone to be rescued, so *there*.' The child stuck out a small, pink tongue. 'It's like throwing someone in water, then saving them from drowning.'

'You're a proper little smart arse, you are.'

'I'm exceptionally clever for me age, which is ten. The teachers say I'm a prodigy.'

'Lucky old you. What's your name?'

If she knew it's name, it would reveal its sex, otherwise it was like talking to a minuscule eunuch.

'Sam,' replied the child.

Donna ground her teeth, no wiser. 'What's that short for?'

'Samantha. What's your name? It's only fair you tell me now that you know mine.'

'I'd no intention of not telling you. It's not exactly a state secret. Me name's Donna.' She realised straight away that she should have given a false name to this wise girl-child whose house she'd recently burnt to the ground. As the night progressed, she seemed to be landing herself deeper and deeper in shitty situations.

'What are you doing?' Samantha enquired.

'Sitting on a wall, obviously. I'm waiting for someone. What about you? Where are you off to?' It was rather late for a child of only ten, albeit a prodigy, to be out on her own. She asked the question reluctantly as she preferred not to become involved in the small girl's personal affairs.

'I'm off to stay with me daddy, me *real* daddy, not the one back there.' She nodded contemptuously towards the way she had come. 'Me *real* daddy loves me, not like the other one. *He* just tolerates me to please me mammy, and *she* forgets about me half the time, because she's too busy with the kids she had by *him*.'

'There'll be a search party out looking for you any minute,' Donna warned.

'No, there won't. I'm supposed to be sleeping with a neighbour who thinks I'm in bed. These aren't my clothes, I stole them and I pinched some money too. The rest of the family stayed together. No one cares that I might be suffering from acute trauma. They just wanted me out the way.'

'Are you suffering from acute trauma?'

'No, I found it all very exciting.' Samantha sniffed and it sounded a touch pathetic. 'Even so, I'd quite like to see me real daddy.'

'Where does he live?'

'In a little village called Culmarnock Bay on the coast. It's not far from Dun Laoghaire.'

'Isn't that miles away?' Donna frowned, unexpectedly feeling sorry for the tiny loveless child. She hadn't exactly been showered with love herself at the same age.

'Miles and miles, but it doesn't matter. I took enough money for the bus.' She patted the haversack.

'There mightn't be a bus at this time of night.'

'Then I'll sit in the bus station till morning.'

'You can't do that!'

'Yes I can. What's to stop me?' Samantha said pugnaciously.

'The bizzies, for one. You're bound to be noticed, being only ten, like, and sitting around all night on your own. Someone will report you. Isn't your daddy something in the Gardai? The other one, not the real one.'

'I'm very sensible. I'll be perfectly all right on me own.'

'People won't know that. Come on,' Donna said kindly, holding out her hand. 'Let's take you back to that neighbour. You can go and see your daddy tomorrow.'

The girl ignored the hand. 'I mightn't be able to get away tomorrow. And you'd be mad, going that way. You'll be recognised. It said on television that the saint had disappeared out the hospital. Everyone's saying prayers so you'll be found. They've issued a description, but it doesn't sound a bit like you.'

'Soddin' hell!' Donna exclaimed, just as a taxi drew up outside the theatre and a tall man in a check suit with Marilyn Monroe hair got out. She waved to the driver as he did a U-turn in the road and he stopped.

'Come on,' she said impulsively to Samantha. 'Get in. I'll take you to your daddy. Culmarnock Bay,' she told the driver.

'Are we going all the way by taxi?'

'Why not!' It wasn't her money she was using. 'I'm worried about you. I don't like leaving you on your own.'

'So you should be,' Samantha said shortly, 'worried,

that is. If it wasn't for you, I'd be fast asleep in me little bed, sleeping like an angel and dreaming lovely dreams.'

'I bet you've never looked like an angel in your life.'

'Neither have you.'

'I've never claimed to.'

'I'm not sure I like you very much.'

'I'm quite sure I don't like you,' Donna snorted. 'You were horrible earlier. "Tell me something funny about dead people." What a thing to say!'

'I'm horrible a lot of the time,' Samantha admitted gravely. 'I do it deliberately. According to an article I read, it's a way of drawing attention to meself because most of the time I'm ignored.'

'Couldn't you draw attention to yourself by being nice?' Donna suggested helpfully.

'It doesn't work. No one's interested in nice people.'

'You're probably right,' Donna acknowledged after a few moments' thought.

'Mind you, I'm not *always* horrible,' Samantha conceded, somewhat regretfully. 'I have to pretend to me mammy that I like me other daddy, else she'd be upset. She doesn't realise I'm an intensely unhappy child.'

'Join the club. I'm an intensely unhappy adult.'

'Is there a club for unhappy people?' Samantha said eagerly. 'I'd like to join.'

'You're already a member, kid. It's called the Human Race.' The conversation was getting too deep for Donna's still-fuddled brain which was urgently in need of a few quick fags to clear it. She decided to change the subject. 'Why don't you live with your real daddy all the time,' she enquired, genuinely interested.

'Because me mammy won possession of me in a court of law when they got divorced,' Samantha said, looking sad. 'We lived in England then. Me poor daddy didn't stand a chance.'

'Why not?'

'He was in prison.'

'What for?'

'Making bombs,' the girl said fondly. 'He's very good at making bombs is me daddy.'

'Is he still at it?' demanded an alarmed Donna.

'No, now he writes poetry instead. He went from the ridiculous to the sublime, as me other daddy's fond of saying.'

'I'm relieved to hear it. Is he expecting you by any chance, your real daddy?'

'It wasn't possible to call him from the neighbours.'

'Would you like to use my mobile and call him now?'

'Thank you, but no,' Samantha said with a surprisingly sweet smile. 'I'd sooner give him a nice surprise. We won't be long getting there in the taxi. You'll come and meet him, won't you? I've never brought a friend before and I think I like you, after all. I like the way you're not buttering me up, trying to get on me right side, so I won't dob on you about the fire. Daddy'll be dead pleased I've got a friend. Later on, he'll bring us back to Dublin in his car.'

'If you want. What's his name, so I'll know what to call him, like?'

'Michael McDougall,' Samantha said proudly. 'He was known as Mad Mick in the old days.'

Donna shivered. 'I've heard of him.' She recalled a great, black-bearded man from the newspapers and the television news about five years ago. He'd been caught trying to blow up the Houses of Parliament and had received a long prison sentence, though had been released a few years later under the terms of the Repeal of Terrorism Act. 'Perhaps it would be best if I didn't meet him, after all,' she said hastily. 'I'll drop you off at his house and come straight back in the taxi.'

'There's no need to worry yourself,' Samantha soothed. 'He's a reformed character. If he takes to you, he'll write you a poem.'

'What if he doesn't take to me?'

'He still won't do you any harm. He'll just make us a cup of tea and we'll have a lovely long chat.'

'I'm looking forward to it.'

Half an hour later the taxi dropped them off in a badly lit village, where the Irish Sea glistened ominously only a short distance away and the waves could be heard lapping angrily on to the shore.

Donna paid the driver, by which time Samantha was already halfway along a path that sloped down to the water, towards a row of small terraced houses that seemed to be perched perilously on the edge of a cliff.

'He lives in the end one,' she announced. 'There's no lights on and the curtains are drawn, so it means he's either in the kitchen or he's gone to bed.'

'What if he's out?'

'He hardly ever goes out at night, but if he has, I can let meself in, I know where he leaves the key, then we'll wait.'

'Is your real daddy a smoker?' Donna enquired anxiously.

'He smokes even more than the other one.' She stopped and put her hands on her hips. 'I hope you're not intending to set *his* house on fire!' she said sternly.

'You can keep an eye on me, make sure I don't.'

They arrived at the end house which was in total

darkness. Samantha removed a plant from its pot and fished out a key. The front door opened on to a narrow hallway which led to another door at the back.

'Daddy!' Samantha called. 'It's me.' She opened the end door to reveal a small, shabby kitchen. Three men were sitting around a table on which were, (a) a plate of chocolate digestives, (b) about a dozen cans of beer, (c) three hand guns, all different, (d) two baseball bats, both the same, (e) what looked suspiciously like a home-made bomb, and, (f) the most welcome sight of all as far as Donna was concerned, an overflowing ashtray.

The men looked up, jaws dropping with amazement, but not with fear, Donna noted. One reached for a gun, the second for a baseball bat. They stood up menacingly, eyes hard and alert, ready for trouble. The third man also stood, towering over the others, filling the room, and Donna recognised Mad Mick McDougall, looking curiously gentle without his beard. His face split into a wide smile when he saw his daughter who had eyes only for her dad. She ran to him, and was enveloped in a pair of huge arms and hoisted skywards, while in a trice the table was cleared of everything except the biscuits, the ashtray, and a few cans of beer. The two men returned to their chairs.

'I've missed you, Daddy,' the little girl cried.

'I've missed you too, Sammy.' The big man tenderly stroked his little girl's curly hair, showering kisses on her face. He adjusted the round spectacles that had been dislodged, recovered the baseball cap from the floor. 'What are you doing here? It's desperately late for such a wee girl to be out and about. You should have rung first, me darlin', said you were coming.'

'I couldn't, Daddy. I'd been put with some neighbour

because our house burnt down to the ground. At first, me other daddy thought it was you that did it, but mammy convinced him it couldn't possibly be. She said you'd never burn little children alive.'

'That's nice of her,' Mad Mick said drily. 'And who's this you've brung with you?' He turned his gaze on Donna.

'She's me friend. Her name's Donna.'

'And what's Donna doing here?' The dark blue eyes narrowed suspiciously.

'She brought us all the way from Dublin in a taxi, Daddy. She's an intensely unhappy person, just like me. She told me so on the way, except I'm not unhappy, not now I'm with you.'

'And what cause has such a smart and elegant young lady to be unhappy?' enquired Mad Mick, smiling all of a sudden, as if he had decided he very much liked what he saw.

Donna was taken aback by the warmth of the smile. She couldn't think of an answer and blushed instead in response to the triple compliment – the 'smart and elegant', the 'young', not to mention the 'lady'. She felt extraordinarily envious of Samantha for being enclosed in such a strong pair of arms as she wouldn't have minded a hug off the poetry-writing ex-terrorist herself, though perhaps the 'ex' wasn't appropriate, considering the contents of the table when they'd come in.

'Give us half an hour upstairs with Donna, and *I'll* make her happy,' the younger of the seated men declared in a leery voice. He was a weedy individual with a heavily spotted chin and long, greasy hair.

'Give us half a minute with Donna, and she'll never be unhappy again because she'll be fuckin' dead,' growled the other, a much older man with burning eyes and an angry, red face. 'We've got to get rid of her, Mick. She's seen our faces, she's seen the stuff. She can never be trusted to keep her gob shut. This is a nice kettle of fish we've been landed in for Christ's sake. You never said the kid might come and bring a fuckin' friend.'

'There's no need to worry,' Donna assured him. 'I've got a terrible memory, particularly for faces.'

'Why is the man being horrid, Daddy?' Samantha looked alarmed. 'Have we come at an inconvenient time?'

'Not at all, me darlin'. You and your friends are always welcome in this house.'

'You won't let him kill Donna?'

'I won't let him even try.' Mad Mick turned on the man with the angry face and said calmly, 'You can shut your own gob, Calum O'Connor. You're forgetting that I'm a reformed character, that tonight I'm not intent on harming anyone except the bad guys. Our dear country would thank us if they knew the facts. I might even write a poem about it afterwards and have it published for all the world to see.'

'Yuck, Mick. You make me sick nowadays,' Calum said disgustedly.

'And you, Ludo,' Mick continued as if Calum had never spoken, 'don't start getting nonsensical ideas about taking Donna upstairs, or I'll slit you from your gizzard to your zatch. She's me darlin' little daughter's friend and not that sort of girl.'

'Your darlin' little daughter would like a cup of tea, Daddy,' Samantha simpered, 'and Donna's longing for a ciggie.'

'Give the nice girl the baccy, Calum,' Mick com-

manded with the confident air of a man used to giving
orders and having them obeyed, 'so she can roll her own.
Would you like a cup of tea as well, Donna?'

'I'd prefer a beer.'

'Then a beer you shall have. You're a girl after me
own heart, you are, with more knobs on than I can count.
Calum, find a beer for Donna, the decent sort, not that
shit from the post office. Ludo, make my Sammy a cup of
tea; milk, one sugar.' Still holding Samantha in one arm,
Mick dragged a kitchen chair over to the table. 'And you,
Donna, sit down and take the lovely weight off your feet.
Make yourself at home now.'

'Thank you.' Donna sat down and Mick seated
himself next to her with his daughter cuddled on his
knee.

'What's all this about a fire I'd like to know?'

'It's no good asking Donna,' Samantha said, sweetly
innocent. 'It's nothing to do with her. We only just met
after she found me wandering the streets of Dublin
looking for a bus. I think it might have been me other
daddy's fault, the fire. He's forever going up to the
bedroom for a smoke, because you know how much
mammy doesn't like it. He probably left a burning ciggie
in the ashtray and it fell off while they were at dinner,
setting light to the carpet. I'll suggest it to me mammy
once I'm back home.'

The child could have lied for Ireland, thought Donna
giving her a look of gratitude mixed with respect. She could
never have come up with such a great story herself on the
spur of the moment. It meant the saint was off the hook, and
had been replaced by a senior member of the Gardai.

'Irresponsible bastard, your other daddy,' Mick
grunted.

As Donna began to roll a cigarette, she cast a surreptitious glance at the face of the huge, powerful man beside her. His nose had been considerably battered over the years, there were two scars on his chin, and a fine, white line on his left cheek that she suspected had been done by a razor. Oh, but the blue of his kind, gentle eyes was that of the Mediterranean sea at dusk – Donna had once holidayed in Barcelona and remembered the colour well. It was a handsome face, as powerful as his frame, despite the scars of the battle he had fought – a battle of his own making.

As she continued to stare, something began to happen inside her stomach. It was as if two bears were having a fight, punching and kicking each other in time to music – a marching band, playing very loud, particularly the drummer, or several drummers. She was also having trouble breathing. Yet despite this inner turmoil, her head had cleared, she was very calm, at least outwardly, her blood was gurgling cheerfully through her veins, and she felt safe and quite at home in this ordinary little kitchen of the house in Culmarnock Bay with the sound of the sea churning away outside. Which was more than surprising, considering that one of the men in the room had recently threatened to rape her, another had her murder on his mind, and there was a small arsenal beneath the table at which she sat.

Why did she feel so free from fear when she was surrounded by danger?

Because she knew, she felt convinced, that Mad Mick McDougall would never let anything bad happen to her, never, not in a million years. He liked her. For a person more accustomed to being loathed, such awareness came as a pleasant surprise.

Then the mind-boggling and amazing realisation dawned that she was in love with Mick. She had fallen in love with him at first sight, something that, until now, Donna? – she still couldn't remember her surname – had regarded with cynical disbelief. The marching band in her stomach broke into a run.

'We'll have to get going soon, Mick,' Ludo said. 'It's nearly half past twelve.'

'Then get going we will.' He gave Samantha a little squeeze and put her on the floor. 'Will you do your daddy a favour, darlin'? Go upstairs and fetch me black woollen gloves out the top dresser drawer.'

'All right, Daddy.' Samantha trotted away.

'There's gloves here, boyo, leather ones, much better than wool.'

Mick rolled his eyes impatiently. 'You're an eejit, Calum O'Connor. I only wanted our Sammy out the way so she won't see the stuff being packed in the bag. Get a move on, quick, the pair o'yis, before she comes back.'

'Who'll be looking after Sammy while we're away?' enquired Ludo.

'Donna will, won't you, darlin'? We won't be gone more than two hours.'

'I'll be pleased to.'

'Oh, no, Mick. Oh, no, I'm not having that.' Calum shook his head emphatically. 'We don't know who she is or where she's come from. I'm not prepared to leave this house with her still in it. Sammy had never met her before tonight. She might be in cahoots with your ex-wifey's new husband in the Gardai, and the minute we're gone, she'll pick up the phone and call him. Is it not a bit more than a coincidence that she turned up tonight, pretending to be a friend of Sammy's? I still think we should kill her. Even if she's in cahoots with no one at all, I don't trust some strange, unknown woman to keep her trap shut for the rest of her breathing days.'

'Don't be daft, Cal,' Mick said contemptuously. 'There'll be no one killed under my roof, never again, because I'm no longer a murdering man, and I've never killed a woman, anyroad.'

'What about the British Houses of Parliament?' Ludo put in. 'You tried to blow the place to smithereens and there's women there.'

'Not on Christmas Eve, there isn't. The place was empty. All right.' Mick slammed his sledgehammer fist on the table. 'All right, if it'll stop you from moaning and groaning, Calum, we'll take Donna with us, that's if she doesn't mind. Sammy can stay the time with Fionnuala Murphy along the street.'

'I don't mind,' Donna said helpfully. She would have gone anywhere in the world with Mad Mick McDougall.

'What about afterwards?' Calum persisted. 'She's seen our faces, she knows where you live.'

'Afterwards? Afterwards?' Mick said in a thunderous voice and with a magnificent smile. 'Why, afterwards I'm going to ask Donna if she'll marry me. If she ses yes, then I'll be the happiest man in the whole of Ireland. No, and I'll cry meself to sleep for the rest of me wretched life.'

'It's "yes",' Donna cried. 'Yes, yes, yes.' The marching band collapsed in a dead faint and a dizzying sensation of pure happiness flooded through the thin, dried up body of the nurse.

'There!' Mick beamed at everyone in sight. 'I'll kiss you later, darlin', after the job's been done and these boyos have gone. As for you, Calum O'Connor, if you're thinking you'll be me best man, then you can think again. I'm not having me bride sitting next to a fella who wanted her dead, not on the day of her wedding, I'm not.'

'Congratulations,' said a bored Ludo. 'Can we go now?'

'I'll just sort out our Sammy, then we'll go.'

Chapter Thirteen

For at least ten minutes Pauline lay shivering on the floor of the Mercedes until Sydney and Roxy returned from their unsuccessful attempt to find the intruder, in other words, herself, in the farmhouse grounds. She prayed Tony wouldn't come to the car to see them off because he was bound to notice her when the doors opened and the light came on.

But Tony must have stayed some distance away. She heard him shout, 'Good luck. I'll see you later. Give us a ring when the job's been done. I'll be waiting.'

'Rightio, boss.' The front seats creaked when the two men got in, the doors slammed, the light went off. Pauline breathed a silent sigh of relief, and prayed she wouldn't cough or want to sneeze or that her stomach wouldn't start rumbling. It had been midday when she'd last had something to eat.

For a long time, neither man spoke as Roxy drove swiftly along the silent country lanes. Then Roxy said in his cultured tones, 'I don't understand what this is all about. Why do the Yanks want to sabotage a computer company in Dublin?'

'It wasn't always in Dublin,' Sydney replied chattily, obviously not averse to a bit of a jangle. 'It's an American firm, used to be in Chicago, started five years ago with funny money, if you know what I mean.'

'Mafia money?'

'Mafia money.' Sydney chortled. 'It's a good way of laundering the stuff and the profit comes out entirely legit. There was a consortium of eight guys behind it with Tony at the top investing the most. The company employed about twenty of the biggest, fuckin' computer brains in the world as well hundreds of support staff. One of the brains invented this chip, it smells, or something daft like that, and before long the profits were rolling in. Then the press started to nose around. There were rumours that Red Box Computers was a cover for you-know-who, though no proof. Tony would have made sure there'd never be proof. Even so, the brains went ballistic and threatened to resign en masse. They didn't have to worry about finding another job, not like ordinary people.'

'Did they resign?'

'I'm coming to that, aren't I?' Sydney said irritably. 'They might have done, except each one got a quiet message, along with a big jump in their pay, that if they cared about their families, it'd be wiser for them to stay and keep their traps shut. It was a message they couldn't refuse.'

'Sounds just like *The Godfather*,' Roxy said in an awed voice. Pauline had thought exactly the same thing earlier.

'It's exactly like *The Godfather*,' Sydney agreed. 'For a whole year, it seemed the message had struck home. The brains kept working as if nothing had happened. Then, one day, just after Easter last year, the staff arrived at Red

Box ready for work, but there was no sign of the brains. Apparently, they'd disappeared. Tony was fucking mad, I can tell you. Turned out, months later, that they'd done a bunk and the whole crowd of 'em had moved to Dublin, set-up their own company, called it Guava Tech. By the time Tony found out, the firm was well-established, making money hand over fist. It was then that yours truly entered the picture.'

'How come you know Tony?'

'He used me to look for that Nicky bitch in London, the one who ran off with his kid. I'm a private detective,' Sydney said modestly. 'Properly licensed, got a permit for a gun.' There was the sound of something being patted – no doubt the place where he kept the gun, thought Pauline, cowering terrified on the floor behind, knowing the gun would almost certainly be used on her if she was found and they realised she'd been listening to all this highly incriminating stuff. If so, she'd claim to be deaf. It was worth a try.

'Came highly recommended, I did,' Sydney went on importantly. 'I'd worked for these Mafia guys before whenever they needed a job doing in the old country. Tony wanted his own back on Guava Tech. They'd double-crossed him and weren't going to get away with it. Tonight, he's gonna give 'em one big fright and blow their fuckin' factory sky high.'

'So, that's what it's all about, revenge,' Roxy mused. 'Though I don't see the need for Tony to have come all the way to Ireland. I thought people like him preferred to keep their noses clean and stay well away from the action?'

'He's only here because I happened to see Nicky in Dublin with his kid. I'd given up finding them by then.

Tony was on the next plane over the minute I told him. He's soppy about that kid.'

'It reminds me a bit of Achilles.'

'Who the fuck's Achilles?'

'A character in Homer's *Iliad*. He was a Greek god, invulnerable except for one thing, his heel, so that's where Paris directed his little old arrow and the poor guy kicked the bucket. Have you never heard of Achilles' heel?'

'I thought it was a medical condition, like tennis elbow.'

'You could say Harry is Tony's Achilles' heel, his weakness,' Roxy said thoughtfully. 'He's taking a big risk, coming over to get Harry back. The kid could be his undoing. You should have put tonight off till Tony had gone back to the States.'

'That wasn't possible,' Sydney replied testily. 'These things can't be set-up on the spur of the moment. There's three other guys involved. Tony wanted to strike at the very heart of the place, so I had to find a lock man to let us in. Guava Tech's security system's so complicated it would need a genius to de-activate the fuckin' thing.' He sighed wistfully. 'Not like those good old-fashioned burglar alarms that you could bugger up in a jiffy. When I was a youngster, I broke into hundreds of buildings. I was never caught, not once.'

'I'm not surprised you became a private eye. It must be an advantage having such personal experience of the criminal mind.'

Sydney didn't answer straight away, possibly unsure if this was a compliment or an insult.

The car slowed down, almost stopped, and Pauline wondered if she should try to open the door and run away. But if it made a noise and turned out to be locked from the inside, then she'd had it. Anyroad, it was no use getting out while they were still in the countryside. Roxy would catch up with her in no time. If she was going to risk it, it would be best to wait until they reached the city where people were around.

Oh, Lord! Now she had cramp again in her foot. It was pure agony and she nearly groaned aloud. Dare she reach down and massage it? No, she decided, she'd just have to put up with it. Any movement might be noticed by the men in front. She said a silent prayer to St Christopher instead, the patron saint of travellers, and asked him to see her safely home. She had thirty-seven Class 4 essays on the subject, WHY I WOULD LIKE TO BE A SWAN, to correct before Monday morning, a task that she hadn't been looking foward to, but now seemed particularly appealing. She wondered what Dennis was doing in Spain? Probably having a whale of a time and, by now, tucked up snugly in bed with the dusky señorita he'd danced with.

Some lousy hen party this had turned out to be. She'd never go on another.

'I found this guy, Ludo,' Sydney was saying, 'used to belong to some fringe terrorist organisation. Nowadays, he works nights for Guava as an electrician, though not tonight, being Saturday. It's the only time the place is empty. But he's got a smart card that lets him in and he knows how to disarm the security system and switch off the cameras. It was Ludo who located the explosives expert for me, and the tough guy for protection. They're both old mates of his.

'I thought you were supposed to be a tough guy,' Roxy said a trifle cattily.

'If you're not fuckin' careful, I'll show you how tough I can be,' Sydney sneered. 'I'm tough when the situation calls for it, and I'm also smart. Which reminds me, I don't want any sign we've been near Guava Tech tonight. No fingerprints, so keep your gloves on. This is going to look like a terrorist operation – that's what we want the Old Bill to think – but the computer brains will know better. They'll know straight away it's a message from Tony.'

'How?'

'They just will, believe me. They'll know the same thing will happen if they start up again. At precisely three o'clock this morning, Guava Tech will become confetti and there'll be three dead bodies found in the wreckage; Ludo and the other two guys. Two of 'em will have a bullet through their heads, the third will look as if he was killed in the explosion – and he'll have the gun that shot his mates in his hand.'

'Clever,' Roxy said admiringly. 'Who's going to do the shooting?'

'Me. I'll put this gun out the way in case we're frisked, and use the one I've got hidden in my hair. It's only a little women's thing, but just as deadly as the male.' The glove compartment was opened and clicked shut. 'It's your job to batter the third guy with something – a computer, a chair – so it looks as if he was killed by falling debris.'

'That'd be nice. Thank you, Sydney.'

'Don't mention it, kid.'

'There's just one thing. I'm not sure if I heard right, but did you just say you had a gun hidden in your hair.'

'Yeh. It's Tony's. It was his idea I conceal a gun in my bun. I mean, no one ever frisks your head.'

The men lapsed into silence just as orange lights began

to flash into the car. They were passing streetlights, Pauline realised. They must be on the outskirts of Dublin. Her relief was mixed with fear. If Sydney or Roxy glanced behind, they'd see her easily.

'Oh, I say!' Roxy suddenly remarked. 'Those curves look familiar.' The car slowed to a crawl.

'What curves? What the hell are you talking about?'

'The curves on that woman in front. It's the girl I picked up earlier. Tracey her name is.'

'Why are you slowing down?

'I'm going to give Tracey a lift.'

'Are you fuckin' crazy or something?' Sydney shrieked. 'The last thing we want is a passenger. Hit the accelerator, kid, or there'll be trouble.'

'You're too old-fashioned by a mile, Sydney.' Roxy laughed derisively. 'You're like the burglar alarms you mentioned earlier. And no one calls the police the "Old Bill" any more. I'd like a bit of serious fun with Tracey once the job's over. You can have fun too – if you're up to it.'

'And what if Tracey doesn't want fun with you, stupid?'

'She won't be given much choice in the matter.'

'And you don't think she'll go to the police, the fuzz, the filth, or whatever you prefer to call them, when you've finished having your fun, give them our descriptions, tell them we took her to Guava Tech?' Sydney screamed. 'And they won't connect us with what happened in Guava Tech? We'd be found in no time.'

'Tracey won't be in a position to tell anyone anything by the time I've done with her. She'll be up with the angels where she belongs.'

The car stopped. A horrified Pauline heard the window whirr as it rolled smoothly down.

'Hi,' said Roxy. 'It's Tracey, isn't it? Remember we met before? I dropped you off at the hospital.'

'Oh, hello,' Tracey replied. She sounded quite cheerful.

'Where are you off to?'

'A club in town. It's a waste of time waiting for a taxi. I was going with a friend but she seems to have disappeared.'

'Would you like a lift? We have to go somewhere first, but we won't be long, then we'll drop you off right outside the club door.'

Tracey didn't answer immediately. Pauline prayed with all her heart she would refuse. Say no, Tracey. *Please* say no.

'All right,' Tracey said.

'Hop in the back then. The door's open.'

'Ta.'

The door opened. Tracey's face expressed astonishent and disbelief, as well it might, when she saw Pauline lying on the floor. Pauline put her finger to her lips and shook her head, at the same time wishing she'd had the foresight to leap out and make her escape — both their escapes.

Tracey climbed into the car, positioning her feet carefully on either side of her friend's face. 'This is very kind of you,' she said to Roxy in a surprisingly normal voice.

'Think nothing of it. We won't be going much out of our way, will we, Sydney?'

Sydney muttered something incomprehensible.

Tracey began to remove her pink, boxy jacket. Roxy must have been watching through the rear-view mirror. 'What are you doing?' he asked.

'Taking me coat off. It's hot in here.' She laid the coat

over Pauline's bottom half, then dangled her hand over the edge of the seat.

Pauline clutched the strong fingers, grateful for their warmth, knowing that now they were going to be all right. As soon as the car stopped and the men had gone to do their dirty work, she and Tracey would run for their lives – and the first telephone box they came to, she would make an anonymous call to the police and tell them of the plan to blow up Guava Tech. Pauline would never cease to remain a responsible member of an increasingly irresponsible society, no matter how dreadful the circumstances might be.

The car *was* warm, and she hadn't noticed before how lovely and thick the carpet was. What's more, her cramp had gone, and her head seemed to fit quite comfortably between Tracey's feet. Before long, Pauline was asleep, and didn't wake up until she felt her shoulder being shaken urgently.

'What's going on, Pauly? Why the heck are you hiding on the floor?'

'It's a long story, Trace,' Pauline hissed. 'Too long to tell you now. Where's Roxy and Sydney?'

'Gone. They said they wouldn't be long.'

Pauline managed to heave herself on to the back seat. 'Me legs are completely dead.' She began to rub them, bring them back to life and noticed she only had one shoe. She'd flung the other away in the orchard. 'We've got to get away, Trace. Immediately, before they come back, because then they'll kill us.'

'Don't be a soft girl, Pauly. Is your head as numb as your legs or what?'

'I'm not being soft. They're dangerous, Trace. They're about to kill three other men. I need to find a phone box.'

'What other three men?'

'I think that must be them coming now.'

They were parked behind a wire fence surrounding a small factory, no bigger than a house, but across the road, through the wire, could be seen a long two-storey building, functional and very modern, with wide, smoked-glass doors. The building was floodlit and there was a name over the entrance in large gold letters: Guava Tech.

It was clearly an area, a business park, that was hardly used out of office hours. There was no traffic, apart from themselves, and a large van which had just turned into the fenced off area and parked beside them. Pauline pushed Tracey out of sight and slid down as far as she could while keeping an eye on the scene.

She was surprised when four people got out, not three as she had expected. Even more surprising, one was a woman who looked oddly familiar. They crossed the road towards Guava Tech.

'You can sit up now,' she said to Tracey. 'You know, that woman looks ever so much like Donna. But it can't possibly be. Donna would never wear such a peculiar get up.'

Tracey yelped. 'It *is* Donna. They're Mark Costello's clothes. I stole them for her in the hospital.'

'You *stole* them! That was very wrong of you, Tracey.'

'Oh, shurrup, Pauline. This isn't the time to get on your high horse. Christ Almighty, Donna's just linked that big guy's arm! What's she up to? Who *are* those men?'

'They're sort of terrorists. They're about to blow up that factory.'

'With Donna's help?' Tracey shook her head incredulously. 'Donna's done some awful things in her life, Pauly, but she'd never willingly sink *that* low.'

'I don't know why she's with them,' Pauline said helplessly. Her head was spinning. 'I don't know anything about anything any more, apart from the fact that those men are going to kill those men.'

'Which men are going to kill which men?'

'I told you before. The sort of terrorists have been hired by Sydney to blow up the factory because Tony Bianco wants to get his own back on the brains. Oh, it's too complicated to explain, but the Mafia are behind the whole thing.'

'The Mafia! You know, Pauly, you should never have watched *The Sopranos*. It's gone to your head.'

'It means,' Pauline said slowly, ignoring the remark. 'That. Sydney and Roxy will kill Donna.'

'Does it?'

'We've got to stop them.'

'Have we? Oh, all right, then,' Tracey said practically.

She must have decided to humour her, thought Pauline, or maybe she was worried there might be a grain in truth in what she'd said. Besides, there hadn't been a moment of doubt that Tracey would stick by her.

'We'd better follow them. They've gone round the back. There's a man called Ludo who has a security card to get in.'

'How do you know all this stuff?'

'Sydney and Roxy discussed it while I was hiding behind.'

'Are you sure you didn't fall asleep and dream the whole thing? Or have you been drinking more of that Irish lemonade?'

'Neither,' Pauline said huffily, getting out the car. On impulse, she opened the passenger door and took Sydney's gun out of the glove compartment.

'What's that?'

'Never mind.' She shoved the gun in her pocket. There was no way she would use it, but she felt better knowing it was out of Sydney's reach. 'You might also like to know that Roxy had no intention of taking you to a club. He was going to have some fun first before he killed you. It's true,' she persisted when Tracey made an incredulous face. 'Anyroad, even if every word I've said is a lie, you can't deny the fact that Donna's just gone into that factory with three strange men. For that reason alone, we need to find out what's going on.'

'Hopefully, that's what we're about to do,' Tracey replied linking Pauline's arm as they went across the road towards the brilliantly lit building housing Guava Tech.

The floodlights must have been all for show as the rear of the factory was in darkness. They found a fire door that wouldn't budge, then a smaller door which opened when Pauline gave it a little shove. Voices could be heard inside. The women looked at each other, Pauline the most frightened of the two — she knew exactly what Sydney and Roxy had planned.

Throwing back their shoulders, they went in and followed the sounds, along parchment coloured corridors lit by an occasional eerie blue bulb embedded in the ceiling, around corners, their footsteps making no sound on the thickly carpeted floors. One of the Irishmen had a great, booming laugh that echoed majestically throughout the building.

They were getting nearer to the voices. At the end of the next corridor, they saw a light shining through a small window which turned out to be in a door. Pauline crept towards it and peeped through, into a large room with parchment walls and a round, doughnut-shaped table that could have seated twenty.

Her eyes searched first for Donna. She was seated on a chair, smiling slightly, her gaze fixed fondly upon the big man whose arm she'd linked – a fine-looking man, with black curly hair and a rugged, handsome face. He was crouched on the floor fiddling with a blue metal box that had a series of switches, leads, and a row of green, illuminated figures.

A bomb!

Donna was gazing fondly upon a man who was setting a *bomb!*

What was happening to the world? What had happened to Donna?

Oh well, Pauline thought despairingly, this wasn't the time to dwell on moral uncertainties, not when a quadruple murder was about to be committed.

The other Irishmen, one youngish with a spotty chin, the other middle-aged, were standing with their arms folded, faces alert, watchful. The older man looked very grim with hard, merciless eyes, presumably the tough guy. The scabby-chinned one must be Ludo. The big man, the object of Donna's adoration, was obviously the explosives expert.

Roxy seemed very on edge. He was leaning on the back of one of the stout metal chairs that encircled the table, holding it so tightly that the knuckles on his well-kept hands showed white – Roxy had his weapon ready.

By contrast, Sydney appeared relaxed. Like Donna, he was seated, idly scratching his neck, his hand only inches away from where he'd secreted the little gun.

Tracey whispered impatiently. 'What's happening?'

'I think the bomb's being primed or whatever it is you do with bombs.'

'Let's have a dekko.'

'No.' It would only waste time.

The big man got to his feet. 'There!' he bellowed. 'That didn't take more than a wee minute. We've all of us got nearly two hours to get well out the way. I suggest we don't hang about. Calum, Ludo, come on boys, let's get going.' He held out his hand to Donna. 'And you too, my lovely girl.'

Donna stood.

Roxy lifted the chair.

Sydney began to fiddle with his hair.

Was she supposed to just stand there, Pauline wondered wildly, and watch while four people were murdered, one of them a friend whom she hadn't liked much but didn't wish any harm? How could she exist for the rest of her life knowing that she'd let this happen? She *had* to do *something*. It was no use shouting a warning when Sydney had a gun and the others were unarmed.

Tracey gasped, 'Holy Shit!' when Pauline took the gun out of her pocket, unlocked the safety catch – she'd seen, it done a million times in films – opened the door a crack, aimed the gun at Sydney's feet, closed her eyes, and fired.

There was an unearthly scream and, when Pauline's eyes opened, it was Roxy who was hopping like a crazy man around the room, blood dripping from his well shod foot, and an astonished Sydney was drawing a little silver revolver from out of his bun.

The other four people in the room were too startled to move, even the tough guy whose job it was to keep an eye out for such things as stray bullets fired from an apparently closed door.

Meanwhile, the sight of blood had done something to Pauline, the normally prim and modest school-teacher. She could taste it and, like the shark, her taste buds had been alerted and she wanted more. But, unlike the shark, it wasn't just any old blood she was after. It was time the world was drained of *bad* blood and now she had the opportunity to do her little bit towards it.

Her lips drew back in a snarl. Kicking open the door, she burst into the room holding the gun in both hands with the barrel pointed at Roxy on the logical assumption that this time the bullet would hit his mate.

'Take that, you fucker.' She fired and the bullet thumped into the wall behind Sydney's head. He jumped up, hands held high in surrender, and the little silver gun dropped to the floor.

'You!' he spat.

'You!' groaned Roxy.

'Pauline!' gasped Donna.

'Donna!' Tracey rushed into the room and flung her arms around her fellow nurse.

'What the fuck's going on?' roared Calum.

'Are these two fetching young ladies friends of yours, darlin'?' the big man enquired of Donna.

'Yes, Mick. The one with the gun's Pauline and the other's Tracey.'

'Would you mind asking the delightful Pauline why she's shooting at people left, right and centre? And if she's finished for now, would she mind putting the gun down? She looks a bit too wild-eyed for my liking. I'm worried she might shoot us all.'

KATH KINCAID

'They were going to kill you,' Pauline said in a deep, gruff voice that no one had ever heard before. 'He'd hidden a gun in his bun. See!' She picked up the little silver gun and waved it in the air.

Everyone ducked.

Roxy fainted.

'And where did the other gun come from, darlin?' Mick asked.

'It's *his*.' She nodded towards Sydney, who had decided to lie on the floor out of harm's way. 'He left it in the car because it's licensed. He was going to shoot two of you with the the little one, then *he*,' she pointed at Roxy, 'was going to batter the third with a chair or something and put the gun in his hand so it looked as if they'd shot the others when your bodies were found after the building had exploded.' She frowned. 'Does that make sense?'

'Perfect sense. You're a nice, brave girl, going to so much trouble on behalf of strangers.'

'I'm not a girl,' Pauline snarled in her new voice. 'I'm not a lady, either. I'm a woman. And although I wouldn't have wanted to see you dead, I'm only here because of Donna. As far as I'm concerned, I don't care if you all rot in hell for the rest of your miserable lives.'

Calum made a treatening move in Pauline's direction, but she pointed both guns at his face. 'Don't even *think* it,' she growled menacingly, and Calum, the tough guy, meekly backed away.

'But you've got it all wrong, Pauly,' Donna cried. 'This,' she waved her arm around the room, 'is all a set-up. Guava Tech know all about it. The plan was to leave those two creeps behind after the security system had been turned on again. There's no way on earth they

could have got out. Once we were safely away, the
bizzies would get a call to say there was a bomb on the
premises and they'd assume the people responsible had
accidentally shut themselves in.'

'They're only nominally responsible,' Pauline said
stiffly. 'It's the Mafia who's really behind it, someone
called Tony Bianco.'

Mick looked at her in surprise. 'You're certainly a
well-informed young lady – young *woman*.' He hastily
corrected himself when the gun in Pauline's right hand
jerked in his direction. 'Guava Tech had already guessed
Tony Bianco was involved, that he was sending them a
message in the form of a big fat bomb.' He sighed, and
Pauline was caught in the blast and nearly blown off her
feet. 'It's a pity we couldn't have caught the organ
grinder, not just his monkeys, but people who know
him say Tony gives the orders, but stays well out the
away.'

'You'll find Tony Bianco in Bray. The house is called
Orchard Farm.'

Sydney, lying on the floor, lifted his head and said in a
quavery voice. 'I hope Tony won't think it was me who
told you that.'

Mick raised his bushy eyebrows appealingly at Donna.
'Would you mind taking both the guns out of the hands
of your dear friend? They make me feel uneasy. I'm
worried I might look at her the wrong way and get a
bullet through me eyes.'

Donna gingerly prised Pauline's stiff fingers off the big
gun and gave it to Mick, who grunted, 'Ta, darlin'.' He
made it safe, emptied the remaining bullets and put them
in his pocket, then wiped the weapon clean with a
hankie. 'This needs leaving behind. These two boyos

will have to come up with an explanation as to why one of 'em got shot in the foot.

'I'd like to keep this for a little while.' Pauline clicked the safety catch of the little silver revolver. 'It's made especially for women.'

'You can't take it on the plane,' Donna warned.

'Don't worry. I'll dump it before we get on the plane.' Pauline felt more comfortable with the gun in her possession. Who knew what might happen in the hours before the plane took off and she was safely back in Liverpool?

'Is everyone ready?' Mick boomed. 'That bomb's ticking away and I want us well out of the vicinity before I make that phone call. I'll tell 'em where Tony Bianco's holed out, an' all.'

'Then for fuck's sake, *go,*' urged a nervous Sydney. Roxy was still in a dead faint.

They hurried out of the building and the three women and Mick piled into the back of the van. Calum sat behind the wheel and they waited for Ludo, who was re-activating the security system that would turn Guava Tech into a fortress that no one could get in or out of.

Ludo appeared and got into the van beside Calum, who enquired, 'Where to?'

'The Green Lizard,' Tracey announced. 'It's a club. I promised to meet some theatrical producer there. It's where me and Donna were headed, hours ago.'

Donna said, 'I'd still like to go, if Mick will come with us. Mick, by the way, is my fiancé.' Donna tossed her strangely turbaned head. 'We're getting married as soon as we can.'

'Congratulations,' Tracey said warmly.

'I hope you'll be very happy,' Pauline croaked. She

suddenly felt enormously tired. Her voice had almost gone, she had no energy left to think, just enough to breathe, to keep herself going until she locked the door of the hotel bedroom and went to sleep, nursing the little silver gun.

'And is the delightful Pauline coming with us?' shouted Mick. 'She deserves toasting with champagne. If it hadn't been for her, all of us might be dead.'

'Hear, hear,' the company echoed, including the tough guy.

'Tired . . . dirty . . . only got one shoe . . . need sleep.'

'Poor thing! You can hardly hear her, she's so worn out.'

'We'll take her to the hotel first.'

The van was bumpy, the journey seemed to take for ever, but Pauline was sustained by the thought she would shortly be in her warm, comfortable bed.

When the van stopped. Mick lifted her out, and despite her tiredness, Pauline felt a flutter of envy for Donna, who was about to spend the rest of her life within this man's lusty, powerful arms.

Tracey came with her into the hotel and went to get the key from Reception. She returned, seconds later, looking puzzled.

'The clerk said the key's been taken. There's already someone in your room. Of course!' Her face cleared. 'It'll be either Emma or Rosemary.'

No, it wouldn't! Pauline's fudgy brain had almost ceased to function, but it would have to die before the memory of last night's snores had been forgotten. It was Donna who'd shared the room. Someone else must have asked for the key.

Who?

Pauline had no idea. Perhaps the clerk had made a mistake. Anyroad, she didn't care if the whole of Dublin was in her room as long as they'd let her sleep.

She refused Tracey's offer to come upstairs and help her into bed. 'I'm fine. You go and have a good time.'

'Are you sure?'

'Positive.'

Tracey kissed her cheek. 'You were a brick tonight, Pauly. A proper heroine. I didn't realise you had it in you.'

'Neither did I.' Pauline went over to the lift and pressed the button. Tracey waited for the lift to arrive, gave a little wave, and left.

The fifth floor corridor was empty, not surprising at such a late hour. Pauline's legs were beginning to give way, but she managed to make it to room 58. Not a sound came from inside. She turned the handle, found it locked, so knocked softly – even in her current exhausted state, Pauline had regard for the people in adjacent rooms who would be asleep. Seconds later, the door was flung open and she was dragged inside and thrown on to a bed.

'I've been waiting for you,' sneered Tony Bianco.

A terrified Nicky was cowering on the other bed, Harry held tightly in her arms. The little boy was still in his pyjamas and looked as if he had been crying.

Lucy was there, Tony's wife, leaning against the wall, wearing a a bored expression, a white trouser suit and a fur coat that might possibly be mink.

'You forgot to tell me that Tony knew the hotel where you were staying,' Nicky said bitterly. 'I thought this was one of the few places in Dublin where me and Harry would be safe.'

'I'm so sorry. I'd forgotten. It's been such a confusing night . . .' Pauline's voice trailed away. She had never felt so wide awake. This was terrible! She'd helped Harry out of the frying pan, only to land him in the fire. 'Why are you here?' she asked Tony.

'I came looking for you,' he replied. 'No one two-times Tony Bianco and gets away with it. Nicky was the only person who could have taken Harry, and you were the only one who knew where he was. Finding the bitch here with my kid was a bonus.'

His face was twisted with hate. He looked nothing like the handsome, charming man she'd met earlier. Should she tell him what had happened at Guava Tech? Not yet, Pauline decided. He'd find out soon enough.

He grinned, baring his lovely, white teeth. 'You, Pauline, are going to take a little trip.'

'Where to?'

'A little trip out the window. There's a balcony out there, only a little one, very dangerous in my view. It would be easy for someone to open the window and fall out. They'd think you'd gone for a little walk in your sleep.' Across the room, Lucy tittered.

'You'd do that in front of Nicky and Harry?' Pauline said in a shocked voice. She wanted Harry out of the way.

'Nicky,' Tony tossed his head towards the bathroom. 'Take my boy in there.'

The woman hurriedly complied. The bathroom door clicked shut.

'If you're thinking that bitch will spill the beans,' Tony sneered, 'then don't bother. In a few hours, me and her are flying to London where she's gonna give me back my tapes and promise never to mention my name again. Otherwise, one day soon that nice new husband of hers will find himself dead. By then, Lucy will be on a plane to New York with Harry.' He made a Tarzan-like gesture, beating his fists against his chest. 'Tony Bianco always comes out on top,' he crowed.

'Not tonight, he doesn't.' There seemed no point beating about the bush. Pauline took the gun out of her pocket and shot him.

Chapter Fourteen

'Isn't this the gear?' yelled Tracey in the Green Lizard, her hips swaying seductively to the music blaring out of the giant speakers overseen by a maniacal disc jockey. The Castaways had finished their stint hours ago and gone home.

The floor was packed, but they'd managed to find a little space of their own. Mark Costello was nowhere to be seen. Tracey hoped he'd already met up with Geoffrey Bannerman from Stellar Television, signed the contract, and gone home, a happy man.

'It surely is the gear,' said Mad Mick McDougall, who had no need to yell, his voice box being just as powerful as the biggest speaker in the world. 'I was only a lad when I last enjoyed meself so much. How about you, darlin'?'

'It's great,' gasped Donna. 'Though I couldn't half do with a long, cool drink.'

'In that case, darlin', you shall have one. There's a great, huge queue by the bar, so I'll see you over there in ten minutes.'

He danced away, surprisingly light on his feet for such a big man.

'He's nice,' Tracey screamed.

'I love him,' Donna said as simply as a person could while shouting at the top of their voice.

'I'm thrilled to pieces you've met him. D'you think Pauline will be all right on her own? I should have stayed with her.'

'She'll be fast asleep by now.'

'I suppose so. It's been a funny old weekend, Donna.'

'Dead funny. I was more than sorry I'd come – until I met Mick, like. I might not come back to Liverpool with you, Trace.'

'You mean, not give in your notice at the hospital?' Had it been anyone else, Tracey would have disapproved. But Donna wouldn't be missed, either by the medical staff or the patients. Indeed, her non-appearance would be greeted with relief all round.

'No one'll care if I give me notice in or not,' Donna said intuitively. She suddenly twisted her head. 'I think I just saw Emma over there.'

'Where?'

'Dancing with a feller with blond hair. See, by the stage.'

Tracey peered through the dancers on the crowded floor. 'So it is! Let's go speak to her.' It must have been Rosemary in the hotel.

They pushed their way through the crowd. Emma's face was bright red and covered with perspiration. She greeted them with a shriek of disbelief. 'So, you found your way here, after all. This is our party,' she explained when they both looked puzzled. 'We went to the wrong pub, Maloney's. Eileen O'Brien was waiting for us in Mahoney's downstairs.'

'Eileen's here?'

'Over there somewhere.' Emma waved a vague hand. 'Oh, this is Jack. He's . . . he's a friend. Jack, this is Tracey and Donna.'

Jack stopped dancing and shook hands politely. He was very good-looking, Tracey thought, and rather nice. He and Emma seemed close, almost as if there was something between them – odd, considering Emma was getting married to someone else in less than a week's time. And Donna had also met the man of her dreams in the form of Mick, who was also good-looking and rather nice. But Tracey felt not even the slightest twinge of envy that Donna and Emma had copped off and she hadn't. One of these days, she thought serenely, she was bound to meet someone.

'Have you had a good time, Trace?' screeched Emma.

'Well, more interesting than nice,' Tracey opined. 'I'll tell you all about it tomorrow.'

'How about you, Donna?'

'More ghastly than interesting, but it had a happy ending.'

'Mine's been dead weird. Anyroad, now you can both relax and enjoy yourselves.'

'Not before time,' agreed Donna, just as a small, green-clad figure came flying through the air and landed on her back, bringing her crashing to the ground. Emma, Tracey, and several other women nearby screamed, though most of the revellers continued dancing, unaware anything untoward had happened.

'So, you're the one who stole my clothes,' spat Mark Costello, eyes burning with anger and frustration. He'd been waiting hours for Geoffrey Bannerman to turn up, but the bastard must have had second thoughts about the job on television. The girl, Tracey, had left the theatre hours ago on her way to the Green Lizard where she'd promised to meet him, but had only just arrived. He couldn't find his friend, Peter, or indeed any friend at all. He was penniless, phone-less, thirsty and longing for a drink. Not only that, he was wearing an utterly stupid costume and everyone was looking at him as if he were mad – not even the most dedicated of doctors attended social events ready to operate on a stray appendix or the odd dicky heart. He had hidden himself in a corner, embarrassed and unhappy, and now he *felt* mad. He was ready to kill when he saw the woman who had spoilt half his night by pinching his clothes dancing with Lady fucking Agatha, who had spoilt the other half by ruining his precious play.

'Mark. Mark.' Lady Agatha was trying to pull him away. 'I've been looking everywhere for you. I thought you'd gone. Where's Geoffrey?'

'Bugger Geoffrey. Why is this fucking woman wearing my clothes, that's what *I* want to know?' He banged Donna's head on the floor, screeching, 'Why, why, *why*?'

'Is that some eejit manhandling my darlin' girl?' a voice roared, and Mad Mick McDougall, swollen with rage and looking twice his normal already abnormal size, barged his way through the indignant dancers who resented being pushed so carelessly aside. He lifted up the inadequately built theatrical producer with one hand and swatted him away with the other. Mark landed comfortably in Tracey's plump arms.

'Hey, that's not fair!' protested Jack, who was mildly drunk. 'He's smaller than you by a mile.'

'He touched my woman,' Mick growled. He tenderly picked up an only mildly stunned Donna. 'Are you hurt, darlin'?'

'No,' said Donna shiftily. The poor little guy had a point. She had, after all, been in receipt of his clothes.

'It's still not fair,' Jack maintained bravely. 'In future, pick on people your own size.'

'He *did* throw himself upon the long lady and bring her to the ground,' commented an interested male onlooker. 'In my opinion, the wee one deserved all he got.'

'Oh, you think so, do you.' Jack approached the man in lieu of the giant Mick and pushed him in the chest.

The man pushed him back. 'Are you after a fight, lad?'

'Don't you *dare* push him!' Emma slapped the onlooker's face.

The onlooker's girlfriend slapped Emma.

Donna hit the girlfriend.

The girlfriend hit Jack.

Mark escaped Tracey's arms and hit everyone in sight. Except Mick.

Everyone was too frightened to hit Mick.

They hit each other instead, and like a disease, the hitting and pushing quickly spread, until all the people in the room were hitting and pushing each other.

The music stopped, but no one noticed.

The maniacal disc jockey called for order, but no one heard.

Eileen O'Brien phoned for the Gardai, unaware it was her ex-nursing friends and *their* friends who were the cause of the commotion. She then went in search of Emma and Jack.

Emma was looking for someone to hit next. Jack was rolling on the floor thumping a man whose jumper he didn't like.

'Come on,' Eileen said urgently. 'The Gardai are on their way, but we can get out the back.'

'Not till I've found Tracey and Donna.'

'Oh, so they've deigned to turn up, have they!'

Within minutes, eight people had departed from the mêlée, Eileen O'Brien at their head, followed by Emma and Jack, Donna and Mick, Tracey, with Mark Costello tucked under her arm, and, bringing up the rear, a haughty-looking woman with frozen blonde hair wearing an electric blue suit, a black leather handbag hooked importantly over her arm.

Outside, Tracey put Mark down, and Mick immediately signalled a taxi. He was no longer a wanted man, he explained, but he'd prefer the law didn't find Mad Mick McDougall in the vicinity of a riot. 'They'd be glad of an excuse to nab me.'

'I'll come with you.' Donna bade them all a temporary goodbye and promised to be at the hotel next morning to see them off. 'Anyroad, I'll be in Liverpool next Saturday for Emma's wedding. Me and Eileen can go together.'

'I'd like to see how Father Jack is,' Emma said in a small voice. 'I'll never go to sleep feeling the way I do and it's hours before the plane takes off.'

'See you Saturday, Em,' Eileen called as Jack and a strangely stiff-faced Emma climbed into a taxi. 'I wouldn't be at all surprised if that wedding wasn't called off,' she said in an ominous voice to Tracey when the vehicle drove away.

'D'you think it's that serious?'

'You don't look at a feller the way Emma was looking at Jack, then marry some other feller altogether.'

'Her mum will do her nut.'

'Doesn't anyone recognise me?' enquired the woman

in the blue suit. She removed her wig when everyone shook their heads. 'It's Geoffrey. Geoffrey Bannerman. I thought it was supposed to be a fancy dress party. Felix and I had to ring all over the place to borrow costumes. He came as Joan Collins. Last I saw of him he was being attacked in the Ladies' loo.'

'And who are you supposed to be?' enquired Eileen.

'Can't you guess? I'm Mrs Thatcher.'

Mark Costello burst into tears. 'I thought you'd forgotten about me.'

'As if I would, dear chap. I've got the contract in my handbag. Where can we go to sign it? You'll need to read it over carefully first.'

'My flat,' suggested Mark. 'It's not far away.'

'Ideal.' Geoffrey raised his arm to hail a cab.

Tracey shook Mark's hand and wished him all the luck in the world. 'I'll keep me eyes peeled for your name on television.'

'I should hate another man to suffer the way I did, so suggest you keep well away from amateur dramatics in future,' Mark advised with a smile.

'I never usually have the time.'

Eileen linked Tracey's arm when the two men had gone. 'Shall I walk back with you to the hotel? It's not far.'

'That'd be nice. Come in and have a jangle. There's a kettle and stuff. I'll make a drink.'

'Where's Pauline and Rosemary?'

'Back at the hotel, fast asleep. Oh, Eil! You wouldn't believe the night we've had. I'll start at the beginning, shall I? You know that pub, Maloneys? Well . . .'

★   ★   ★

Pauline had aimed for his right shoulder and hit him in the left. Tony's face was a mask of disbelief when the bullet struck him.

'Would you like another?' she enquired.

He numbly shook his head. Lucy waved her arms, indicating she wanted no part of things. She opened the door and could be heard running along the corridor towards the lift.

There were other noises. The shot must have woken up some of the guests. Soon, people would come.

The next hour was turmoil. The manager of the hotel arrived in his dressing-gown, shortly followed by half a dozen members of the Gardai. An ambulance was called and Tony was taken away. Nicky and Harry came out of the bathroom. Nicky asked if she could call her husband. 'I didn't have time before.'

'Where did you get the gun?' the policemen who seemed to be in charge enquired of Pauline. He introduced himself as Sergeant Connor.

'It belonged to Tony Bianco. He left it lying on the bed. He thought I wouldn't have the nerve to use it.'

'Tony Bianco!' He turned to his colleague. 'Isn't that the guy . . .?'

'Yeah, the one wanted in connection with the bomb planted earlier tonight at that computer place. They went to some farm to look for him, but there was no one there.'

'That's because he was here instead,' said Pauline. 'He was going to kill me.'

This was met with a disbelieving eyebrow. 'Really!'

Nicky interrupted. 'He was going to throw her out of the window. Look, can someone take Harry down to the lobby and buy him a Coke? I don't want him listening to all this stuff.'

'Well, ladies, now you can begin,' said Sergeant Connor when a reluctant Harry had been led away, so Nicky told the story that Pauline was already familiar with, starting with going to work in America and meeting Tony Bianco, right up until the events that had occurred that night. Then Pauline took over and described what had happened to her, skirting around everything to do with Sydney, Roxy, and Guava Tech.

'At the farm, after Nicky had rescued Harry, I just made a bit of a noise for a while, as a distraction like, until I heard her car start. Then I managed to hitch a lift back to Dublin.'

'You were very brave,' Sergeant Connor said admiringly. 'Now, I'd like you both to come to the station and make a proper statement.'

'Can't I come in the morning?' Pauline pleaded. 'I'm dead tired.'

'Okay.' He looked sympathetic. 'I'll send a car for you at ten o'clock.'

'I'm catching a plane at eleven.'

'I'm afraid that's not possible, but don't worry, I'll make sure you get a later one.'

Ralph came rushing into the room. 'Nicky, darling, I've been searching everywhere. Seamus stayed in Marlay Park. He's still looking for that damned house. Where's Harry?'

'Downstairs.' Nicky ran into his arms. 'Oh, Ralph, it's all over. Tony's going to jail. He'll never bother us again.'

Knowing Tony Bianco, Pauline wouldn't have taken that as gospel, though didn't say so. Perhaps they'd realise that themselves in the not too distant future.

Half an hour later, everybody left, and the room that had been so noisy and full of people, suddenly felt unnaturally quiet and strangely empty. Pauline had a quick shower, changed into her sensible nightdress, and got into bed.

After ten minutes of tossing and turning, she sat up and turned on the bedside lamp. Her body was weary, yet her mind was wide awake.

Would she ever feel the same again after tonight? She doubted it. Earlier, in the car with Sydney and Roxy, she'd thought about the essays she had to mark. Then, she'd longed to be home, sitting at her desk, working.

But now she wasn't sure. The house would be as quiet as this room, Dennis out somewhere, the only company the television and her work. She only came alive when she was at school, when she was Pauline, the teacher. Pauline, the person, hardly existed, wasn't real any more.

She could divorce Dennis. She was a Catholic, a good one, but it didn't seem right to sacrifice the rest of her life for a rule that hardly applied nowadays, not even to many Catholics she knew.

Perhaps it was the night, the things she'd done, so many people calling her 'brave', that made Pauline impulsively reach for the telephone directory beside the bed. She searched for the number for the International Operator, picked up the phone, took a pen out of her bag, and dialled 114.

'I'd like the number of the Hotel Orquidea in Lloret de Mar, Spain, please.'

'Hold on, Madam.'

She wrote the figures down, hands shaking. Dennis would think her mad, but she didn't care. It had been a good marriage once, and it deserved one more try.

'Hotel Orquidea.'

'Can I please speak to Dennis Gallagher. I don't know which room, but he's with Matthew Roper's party.'

'One minute, madam.'

'Hello,' came Dennis's sleepy, surprised voice.

'Dennis, it's Pauline.'

'Pauline!' He woke up. 'Has something happened? What's wrong?'

'I'd like us to try for another baby.'

'Y'what?' He sounded annoyed. 'You rang up all the way here in the middle of the night to say that! Are you drunk or something?'

'No, Dennis. I'm perfectly sober. A few minutes ago, I contemplated us getting divorced. If that's what you want, then we'll start proceedings tomorrow. But I'd sooner not. I'd sooner spend the rest of me life with you and our children. I'm only thirty-five, young enough to have two babies, even three.'

'Are you *sure* you're all right, Pauline?'

'I'm fine. Which is it to be, Dennis? Divorce or babies? It's up to you.'

There was silence for several seconds, then Dennis said, quietly, sadly, 'I still miss our Jamie, Pauline.'

'Me too.'

'Nothing's been the same since he died.'

'I know, Dennis. We drifted apart instead of clinging together.' They'd grieved separately and alone.

'Look, can we talk about this tomorrow?' She imagined him scratching his head, thinking.

'No!' Pauline was adamant. 'I want a decision now. You've got to say yes or no, or I'll never go to sleep.'

'What if I say no?'

'Then I'll go to sleep knowing where I am.'

'I don't suppose it would hurt to try again,' he said

thoughtfully. 'Shall I meet you off the plane? We're leaving at half eight, so we'll be in before you.'

'I'm not sure what plane I'll be getting. I've been delayed.' This wasn't the time to tell him she'd shot a man – two men, counting Roxy. 'It's very complicated, Dennis. I'll tell you all about it when I see you.'

'Okay, Pauly. Cheers for now.'

He hadn't sounded as enthusiastic as she would have liked, Pauline thought as she put back the phone. But then, she'd taken him by surprise and he hadn't been exactly *un*enthusiastic, either.

She lay down, pulled the bedclothes around her shoulders, and fell into a relaxed and peaceful sleep.

A fight was taking place in the kitchen of the priest's house when Emma and Jack went in. Kate and Grace O'Reilly were sitting companionably shoulder to shoulder at the table opposite the horse-faced woman and the grey-haired twins Emma had seen arrive earlier. There was no sign of the other Jack.

'Once and for all, you're not seeing him,' Kate screamed. 'He's not up to being faced with these two daft creatures, not on top of you an' all.'

'I agree,' said Grace.

'Mam!' Jack spluttered. 'It's gone half past three in the morning. I thought you'd be in bed by now, yet you're still carrying on like an insane bloody parrot. Who are these people?'

'This is Beattie something-or-other, and these are her girls. Least, *she* calls 'em girls, but they'll never see fifty-five again. If what she ses is true, she was at it with the father before I was even born.'

'I was Father Jack's housekeeper when he was no more than a lad just out the seminary,' Beattie explained in a grating voice. 'I heard the bugger was about to become null and void and I thought he'd like to set eyes on his own flesh and blood before he expired altogether. These are his girls, Mollie and Millie.'

'More like Pinky and Perky if you ask me,' Kate said in a stage whisper.

Grace tittered.

'*Mam!*'

Kate looked ashamed, but only slightly. 'Well, I'm fed up to the teeth, son, if you must know. The house has been like a railway station all night long – there's still some tramp asleep in the hallway and a couple of drunks nestled amidst the graves. Then Grace and the other Jack arrived – not that I minded them a bit.' She patted Grace's arm. 'Oh, no, I didn't mind Grace and her lovely boy at all, but now this person's turned up with the ugly sisters demanding to see Father Jack. The poor man's fast asleep, but even if he wasn't, the shock of seeing these three would kill the poor feller.'

'*Mam!*'

'Would that matter,' grated Beattie, 'seeing as how he's already got one foot inside death's door?'

'Of course, it would matter. No one would be happy finding they'd spawned the twins from hell. And who said anything about death's door? Last time I looked, Father Jack was as fit as a fiddle.'

'*Mam!*'

So far, the twins hadn't spoken. They were exceptionally plain, thought Emma, though not quite deserving of Kate's reckless insults. Their faces were round and doughy, with pale, vacant eyes, and noses merely little, shapeless lumps. A different hairstyle might have been an improvement, but their grey hair was precisely parted and they wore a slide on the longer side to keep it in place. Their frocks were the sort Emma's grandma used to wear; made of stiff crimplene with a loud, geometrical pattern. They were nothing like as ugly as their mother, who undeniably bore a strong resemblance to a horse. What's more, she didn't seem a very nice person, though Kate, in her present mood, was unlikely to bring out the best in anybody.

'Are they married, your girls?' Kate demanded.

'No.' Beattie tossed her mane. 'They preferred to stay with their mam.'

'You shouldn't have let them stay. That's being selfish, that is. What d'you think, Grace?'

'It is so.' Grace nodded her agreement. 'I would have been most upset if Jack had stayed at home with me. Purely for his sake, mind.'

'They've led sheltered lives, my girls,' brayed Beattie. 'They didn't have the opportunity to meet fellers, otherwise I'd have been glad to see the back of the pair, believe me.'

'That's not true, Mam,' one of the twins protested in a high, sweet voice. Her eyes had come to life and she looked hurt. 'Timothy Keogh asked me to marry him, but you wouldn't let us because you said he was a faggot.'

'And Ardal McShane kept on and on at me to get married, but you said he was a no good piece of shit,' claimed the other twin in the same voice.

Emma waited for an explosion from Kate, but Kate was looking at the two women with nothing but sympathy and kindness in her green eyes.

'It's not too late to get married now,' she said warmly.

'Why don't you go to England and find yourselves jobs? Buy some decent clothes and a bit of make-up, and do something with your hair. You're not bad-looking women, if the truth be told,' she finished, thus contradicting everything she'd said before.

'But what about me?' Beattie exploded.

'You'll just have to get on with things, the way all of us women do. It's a sin to have children just to keep you company for the rest of your life.'

'Hear, hear,' murmured Grace.

Beattie sniffed. 'My girls can leave whenever they like. No one's stopping 'em.'

The twins gave each other a delighted smile, transforming their plain faces. 'Ta, Mam,' said one.

'We'll go tomorrer,' said the other.

'Shall I make us all a cup of tea?' Grace offered. 'As long as it's all right with you, Kate?'

'It's fine with me, thanks all the same, Grace.' Kate turned her sympathy upon the older woman, who looked shocked and depressed, no doubt contemplating her suddenly shattered life. 'How about you, Beattie? Would you like a cup of tea?'

'I wouldn't say no.'

Emma signalled to Jack that she was going upstairs. He followed her into the hall where the tramp was peacefully asleep.

'I'll just take a peek at Father Jack,' she told him, 'then I'll go back to the hotel.'

'And that's it then?'

'What else did you expect?'

He pulled her down so they were sitting at the bottom of the stairs and put his arm around her shoulders. 'I expected much, much more than that,' he said in a thin, sad voice. 'I expected you to say you loved me, that you wouldn't be marrying Matthew on Saturday next, but me instead. I expected us to spend the rest of our lives together.'

'That's too much to expect, Jack.'

'Not long ago, you said you were my fiancée.'

'No, Jack. *You* said I was your fiancée. I said I felt confused.'

'Are you still confused?'

'Yes. No. I don't know.' When it came right down to it, she had neither the courage or the hardness necessary to let her parents down, to hurt Matthew as he would be hurt, to tell her friends the wedding was off, return the presents that had already been sent. And think of all the money that would have been wasted! The cars, the hotel, all sorts of things had been booked, the flowers, the cake, and other things had been ordered. Her lovely, very expensive wedding dress would be no good at all, because she could never bring herself to wear it to marry Jack, when it had been bought to marry Matthew.

And then there was the house, the new one in Woolton they'd put a deposit on. They'd already seen the carpets they would like, spent a lot of time deciding what sort of furniture would look best. Mam had offered to have the curtains made. Emma had been looking forward to getting everything just right for her and Matthew to live in.

Oh, but she wished she had the nerve to cancel every single thing, to throw her arms around Jack and tell him that she loved him. But she knew if she did that, she would be lost. There would be no going back. Everything would change, not in the slow measured way she'd always planned, but bumpily, unevenly. Where would they live? Did Jack earn a living wage? Could they afford to have children in a few years' time as she had intended to do with Matthew?

Did those sort of things matter when you were in love?

Emma wasn't sure.

She decided to talk to the wise, old priest one more time. He would give her the necessary courage, convince her, somehow, that choosing Jack was the right thing to do. He had the gift, Father Jack, of making her believe in herself.

Without a word, Emma got to her feet and went upstairs. He'd probably welcome being woken up and asked for advice.

She knocked softly on the door and went in. He was lying perfectly still with a beatific smile on his deceptively saintly face, his arms crossed over his chest.

He was *too* still! Emma placed her hand on his creased brow. It was cold. She uttered a small, soft sigh.

'Has he gone?' Jack asked from the door.

'Yes. He was right, after all. He said he was born at half past three in the morning, and it's just gone quarter to four.' She avoided his eyes. 'We'd better go down and tell the others.'

Chapter Fifteen

Sunday morning. A beautiful day. The world looked fresh and newly washed, the air felt tangy, and a pale, lemony sun shone like a dusky jewel in the pale, blue sky.

The night before last five women had occupied rooms 58 and 59 in the Arcadia hotel in Dublin. But twenty-four hours later, only three remained. They knew what had happened to Donna, but where was Rosemary?

Nobody knew.

The hotel staff hadn't seen her. On their way back from Mass, Emma suggested to Pauline that if she hadn't turned up by the time they left for the airport they should alert the Gardai.

'It's all right,' said Pauline. They were walking under a tree and she ran to catch a leaf, the very last one. It was pure gold and felt strong and leathery. Emma looked at her in surprise. It was a very un-Pauline-like thing to do. 'I'll tell the Gardai. They're sending a car for me later. It means I'll have to catch a later plane than you and Trace.'

'Why, Pauly?' Emma seemed very subdued and not at all her usual sunny self.

'I'll tell you some other time.'

'I've got things to tell you later.'

So many stories to tell, later or some other time.

Tracey was waiting for them in the dining-room and confessed she could eat a horse for breakfast. Pauline agreed, but Emma didn't feel like more than a piece of toast.

She felt incredibly sad, Emma. Would she make it to next Saturday without breaking down? she wondered. She almost hoped she wouldn't, that she'd weaken, and one day, one night, when everthing seemed too much, she would call the number of the priest's house and ask Kate if she could speak to Jack – he was staying with her until the funeral was over. Or Jack might answer the phone himself.

And then what would she say?

The number was in her bag, scribbled on a little piece of paper by Jack himself. She thought about tearing it up into little pieces and throwing it away, but it would be a simple matter to get it again from directory enquiries.

If she wanted to, that is.

Emma groaned inwardly. The next seven days – no, six – leading up to the wedding were going to be hell.

Tracey looked remarkably fresh, just like the day, despite having been up all night talking to Eileen O'Brien. Eileen hadn't left till daybreak, and then only because she was shortly expected at the hospital.

All in all, now that it was over, she'd quite enjoyed the weekend. It all added to life's rich pattern, as her mum was fond of saying, not that there was anything rich or remotely resembling a pattern about her mother's untidy life. Tracey would put the memory of the weekend away in her neatly ordered brain and take it out to look at whenever she felt like a thrill or a laugh.

As from next weekend, things in Liverpool were going to be different. Emma would be married, Donna was getting married soon and staying to live in Ireland. Rosemary and Pauline already had husbands. She would be the only one of the group of friends who was single.

She felt a moment of sadness, because even the most optimistic of people can be frightened by change. Almost immediately, she cheered up. She'd make new friends, she was bound to. As a treat, she'd take mum on a little holiday, and the obvious place to go was Dublin. She'd seen hardly anything of it and had the feeling she'd like the place when she saw it properly.

The leaf was still in Pauline's pocket.

'Catch a leaf and make a wish.'

She'd done it when she was a child, running through Sefton Park in autumn, catching leaves and making wishes. She couldn't remember if any had come true. This morning the wish had been that she and Dennis would get back together, have at least two babies. And be happy.

This time, next time, they wouldn't think of names, buy tons of babyclothes, and all the other myriad things required. They wouldn't decorate the spare room in advance, put teddy-bear transfers on the walls, not until the first baby was born.

But then, Jamie had been born, and they'd had him nine whole months before he was taken away. People couldn't run their lives always expecting the worst to happen, so next week, they'd buy more transfers and more paint; a nice light lilac or creamy yellow, so it would be suitable for a boy or a girl.

During the weekend, two people had said she was brave. She'd done things she hadn't thought herself capable of. Now she would have to continue to be brave, take chances, as well as pray, like she'd never prayed for anything in her life before, that she'd become pregnant. And she'd urge Dennis to pray too, and if they both prayed hard enough and long enough, this time next year they might have a baby.

No, an*other* baby.

Donna arrived when they were eating their toast and marmalade, still wearing the strange, laddish clothes, and holding the hand of a boyish little girl or a girlish little boy. No one was quite sure. She turned out to be a girl whose name was Samantha.

'She's Mick's.' Donna removed the child's baseball cap and ruffled her fair curls. 'I'm going to become her other mammy. We can't wait, can we, Sam?'

'No.' Sam gazed adoringly through her round spectacles at the tall, lanky figure holding her hand. The other women gaped. In the past, children and old people had been known to cry at Donna's approach. Something magical must have happened in Dublin. Perhaps it was the place where she was meant to be, where the real Donna would bloom, now that she had found her true love.

'Mick'll be here in a minute,' she said. 'He's gone to buy flowers for his ex-wife. She nearly had kittens when he rang this morning to say this little madam had done a bunk and was staying with him.'

'She hadn't realised I'd gone.' Samantha sniffed disdainfully. 'The flowers are to get round her, so she'll let me stay with me real daddy more often.'

'That'll be nice,' Pauline remarked.

Mick came bursting into the dining-room bearing a giant bunch of chrysanthemums and beaming at everyone in sight. 'Good morning, ladies. And how's the lovely heroine this fine day?'

Pauline blushed. 'Very well, thank you.'

'I've news for you, darlin'. Guava Tech would like to show their appreciation for you having got them out of such a desperately deep hole last night. They want to know where to send the cheque.'

'To my school. I'll give you the address.'

'And now I must be off, to give these flowers and me dear little daughter back to me old wife. Are you sure you won't come with us, Donna, me luv?'

'I'd sooner stay with me friends a while. I'm not too keen on meeting your ex.' She'd be recognised immediately as the saint who'd rescued the children from a terrible fire. By now, it might have entered one or two heads that the saint had *started* the fire, though Samantha was going to do her best to cast suspicion on her other daddy.

'Understandable,' Mick roared. 'I'm not exactly keen on meeting your ex, either.'

After he and Samantha had gone, Donna ordered another pot of coffee. In a minute, she'd go to her room and get changed into her own clothes, but would miss the bizarre outfit belonging to that cute little guy, Mark Costello. Tomorrow, she'd buy herself black velvet trousers and some glamorous tops. She'd start dressing differently, wear hats. Mick mightn't have fancied her had she been wearing her usual, drab clothes.

She remembered she still had the little guy's wallet and mobile phone, but there was a card with his address and

237

home phone number in the wallet. She'd give him a call just before they left and say everything was in Reception for him to collect. It was an act of kindness that wouldn't have entered the old Donna's head, never in a month of Sundays.

'This reminds me of that song we used to sing when we were kids,' Tracey remarked when she and Emma were in the taxi on the way to Dublin airport, 'the green bottle one. But instead of ten, it started with five. Then, one by one, we fell off the wall, and now there's only us two left.'

If she'd had a bit more bottle, there'd have only been one, Emma thought listlessly. 'Pauline will be along later,' she said. 'I wonder why the police want to see her?'

'Dunno, Em.' Tracey didn't know yet about Pauline's confrontation with Tony Bianco in the early hours of that morning.

'Maybe she heard the shot.'

'What shot?'

'This morning, the waiter said someone had been shot on our floor. They didn't die, or anything, but the police were called.'

'I didn't hear anything.'

'Neither did I. It must have happened before we came back.

Tracey remembered the desk clerk had mentioned there was someone in Pauline's room when they'd returned from Guava Tech. She'd thought it was Emma or Rosemary, but it turned out to be neither. Pauline had had Sydney's gun. It was unlikely there'd been two people with guns last night on the fifth floor of the Arcadia. She shrugged. Pauline had looked fine that morning, exceptionally fine, in fact. No doubt she would tell them all about it in her own good time.

'Once a holiday's over, I can't wait to get back home,' she remarked conversationally, but Emma didn't reply.

'Would you like us to come with you to the police station, Pauly?' enquired the new, kind Donna. They were in the hotel lounge, sitting by the window, so they could see the police car arrive.

'No, I'd sooner go by meself, if you don't mind.'

'I don't mind a bit. I'll just wander round, window shop, like. I'm seeing Mick in Mahoney's at midday, the place we should have gone to meet Eileen O'Brien.'

'I wonder how things would have turned out if we had?' Pauline mused.

'Boring, I expect. It would have just been one long party.'

'I'd have hated that. I'm too old for those sort of things. No one ever asks me to dance.'

Donna wrinkled her nose. 'Nor me. We'd have ended up dancing with each other.'

'That wouldn't have been so bad.' Pauline smiled and their eyes met. It was a bit late now, too late, but she felt that, given time, she and Donna might have become good friends.

'Your car's arrived.' Donna got to her feet. 'Don't forget to tell them about Rosemary, will you?'

'I won't. I'm dead worried about her. Lord knows where she can be.'

'Oh, what a beautiful morning,' sang Monsignor Aloysius Innocent (after the Pope) McGillivray as he drove through the pretty Welsh countryside in the direction of distant Liverpool. It was dark when he'd driven off the boat. He'd stopped for breakfast in a restaurant just past the Menai Bridge, and now his part of the world was just waking up. Autumn flowers were opening to the first rays of the sun. Birds were emerging from the hedgerows, shaking their feathers and twittering furiously.

Of course, being a priest, and it being Sunday morning, he should have been singing something else; a drippy hymn or a soggy psalm. But he was in the mood for something a bit more fleshy, describing how he felt.

'Oh, what a beautiful day,' he warbled, slightly off tune. He'd never had much of a voice. He hadn't had much of a vocation, either, but it hadn't seemed to matter. He'd *acted* the part of a priest, and he'd done it so well, he deserved an Oscar. And if he kept up the acting much longer, they'd make him a bishop. He might even end up the Pope. It was about time they had another Irishman in the part.

The first thing he'd do, as Pope, was change the rule on celibacy. Priests would be *encouraged* to get married. If there was a problem, he'd set up dating agencies. And he'd allow women to become priests, and *they* would be encouraged to get married. Same sex marriages would be all right by him, and there'd be no more restrictions on birth control.

Oh, yes, thought the Monsignor grimly, once *he* was Pope, the Roman Catholic church would see a few changes made.

He turned on the radio and found himself listening to a church service. The Monsignor winced delicately and turned the knob until he found something more cheerful.

For the next few hours, he was happy with his

thoughts and it came as a surprise when he found he was approaching the bridge across the Mersey that led to Runcorn. He was within a few miles of Liverpool. The petition in his briefcase was intended for a fellow priest whose parish was in Tuebrook, but first he would attend Mass at the Metropolitan Cathedral, one of his favourite buildings. He always found it very uplifting.

Perhaps it was the sounds of her hometown, or the smells, or merely the feel of the place, that caused Rosemary to wake up. Or she might have sensed the proximity of Liverpool General Hospital where she worked as a nurse.

What a fantastic sleep! The best ever. And what wonderful dreams! She couldn't remember when she'd last felt so relaxed, so full of life. Ready for anything.

She stretched, leisurely, but instead of empty space, her arms banged against something cold and hard.

She opened her eyes and discovered she'd gone blind.

With a feeling of horror, it eventually dawned on Rosemary that the thing had happened that she'd had nightmares about all her life.

Some stupid idiot of a doctor had pronounced her dead and now she was in a coffin, buried alive!

How long had she been there?

She opened her mouth, screamed for all she was worth, and frantically kicked and banged the lid. It mightn't be too late to make people notice. She imagined the faces of the mourners; her husband, her mum and dad, her brother, her friends from the hospital, lined up around her grave, staring down, wondering where the noises were coming from.

'It's Rosemary, she's still alive,' they'd all cry. Any

minute now, the lid would be torn off. 'Thank God, you're still with us, Rosemary!'

Nothing happened.

Perhaps everyone had gone and the grave had been filled with earth!

But if that was the case, why could she hear traffic? A car sounded its horn and made her jump.

Come to think of it, if she was in a coffin, it was remarkably spacious, if a bit short. She could turn over, raise her feet, move her arms. She banged again and it sounded tinny.

She was in the boot of a car.

Though a slight improvement on a coffin, it was nevertheless an unpleasant place to find herself, particularly when she'd expected to wake up in bed.

Voices! She could hear voices!

Rosemary banged, kicked and screamed again. 'Help!' she yelled.

'Is someone in there?' A tiny, tinny knock.

'*Yes!*'

'Who?' A woman's voice, old.

'It doesn't matter who. Get me out of here. Call the police. Get a spanner. Find the owner. *Get me out!*'

'There's no need to shout, dear. I'll see what I can do.'

Another knock. 'Is someone in there?'

'Yes!' screeched Rosemary. 'Yes, *yes, YES!*'

A matter of minutes later, the police arrived. The boot was prised open, and a relieved, sobbing, exhausted and terrified Rosemary was lifted out. A small crowd had gathered and there was a smattering of applause.

Rosemary rubbed her eyes. 'Where am I?'

'Liverpool, luv,' said a policeman. 'We're right outside the Roman Catholic cathedral.'

'But that can't be!' She'd left Liverpool days ago for another place. She couldn't remember which place, or why she was going, or who with, but could vaguely recall getting on a plane.

'It is, luv. I assure you. Let's get you to the ozzie. You need a good checking over. Do you know who this car belongs to?'

'I've never seen it before.'

When a duly uplifted Monsignor McGillivray emerged from Mass and went over to his expensive, grey car, he found half a dozen policemen waiting for him. He was immediately handcuffed, roundly cursed, and thrown roughly into a van.

It was a totally stunned man of the cloth who was taken to a police station and charged with the abduction of Mrs Rosemary Hunt. He was then transferred to an interview room and subjected to a terse interrogation by a hatchet-faced inspector and his female sidekick, a woman young enough to be the Monsignor's daughter had he indulged in such goings on – he had, as it happens, but had always been careful to take precautions.

'But I've never heard of Rosemary Hunt,' he stammered.

'I don't suppose you bothered to ask her name before you raped her and stuffed her in your boot.'

'I've never raped anyone in my life. For God's sake man, I'm a priest. I didn't stuff her in my boot, either.'

'Did you drug her first?'

'No.'

'Oh, so she quite willingly climbed in your boot?'

'I didn't know she was in my boot.'

'How long did you intend to keep her?'

'Keep her? How could I keep someone I didn't know was there?'

'Where have you come from?'

'Dublin.'

The questions continued until he felt dizzy and totally confused. They looked through his briefcase, found the petition, and must have contacted the media, because after a while he became aware that the corridor outside was full of reporters. He could hear them shouting, pleading for his photograph, an interview, a press conference.

'According to this,' the petition was waved in his face, 'you're dead set against celibacy.'

'Wouldn't you be?'

'Too true, mate, except I'm not a priest. I wouldn't be surprised if these men,' the petition was waved again, 'weren't a ring of sex perverts. Do you use the Internet? How many young women have your crowd abducted?'

'Look,' the Monsignor said desperately. 'My car was left unattended on the midnight ferry from Dun Laoghaire. It could be that's where the poor young lady was put in.'

'Did you stop anywhere else on your way over?'

'No. Yes. Last night, not long before I reached the ferry, I stopped briefly at a pub in Dublin, Maloney's. This morning, I had breakfast near the Menai Bridge.'

'Someone check the passenger list with the ferry company,' the inspector ordered. 'Then put a call in to Maloney's and see if they recognise a description of the woman. Check the restaurants in the vicinity of the Menai Bridge.' He turned to the priest. 'I bet nothing comes of any of 'em,' he spat. 'You're nothing but a sanctimonious prick, hiding behind that dog collar and preying on young girls. You make me sick.'

It was then that the good Monsignor remembered that it was only a matter of hours since he'd imagined himself becoming Pope.

Overnight, Trish, the burly barmaid who worked at Maloney's, had been suffering from desperate pangs of conscience. Say if the woman in the boot died of suffocation, became a genuine corpse? Or the car was parked somewhere dead quiet where her screams wouldn't be heard?

The pangs of conscience came to a head next morning during Mass. After the service was over, she tearfully informed the priest, Father Kelly, what she had done.

Father Kelly immediately telephoned the landlord of Maloney's and demanded that he do something.

'What?' demanded the landlord back.

'Find out where these five women were staying and if the cruelly treated one has caught up with the other four. Alternatively, find out who the car belonged to and tell him he's got a passenger in his boot.'

'How?'

'I've no idea how,' the priest snapped irritably. 'It's your problem, not mine. I'll ring back in half an hour, and if nothing's been done, I'll be calling in the Gardai.'

The priest rang off.

The landlord stared at the phone, desperately wondering where to start. Was he supposed to contact every hotel in Dublin?

The phone rang. The bewildered landlord wondered

if a whole half-hour had passed without him noticing but, to his eternal relief, it was the Liverpool police.

Monsignor McGillivray was released without a stain on his character, though news of his petition was already on the internet and the main item on the television news.

He drove to the Adelphi, followed by a cavalcade of cars containing an avid media. At the subsequent press conference, he flamboyantly undid his dog collar, threw it to the ground, and stamped on it.

'I've just defrocked meself,' he announced to the gleeful reporters. Later, when the whole, horrible business was over, he telephoned the widow Estelle, and asked for her hand in marriage.

She accepted like a shot.

At the hospital, Rosemary was in a side ward surrounded by her appalled relatives. With some prompting, she recalled having flown to Dublin for Emma's hen party. 'We were all dead bored,' she said. 'Friday night we went to bed early. Saturday, we saw this film no one liked. Then we went to some awful pub to meet Eileen O'Brien, but from then on, me mind's a blank.'

'Some friends you've got,' her husband expostulated angrily. 'You'd think they'd have reported you missing.'

'Perhaps they did.' Rosemary resented hearing her friends being criticised.

'Never mind, luv,' her mother said comfortably. 'All's well that ends well – anyroad, it doesn't sound as if you've missed much, does it?'